LIGHTNING IN A MASON JAR

PREVIOUS TITLES BY CATHERINE MANN

Hometown Heroes Series

Forever His Girl

In Too Deep

Pretend You're Mine

His North Star

This Time Around

LIGHTNING IN A MASON JAR

A Novel

CATHERINE MANN

LAKE UNION
PUBLISHING

This is a work of fiction. Names, characters, organizations, places, events, and incidents are either products of the author's imagination or are used fictitiously. Otherwise, any resemblance to actual persons, living or dead, is purely coincidental.

Text copyright © 2025 by Catherine Mann
All rights reserved.

No part of this book may be reproduced, or stored in a retrieval system, or transmitted in any form or by any means, electronic, mechanical, photocopying, recording, or otherwise, without express written permission of the publisher.

Published by Lake Union Publishing, Seattle

www.apub.com

Amazon, the Amazon logo, and Lake Union Publishing are trademarks of Amazon.com, Inc., or its affiliates.

EU product safety contact:
Amazon Media EU S. à r.l.
38, avenue John F. Kennedy, L-1855 Luxembourg
amazonpublishing-gpsr@amazon.com

ISBN-13: 9781662525223 (paperback)
ISBN-13: 9781662525216 (digital)

Cover design by Kathleen Lynch/Black Kat Design
Cover image: © Susan Fox / ArcAngel; © Jose A. Bernat Bacete / Getty

Printed in the United States of America

To all the women who've lived in the shadows

PROLOGUE

1971

Changing my identity and leaving behind everything familiar should have been difficult. Traumatic, even. Except it wasn't. Because from birth, we women aren't tethered to our names. Marriage may turn a Jane Smith into Jane Brown or Jane Jones. Or into Jane Smith Brown Jones through widowhood or divorce, followed by remarriage.

Even the connection to a first name is tenuous when spoken. "Introducing Mrs. John Smith" would be followed with a whisper like a distorted echo . . .

"Her husband's a *doctor*."

"Her baby d-i-e-d."

"She's barren."

As if a woman's entire worth, her sum total sense of self, were tied into her ring finger and uterus. A Mrs. or a mom.

Could those hushed voices be that oblivious to the world exploding with marches and rallies, bra burnings and sit-ins? I wasn't. I cheered those women on from my living room, images flickering across my new color television set, the wooden cabinet kind that dominated its own corner where once a tiny black and white had rested on an antique tea cart.

This was more than simply incinerating cotton and lace. It was like a broken bottle being melted and reshaped by an emerging sisterhood, a revolutionary sorority.

The world was changing, and that bigger, brighter screen gave me an expanded peek. Decorated with family portraits and silk flowers on top, the Magnavox invited me on a nightly news date to watch *them*. I was proud of *them* and all *they* were battling to achieve. I was also thankful for my safe life that protected *me* from being *them*. What a comfortable place to exist, in that cottony swaddle of complacency.

So yes, I expected the changes that began when my father gave away the bride. Giving *me* away to Phillip, as if I were a possession passed over to a neighbor like a handsaw or a charcoal grill—or the tiny black-and-white television—he no longer needed but still thought of fondly. Although if I'd been a brighter color TV, I might have been wanted. Still objectified, but not discarded.

However, I accepted, and at that time embraced, my new identity as Phillip's wife, even if it meant losing a part of myself. No one forced me to walk down the aisle in my mother's white lace gown that itched, with my hair piled on my head, anchored by Aqua Net that stung my eyes and bobby pins that scarred my scalp. Nobody insisted I put aside completing college to start a family right away. I made my own choices. At least I thought I did.

Then I began doubting even my tiniest of decisions. I forgot to buy slaw for supper, even though Phillip insisted he'd written it on the list I'd anchored to the refrigerator with a banana-shaped magnet—a list I now couldn't locate. But no need to be upset or melodramatic. Didn't I know how much he treasured me?

I thought I'd put the credit card in my wallet as always, except it was in the medicine cabinet. No wonder a husband had to sign the application for a Master Charge card. Perhaps he should keep it from now on. If I wanted extra cash, I only had to ask him and he would increase my household allowance. Money that came from my trust fund.

Maybe I just needed rest. I should cancel the cruise to Mexico with his parents. Send our regrets for my class reunion. Leave behind sad reminders of my dead parents and relocate to the country for fresh air, where we could build my dream studio for glassblowing. Didn't I want to get back to my art? Eventually. Once I was myself again.

Except time went by, feeling more and more strange. And as I lost my bearings, my husband retreated from me in ways that unnerved me. Who was he to become the expert on my mental health? And why did I feel better the days when he traveled for work? The weeks when he left for conferences?

By increments my world grew smaller and smaller, until that day, the worst day, when *I* became one of *them*. My cottony swaddle of complacency split open to reveal a light so blinding it sliced through me like the electroshock therapy that followed. Therapy that Phillip had been quick to suggest. Quick to approve.

In the silence that followed came a soul-deep realization. Phillip intended to keep me institutionalized forever and take what was mine for himself. Who knew when he'd made that decision? Surely not from the start. After the miscarriages? The stillbirth? Or simply because he could. Now that my parents were gone, who would stop him?

Except he underestimated me. Or overestimated himself. He could steal the money, my name, even a piece of my sanity. But he couldn't steal *me*. Which meant I had the most important choice of my life, the first I made completely on my own.

I had to run.

The details of how I managed to escape the hospital aren't important yet. Those secrets are carefully guarded, doled out in increments to only the most trusted in what has become my network—my life's work, you could say. To protect those with the greatest need.

All you have to know for now? I embraced the reality of my own making, being one of *them*. Helping the most vulnerable of *them* when they need to run as well.

Ask me who I am or where I'm from? Eloise Carlisle Curtis is a faint specter, ostracized to the dim recesses of my mind. I rarely think of my life in Mobile, Alabama, anymore, of my marriage, of my art. Of my daughter. In fact, it's better that way since a whisper of that time threatens my present, even my hard-won sanity.

Today? My name is Winnie Ballard. I'm from Bent Oak, South Carolina, where I work in the paper mill.

But tomorrow? Well, like I said, I'm not tethered to something so inconsequential as a name.

CHAPTER ONE

2025

Without Aunt Winnie, nothing anchored Bailey Rae Rigby to backwoods Bent Oak, South Carolina, anymore.

Only a month left until she could hitch her vintage Airstream behind her F-250 and hightail it out of this town to Myrtle Beach, where she would fulfill the dream of the woman who'd raised her. She just had to survive the next four Saturdays at the Bent Oak Farmers' Market settling Aunt Winnie's affairs in an estate sale—flea-market style.

How fitting.

Bailey Rae leaped onto the tailgate of her eighteen-year-old truck parked behind her stall. She grabbed a can of bug repellent from her backpack and showered herself in an aloe-scented haze. Pitiful protection against Southern mosquitoes hatching from swamps in an endless horde.

Aunt Winnie had been gone for sixty-seven days.

Tears still welled up without warning at the least reminder of the person Bailey Rae loved more than any individual on the planet. But there wasn't time to grieve. The estate wasn't going to settle itself.

As she hefted a crate of canned tomatoes—five dollars a jar—she could hear Winnie's voice insisting that estate was a hoity-toity word for a barn full of clutter.

"Aunt" had been an honorary title, since Winnie had been more of a mother than the woman who only came around when she didn't have a better offer from a man. Bailey Rae never quite understood why Aunt Winnie had kept her or why child services never intervened. But thank heaven for unexplained blessings. Time to move forward, to leave behind all those painful memories plastered all over Bent Oak like out-of-date wallpaper.

The weight of gossipy stares beat down on her shoulders, fierce as the Southern sun. Heavy. Unrelenting. Weightier than ever on market day, with the field packed full of vendors and early shoppers, even a police cruiser on duty to monitor the expected crowd. She'd long ago learned to pretend indifference, a survival mechanism to withstand the whispers about her mom and Aunt Winnie, not to mention being a reject kid. Still, for some reason, today the small-town, judgy vibe really put her on edge when she needed to focus on unloading the first batch of loot from Winnie's farm.

Her farm now. She blinked away the tears and got back to work.

One box after another. So. Much. Stuff.

How could a person possibly have expected to consume hundreds of jars of home-canned goods? Who needed seven microwaves, twenty-two quilts, and three crates of the same cookbook?

Yep. Buy three jars, get a cookbook for free. With any luck, she would only have a kajillion of them left at the end of the next four weeks.

A muggy breeze drifted through the open-air market at the end of Main Street, which wasn't much more than two blocks with old storefronts. At least a quarter of them sported Space for Rent signs in the front window. The library perched on the other end of the road, a red-brick building that had once been a schoolhouse. And one street back, along the river, the paper mill loomed, a stark steel building. Even with upgrades, it still looked like a relic from a bygone era, and somehow, Aunt Winnie had survived working there for thirty years.

No doubt about it, the town was dying. Well, for six days a week, anyway. On market day, though? Bent Oak came alive.

Farmers and artisans set up their booths. Livestock bleated, watched over by the 4-H kids ready to educate. The scent of hay bales and grilled hot dogs filled the air. A local pickup band tuned their instruments and performed a sound check before warming up with a beach tune, the heartbeat of South Carolina no matter how far from the sandy shores.

Pausing for a water break, Bailey Rae chugged half the bottle, then used the rest to refill Skeeter's metal bucket. The old hound mix peered up at her from under the truck, his leash hooked to a leg of her chair. Skeeter's eyes were two different colors. When he looked up with the brown one, like now, he was all soul. The day promised to be a long one, and she hadn't wanted him to be lonely, so she'd brought him along. He'd been extra clingy since losing Aunt Winnie.

"Hang in there, pup. Before you know it, we'll be living in Myrtle Beach, proud owners of a food truck by the ocean, just like Aunt Winnie always talked about."

It wasn't a big dream. But it was hers now, along with one of those cookbooks for inspiration.

As she scooted along the truck bed to grab another crate, a honking horn drew her attention. A familiar minivan careened across the field on shock absorbers long past their expiration date.

She should have known Winnie's three best friends would show up, even though she hadn't asked. And yes, while it was only one vehicle, they always traveled in a flock.

Of course they had come today. They would want to honor Winnie every bit as much as Bailey Rae did.

The minivan kicked up a cloud of dust as they drove past the 4-H booth and a slushy stand before pulling up alongside her truck.

"Yoo-hoo." Waving, Libby Farrell leaned out of a back window, her thick braid swinging free. "Never fear, the reinforcements are here."

The driver's side door creaked open, with June Evans behind the wheel. It wasn't her van, but she chauffeured whenever Libby's son, Keith, was unavailable to help his widowed mom.

June grabbed the doorframe and hopped out. "Bailey Rae, honey, dry your eyes. The party has arrived."

Barely five feet tall, June sported a neon-pink streak through her bobbed graying hair today. Blue last month. Highlights, lowlights, she changed her hair color on a regular basis. June once said hair was her way of appearing relevant to the students at the community college where she taught women's lit. She still hadn't recovered from the rejection of her submission for a class based on an Ivy League college course called "Feminist Perspectives, Politicizing Taylor Swift."

Bailey Rae lifted her ponytail off her sweaty neck. "Love the rosy stripe. I see you're the designated driver."

Nodding, June hip-bumped the door closed. "Keith had a job interview, but he'll be along shortly."

Keith always had another job interview.

The passenger-side door opened, and a disdainful snort sounded ahead of the woman who'd never thought much of Keith Farrell. Thea Tyler was overdressed as usual in a Chanel-style suit that had been around for at least two decades. Some said she took her role as a councilman's wife a bit too seriously.

Judgmental gossips.

Then the side panel rolled away and a wheelchair ramp cranked out for Libby, frail and holding a picnic basket on her lap. A cane was hooked on the armrest if needed, since her mobility, though limited, was not entirely gone. June guided the wheelchair carefully onto the packed earth.

Thea held a handkerchief as she activated the remote to retract the ramp. "We've brought sweet tea—"

Libby interrupted, patting the basket. "And Southern Comfort for later."

Bailey Rae hopped off the tailgate, then shifted a crate to the table. "Surely you have something better to do with your time than help me sell off all this . . ." She waved toward the boxes under the table and stacked in the back of her truck. "Well, you know what a collector Aunt Winnie could be."

Thea stuffed the handkerchief into her leather handbag, the small type like Queen Elizabeth had always carried. The kind that, no matter how big or small, couldn't contain all the mystery of the aloof wearer. "And that's why we're here. Libby even circled the date on her calendar."

Bailey Rae grieved over how calendars had become more and more a part of Libby's world lately, a memory aid that sometimes worked. Other times, not.

Libby released the brakes on her wheelchair and wheeled herself over the packed earth to the table. Grinning, she patted a jar of peaches. "Don't let Winnie catch you snitching any of these from her stash. She saves those for your Uncle Russell."

Silence fell, cut only by strains of the pickup band playing "My Girl." One minute Libby could recall that the picnic basket contained Southern Comfort, and the next she couldn't remember that Russell had been dead for years and her very best friend had been gone for two months.

Sixty-seven days. No body to bury.

As best they could reconstruct from footprints, Winnie had walked from her cabin to swim in the nearby river, only to be carried away by the current that had claimed a fisherman just this week as well. Her striped sack had snagged on a downed tree, just barely protruding from the muddy water. A tragic accident. Or had her grief over losing Uncle Russell finally led her to that shoreline?

Bailey Rae's fingers clenched around the amber jar. "Aunt Winnie canned so many, she's okay with me sharing the extras."

That seemed a benign-enough answer that would fit in whatever time frame Libby's mind currently embraced.

Thea skimmed her gloved hands along a stack of quilts, the one on top a scrap pattern made with old clothes. "I understand needing to clear out some of Winnie's clutter, but are you sure you want to sell the cabin too? It's not too late to change your mind."

"It's time. I'll still come to visit." Bailey Rae had zero regrets about leaving Bent Oak, but the people . . . this makeshift family of no blood relation . . . she would miss them dearly.

June grapevined to the music, her feet dancing pinwheels in the dirt as she carried a box of wind chimes crafted from kitchen utensils. "Why would she want to stay here? The town's old and dying. Like us."

"Shush your mouth," Thea said. "Bailey Rae, honey, you don't have to sell off everything." Easy for Thea to say, thanks to her husband's generational wealth and her sharp mind for investments. "We'll give you the money for the start-up cost of your food truck."

The wheelchair rattled over rocks as Libby joined them. "Then if things don't work out in Myrtle Beach with the food truck business, you can just pull up stakes on the Airstream and come on back."

They were like Winnie that way. Generous. But something about the way Bailey Rae had lived the first six years of her life made it tough to accept help. Even owning the farm made her as itchy as sitting in a bed of chiggers.

The cabin and three riverfront acres had actually belonged to Uncle Russell, a quiet man with a genius mind when it came to anything with an engine. Everyone assumed he and Winnie were married, but she'd always insisted a piece of paper didn't mean squat.

He'd died six years ago and left the farmhouse to Bailey Rae, with the provision that Winnie could live there for the rest of her life. When Bailey Rae had asked the attorney why the will had been structured that way, the lawyer said it was easier legally. Which didn't make sense. Had Russell been angry with Winnie over not marrying him, even though he never said as much? Bailey Rae had been too busy mourning the great man to untangle his motives.

And now she mourned them both. A double loss that choked her, surrounded by all these memories.

"Thank you, Thea," Bailey Rae said. "That's a truly generous offer. But I'm not moving back, so selling makes the most sense."

"Well, then," June said, even though the fight hadn't left her eyes, "at least we get to keep you until the Fourth of July." She gave Bailey Rae a swift hug, one of those firm kinds that hurt a little as it reminded a person of the tender spots on their heart.

"Ladies?" Thea whispered, which should have been a big red flag coming from the usually assertive woman. She pointed across the field toward the tractor supply store's parking lot.

Squinting in the sun, Bailey Rae saw a pair of teenage boys wearing camo and an air of troublemaking. Both stood in the back of a shiny pickup with a huge crate.

A bolted-down crate filled with an angry wild pig.

A beast charging the grate, tusks gleaming.

Bailey Rae had lived in this town long enough to recognize that those mischief-making boys were about to set that crazed hog loose in the middle of a crowded market.

And people wondered why she couldn't wait to put Bent Oak in her rearview mirror.

CHAPTER TWO

Bailey Rae could already imagine the headline in next week's *Bent Oak Weekly*: Pig Stages Protest at Hot Dog Stand.

She'd had more than her fair share of experiences with the feral pigs that wandered out of the woods to tear up Winnie's garden. Usually, they meandered off on their own. Unless agitated. No doubt, those boys had agitated the piss right out of this beast.

Her heart rate kicked up a notch.

At the other end of the field, the cop car doors swung wide. Two officers piled out, tossing aside their snow cones as they sprinted past stalls and toward the teens. The police shouted a jumble of commands: "Don't do it, boys . . . Everybody stay back . . . Somebody find the game warden . . ."

With a whoop, the camo-clad duo opened the kennel before scrambling to safety on top of the truck cab. The pig—a.k.a. Angry Wilbur—launched out of his cage and soared over the tailgate. He hit the ground, tumbling and squealing.

Drawing all eyes in his direction.

Not. Good. Bailey Rae's pulse slugged harder as she searched for the fastest path to load Libby back into the safety of the minivan.

Skeeter came to life in a roll of gangly hound legs, shooting out from his shady spot under the pickup. He tipped back his head and howled. Every ounce of hound dog in his mixed DNA roared to life, his baying battle cry piercing the air.

The wild pig—or maybe it was a hog, she didn't intend to get close enough to identify—made a slow turn in their direction. Skeeter and Wilbur locked eyes across the distance. The hog's were beady. Skeeter narrowed his glacier-blue eye.

Outright terror for Skeeter and the three vulnerable women kicked her feet into high gear.

"Skeeter, stay!" Bailey Rae ordered, lunging to grab his collar, not trusting the strength of his tether. "Where is that game warden?"

Not in her wildest dreams would she have imagined praying for the new game warden's help. That man had been a spur in her side since writing her a ticket for fishing without a license—on her own land. He'd informed her that while the land was hers, the water and fish were under the state's purview.

And *riiiiip*. He'd torn off her ticket.

A ticket she still needed to pay. Or had he just given her a warning? She really shouldn't have stuffed it to the back of her kitchen junk drawer in a fit of irritation.

Down by the 4-H booth, an engine roared to life just before a truck peeled out across the field. The muddy black pickup sported a SCDNR logo—South Carolina Department of Natural Resources. Tires chewed up the earth as the game warden drove straight toward the wild pig charging onto the field. Cloven hooves plowed the earth as the beast upended a table of watermelons and toppled the garden club's flower sale.

The pickup bore down, closer, until only a couple feet shy of hitting the pig, the game warden blared his sirens and laid on the horn. Startling the pig. Angry Wilbur turned into Confused Wilbur. Accelerating, the truck took tight turns like a horse herding cattle, guiding the pig away from the crowd and into the woods.

Seconds later, three gunshots echoed from the tree line.

The stampeding crowd froze for a heartbeat, then burst into a round of applause for the hero of the day before melting right back into their setting up and shopping. Another normal day in Bent Oak.

Thea dabbed her forehead with her handkerchief. "Wild pigs can be eaten if cooked properly."

Legs wobbly, Bailey Rae sank down beside Skeeter. "Is the councilman planning to dig a trench for a pig pickin' party?"

Thea looked over the rims of her glasses. "Someone needs to let Game Warden Perez know there are a couple of single moms in the area who could use some help putting a meal on the table." She dug in her purse for her cell phone. "I'll call Howard to come field dress the pig."

Her navy-blue pumps punched holes in the earth as she marched across the field, sidestepping split melons.

June patted Libby's hand. "Could you stay here with Bailey Rae and package up purchases?" she asked, navigating Libby's pride and loss of independence. "Thea may need my help."

A smile teased at Bailey Rae. Thea rarely needed assistance.

Bailey Rae pushed to her feet just as Libby's son shouldered through the growing crowd. Apparently, the pig incident was already ginning up extra traffic and potential buyers.

"Mom? Mom," Keith said breathlessly, kneeling beside his mother's wheelchair. "Are you okay?"

Libby patted his cheek. "Of course I am. Did you get the job? With a construction company, right?"

"I start on Monday. Of course, there aren't a lot of hours available..." Approaching sixty, Libby's son wore the disappointments of his life like someone dragging a tractor tire.

Up a hill.

In summer.

He'd been through three divorces, six career changes—none by choice. After the most recent, he'd moved back in with his mother under the auspices of caring for her. But folks in this gossipy town knew he was flat broke.

Wiry, like his mom, with graying dark hair, Keith dislodged the wheelchair from a mushy patch of grass before helping her shift into a seat beside Bailey Rae.

"Here, Mom." He picked up her cane from the ground, a floral aluminum model today. It must have rolled from her lap in the confusion.

Libby draped the cane across her lap and patted Bailey Rae's arm. "Go take a break, have some lunch, kick up your feet and dance a little." She paused. "My son will keep me company so I don't get confused about the prices. Right, Freddie?"

"Mama," he said softly. "I'm Keith."

Confusion only flickered before she smiled. "Of course. You just look like your father."

Did he? Bailey Rae couldn't recall seeing photos of him. Winnie had always said Libby was so heartbroken by his death that she couldn't bear reminders. And soon Libby wouldn't even have those memories. Regardless of what latest failure had brought Keith home, thank heaven he was there to help his mother.

Bailey Rae slid an arm around Libby's shoulders—thinning and hunching with age. "That's sweet. But I'm fine. Although if Keith wants to go wander around, you're welcome to hang out with me."

He glanced back and forth from her to his mom. "If you're sure. Maybe I could pick up food for all of us?"

The question in his tone settled around her, making her realize . . . She reached into the cashbox and peeled off a pair of twenty-dollar bills. "If you don't mind, that would be great."

Keith backed away, waving the pair of bills. "I'll let you get to your customers."

Customers? Oh, right. The pig thing had thrown her off balance. And, truth be told, sorting through so many memories even just packing the truck that morning had been draining.

She dropped into a folding chair and chugged the rest of her water bottle since Libby was already working a sale with Mrs. Watson—the mother of identical twins Missy and Sissy, who had been in Bailey Rae's class growing up. No one seemed to remember the pair's real names anymore. Winnie had always insisted a person's name didn't matter near as much as how they treated others. Which meant Missy and Sissy were worthless as gum on a bootheel.

More than once, Bailey Rae had wondered if Mrs. Watson knew that her precious little darlings used to enjoy chanting, *Winnie Ballard's a cuckoo bird, Winnie Ballard's a cuckoo bird* . . .

Bailey Rae had put up with it until her seventh birthday—which her mother forgot—and then let her fists fly. The Watson girls fought dirty, biting and pulling hair. She'd only managed to break free by headbutting Sissy. Bailey Rae got three stitches, and Sissy had a chipped front tooth.

Sissy and Missy weren't identical twins anymore.

Mrs. Watson lingered over a wedding ring quilt and traced the tiny stitches, her fingers arthritic from decades of teaching piano. "We sure do miss seeing Winnie at the market, but I bet she's smiling down from heaven knowing you're here."

For now. "I'm not nearly woman enough to fill those floral Crocs of hers."

"Winnie would disagree." Mrs. Watson tucked her credit card into the reader and scrawled her signature with her finger on the screen. "Would you mind holding on to the quilt for me until I'm fixin' to leave? I'm supposed to meet my girls and their babies for lunch."

"Of course," Bailey Rae said, rubbing the scar in her eyebrow.

Libby waggled a wave. "If you see Freddie over yonder, could you send him back over with our lunch?"

Mrs. Watson turned, penciled eyebrow lifted. "Freddie?"

Libby frowned, her gray eyes searching as if the memories would materialize. "My boy . . . My boy . . . Keith."

Wrong name again? Libby was having a rough day. Bailey Rae considered calling Keith back to see if he should take his mother home.

"Excuse me," an unfamiliar female voice interrupted.

Bailey Rae held up her hand for the person to wait, scanning Libby's face for further signs of distress or disorientation. But the older woman seemed at peace, thumbing through one of the cookbooks, humming. The Freddie-Keith mix-up had already been forgotten.

Biting her lip, Bailey Rae willed away tears over losing this woman too, in a different way from Aunt Winnie. But a loss all the same. An end to the chapter that had started when the two women came to Bent Oak at the same time, responding to an ad for jobs at the paper mill.

Bailey Rae was more than ready for a fresh beginning of her own. She turned to her next customer. "Yes? If you don't see exactly what you're looking for here, I have more canned foods and quilts in the truck."

A dark-haired woman leaned closer, maybe in her early thirties, with a toddler girl hiding her tiny face against her mother's legs. The young woman looked like she hadn't gotten a full night's sleep in weeks. "I need your help."

Her words were so soft they were almost swallowed by the bustle of shoppers and echo of beach music.

"Sure. This is our price list. And I also have a legend map of the market stalls under here somewhere." Bailey Rae tugged a smaller bin out of a larger box.

"That's not what I meant." The woman's voice was louder, more insistent. Her daughter hugged a tattered blanket, rubbing an edge along her chin in comfort as she moved away from her mother's legs.

"All right." Bailey Rae rocked back on her heels. Given the dark circles under the woman's eyes, maybe lack of sleep was making the young mom edgy. "What can I do for you?"

The young mother flattened a palm on the stack of cookbooks. She shook loose her other hand from her daughter's vise grip and fished in her overstuffed hobo bag. Digging, she withdrew a wallet, sippy cup, a pack of cookies, until finally she tugged free a frayed book of some kind, a pair of socks fluttering to the ground. She eased it onto the scarred tabletop, the volume's cover an older, tattered version of the cookbooks Aunt Winnie had sold for decades.

"I need *help*," the woman repeated, patting the vintage binding, then extending her trembling hand toward the similar volume in Libby's grip. "And this led me here."

1971

"Winnie Ballard, be sure to hold on to this."

As I stood in a back room at the Bent Oak Public Library, I took the packet of papers from Annette Davis. My point of contact. The final stop in my journey.

At first glance, Annette resembled a kindergarten teacher or grandmother sort in her teal polyester pantsuit. Not someone people would suspect. Good. She patted my hand, and I didn't bother correcting her about needing comfort. It wasn't surprising that she would assume I was shaking in my battered sneakers.

Excitement and terror are close kin. Outwardly they resemble each other. Anticipation and fear both flip the stomach, set the heart racing, dilate the pupils, and accelerate breathing. So it wasn't any wonder that people would assume I was afraid. But I wasn't. Not anymore.

Mrs. Davis and I kept our voices low in this tiny storage space. A big rolling bin was full of returned library books, with three shelved carts beside it for sorting. We both sat at a table with hard wooden chairs. The worn and faded top was cluttered with a stack of film strips and a projector.

"Thank you," I said, for more than the stack of papers I fanned out on the Formica tabletop. A high school diploma, a driver's license, a Social Security card, and a birth certificate. I was now a year older, with a different birthday. "Can I ask how documents like this are possible?"

"You only need to know they'll hold up under scrutiny," Annette said in a voice that inspired trust.

"Thank you," I said again, such inadequate words. But the past month had been a lot to process. Sometimes I felt like I was still under the fog of drugs back in the hospital.

Stuck back under my husband's iron-fisted control.

"You should have all you need to complete the job application." Annette tipped her head toward the lone window that framed the view of the paper mill in the distance. The steel beast had recently expanded, advertising dozens of jobs, which offered the perfect cover for new residents. "Check them over. Memorize every detail so you don't pause when you're asked tomorrow morning."

And just that fast, Eloise was gone. Winnie was born.

Annette stepped back behind the book cart, swinging the door open. "Come with me. There's someone I want you to meet before you go to the boardinghouse. You can practice your introduction."

As I followed her past a row of microfiche readers and typewriters, I recited my new name in my head like a mantra. The library felt like a portal between my previous world and the one to come. The air was filled with the timeless, musty scent of old books, paper and leather seasoned by the oils of many hands. Those novels connected people who might never lay eyes on each other.

So how did I get here?

Luck. And a hefty dose of irony that when Phillip attempted to lock me away, he'd actually given me the key to my freedom in the form of a whisper from a cook in the cafeteria of the psychiatric hospital. The cook had escaped *her* past life thanks to a secret network that helped women leave abusive relationships. If I was interested, we could speak later.

Then, as if the conversation never happened, the woman pivoted to spoon mashed potatoes on the next tray. The following day at breakfast, I told her I wanted to have that conversation.

I never knew for sure why I decided to trust the word of a complete stranger, but I was desperate, and something about her story rang true. She told me about a network spanning the country, connected through the library system. And while she couldn't guarantee anything . . . I said yes. Hid in a food delivery truck. Faked a suicide on the beach.

Then started a monthlong, circuitous path meant to cover my tracks to the extent that even each link didn't know anything about the ones prior or yet to come. Sometimes, I had a companion for a single leg. But never the same person.

Now, Annette paused by the children's books section. At first, it appeared empty. After all, school was in session. The table and chairs were all low to the ground, like for kindergarteners. Then I saw them. A mother and a little boy who looked so much like her, he must have been her son.

Not too long ago, I would have been envious of any woman with a child of her own. I wouldn't have been able to see beyond that label of mother. And I definitely wouldn't have seen the vulnerable light in this woman's gray eyes or how her thin shoulders curved inward.

Or how her hands were pressed to a packet of papers on the Formica tabletop. A packet that looked suspiciously similar to mine.

In that moment I realized Annette had supplied more than a janitorial job at the paper mill and a boardinghouse room, she'd provided a friend. That simple connection nearly drove me to tears after so long in isolation, surrounded only by medical staff and people from *his* world, indoctrinated to see me through his distorted lens.

"Winnie," Annette said, "I would like for you to meet Libby Farrell. She's new to town as well and will be working at the paper mill."

"Hello, Libby. I'm Winnie Ballard." I spoke my new name for the first time, half expecting something big to happen, such as the floor opening up and swallowing me. Or people popping out from behind shelves and shouting, "Liar. Fake. Fraud." But it was easier than I thought. I slipped on the name like a new pair of shoes, so much more comfortable than the ones from before.

Libby extended a chapped hand, with a thin gold wedding band on her ring finger. "Nice to meet you. This little man is my son, Keith."

She motioned to the young boy sitting cross-legged on the ground, leaning back against a towering bookshelf. With a pristine stuffed Winnie-the-Pooh doll in his lap, Keith lifted a View-Master to his face and clicked through the circle of images. A stack of extra photo disks rested on the floor beside him.

Would we ever learn each other's names from before? Feel safe enough to trust each other with nuggets of our stories? I couldn't answer that. But I sensed that over the years we would need each other when something triggered memories, bad ones. We would depend on each other to stay sane. Annette was smart that way, knowing how to build a support system to sustain this new life.

Going to a counselor was out of the question for obvious reasons, and quite frankly, I'd had enough of that at the hospital.

"Keith," his mother called, and when he didn't respond, she touched his shoulder. He flinched. "Keith? Say hello to Miss Winnie."

He blinked fast, eyes wide and searching like someone waking up in the morning only to realize they'd forgotten where they were. Silently, he returned to his shiny red View-Master.

His mother smiled apologetically. "He's just tired."

"It's okay," I said. "Change is tough for everyone. I imagine it's especially overwhelming for a child."

My words worked no matter her past, while still protecting my own. I was learning a new language of sorts, speaking in code with benign-sounding phrases laden with undercurrents. The new teacher was this grandmotherly librarian who oversaw this portal full of words.

Had my grandmother ever been a part of changing someone's life this way? Taking such a risk for someone else? If so, she'd never let on.

Could she have, though? My grandmother who'd played cards with me and made pimento cheese sandwiches with the crust cut off. Then, like a whisper meant for library ears only, I realized my grandmother and Annette would not have been allowed to attend the same schools in the segregated South.

The thought hurt. "Mrs. Davis, I don't know how to thank you enough."

"You can't." Annette shook her head and gripped the handle of the rolling cart. "You can only pay it forward."

And we did.

CHAPTER THREE

2025

Bailey Rae eyed the stack of cookbooks on the corner of her vendor table. Confused didn't come close to describing this weird exchange. "Ma'am? You are?"

"My name is Gia." The young mother swallowed hard, as if sharing even her name were some Herculean task. "Gia Abernathy. My daughter and I need a place to stay. *This* led me here."

The woman's words knocked around inside Bailey Rae's head, jockeying for a place to land. Winnie's cookbook had led her here? Maybe she just meant Winnie's reputation for helping folks, even letting them pick out necessities from the overstocked barn. "There's a bed-and-breakfast right up the road. Reasonably priced. A cute little swing set in back. And they serve the best pancake breakfast."

"Not that kind of place." Her face flushed red, her dark eyes darting. "I need, uh, like a shelter."

"Oh, okay," Bailey Rae said, sitting up straighter. "We don't really have anything like that in Bent Oak, but I can ask around—"

"But *this* cookbook says . . ." Her words dwindled off on three quick breaths, the shallow kind.

"Mrs. Abernathy, I want to help you, if I can. Truly, I do." Seeing this mother and daughter sent her empathy into overdrive. She'd been in that little girl's shoes.

Leaving a home with nothing but a backpack after her mother fell out with another man. Warnings to stay quiet so as not to upset Yvonne's newest guy. And, in quiet times, sharing a sleeping bag in the back of the station wagon while Yvonne whispered reassurances that Bailey Rae would survive, just as she had as a kid. Not realizing that the real strength lay in breaking the cycle.

Thank heaven for Uncle Russell and Aunt Winnie, who'd taught her how to steer her life rather than be dragged along by the undertow of her mother's generational trauma. Now, though, she felt adrift without an anchor . . .

"I must have misunderstood." Gia gripped the tattered cookbook, her voice soft, each word separated by another of those hitchy breaths.

Bailey Rae shook off the past and focused on this woman's very present need. "I'm sorry if there's been a misunderstanding. Maybe you're looking for my aunt—Winnie Ballard?" Even saying her name out loud stirred the grief. "If so, I'm sorry, but my aunt passed away recently."

Libby tapped her cane against Bailey Rae's leg. "Loose lips sink ships."

"Luckily, Mrs. Libby, I don't know anything to be blabby about."

Gia frowned in confusion. "*Your* aunt?"

"Yes, ma'am." Bailey Rae nodded. "But since she's passed away . . ."

"Oh no. No, no, no, no . . ." Gia gasped, fidgeting and looking every which way like a bird about to take flight. Her agitation grew along with the rise of her voice.

Even Skeeter lifted his head with a whimper.

Gia clutched her daughter's hand and sagged back against the table, her breaths hitching faster and faster. One tear streamed down her face, then another.

The woman was fast on her way to a full-blown panic attack.

Libby stabbed her cane into the ground and pushed out of her wheelchair, grasping the edge of the table for extra balance as she made her way around the edge to Gia. "Breathe in, breathe out . . . slower.

That's it. Smell the flowers. Blow out the candle. Smell the flowers. Blow out the candle."

Aunt Winnie used to say the same when Yvonne would show up unannounced. Even at the memory, Bailey Rae's chest went tight all over again. Like a beast was parked on her rib cage. And the beast had a name. Fear. Fear that she would be hauled off in her mom's station wagon with everything they owned, headed to heaven only knew where. Sometimes sleeping in the back. Wasn't "camping" fun?

She breathed in the equivalent of a bouquet herself and blew out a few more candles, grounding herself in the present. Gia's fear mattered most now. Bailey Rae's was in the past.

Gia pressed her fingers against the center of her rib cage. "I have nowhere to go, and if Ian finds me . . . I'm scared of what he'll do."

Bailey Rae carried her chair around to the woman. Skeeter loped behind until he reached the end of his tether. "Take a moment to sit and catch your breath. Have you filed a police report?"

Libby snorted. "If you can get one of them over here. They're in Keystone Cops mode directing traffic after that wild pig incident. Thea still hasn't managed to convince her husband to put in another traffic light on Main Street."

What a time for Libby's memory to kick into overdrive.

Gia backed away a step, hitching her bag on her shoulder. "Never mind. I, um, shouldn't have bothered you."

"Hold your horses," Bailey Rae called, desperate for some Winnie-wisdom in navigating the woman's situation. "I'm sure I can figure something out."

Libby snorted again. *Cane stamp. Stamp.* "You're a short-order cook, not a superhero."

Bailey Rae bit back a smile and returned her attention to Gia. "Please wait. Let me text Officer Underwood and see if he can break free. He should be able to steer you toward available resources. And I'll give you my number as well."

It felt good to help in some way. Maybe not at a Winnie level, but assisting all the same. Bailey Rae scrolled through her cell phone until she found the contact info and tapped out a text. Then she grabbed a pen from a Mason jar and jotted her name and number on the back of a market map.

Her phone lit with a response from Officer Underwood that he was sending the game warden—Officer Martin Perez—her way.

Great. Maybe he could write her another ticket.

Sighing, she grabbed a rag doll for the child, channeling Winnie after all in doling out something from the pack-rat collection. The bright-orange yarn hair was rough against her fingertips, simultaneously soothing and abrasive. Like her memories of playing with one so similar, crafted by Libby from a basket of clothes that couldn't be mended.

Everywhere she turned, those phantoms from the past blocked her path forward.

Kneeling, Bailey Rae passed over the doll, yarn hair trailing. "Here you go, sweetie. A new friend to keep you company."

Wide eyes swept upward to her mom. Silent.

Perfectly normal to ask permission from her mother. But the lack of excitement on that wan little face? Far from normal.

The woman dragged in a ragged breath and nodded to her child. "Cricket, be sure to say thank you to the nice lady."

Bailey Rae stood, feeling helpless—a bit like that gum on a boot-heel. She'd done everything she could for the woman. Yeah, Aunt Winnie probably would have done more, but Bailey Rae wasn't like her aunt.

The metaphorical beast on her chest turned into an elephant.

She was right to leave, to put this town and all the elephants behind her. Only then would she be free—able—to become a person worthy of Winnie's second chance. Because right now, Bailey Rae fell way short of the mark.

Martin Perez's favorite days on the job involved no people. Only animals, because animals didn't lie. Today had been flush with people and only one wild pig. And the "people time" wasn't close to an end.

Martin jogged past booths, weaving through the crowd, eyes locked on the cluster of folks around Bailey Rae Rigby's spot. He had hoped his job as a game warden in this sleepy little town would be low key and peaceful, the perfect place to recover from the nightmares spawned by his military career. No such luck.

In theory, he understood that in addition to protecting the wilderness, his job description included educating the public, assisting in backcountry search and rescues, and partnering with law enforcement. He just hadn't expected it all to happen in the same day.

He'd barely had time to shower this morning after spending most of the night wading through alligator-infested swamps searching for a missing boater before heading over to man the SCDNR information booth at today's market.

Then the wild pig happened.

He didn't draw a gun often on the job as a game warden. Not like back in his days as an army cop. But when he did, it took him a good bit of time to clear the numb feeling. Adrenaline had a way of searing nerve endings until all sensation was gone.

Slowing as he drew closer, Martin could sense something was off about the cluster of people. There was a buzz, an energy he recognized on a cellular level from his military days.

Bailey Rae and Mrs. Libby were comforting a dark-haired woman who had tear streaks on her face. A child clung to her mother with one hand, gripping a rag doll in the other not as a treasure but more like a lifeline.

Maybe the mom was just stressed from struggling with a fractious kid. He exhaled. Hard. His instincts must be off this afternoon.

"Good afternoon, Bailey Rae. Mrs. Libby." He nodded to each. "What can I help you ladies with?"

Born in Arizona, he'd given up on understanding why people in the South called anyone older by their first name plus Mr., Mrs., Ms., or Miss. But rarely a surname. It was just the way things were done around here, and to say it differently would only add another unspoken barrier between him and the community he served.

Bailey Rae glanced his way, her auburn ponytail swinging. The softness in her expression faded as she crossed her arms over her chest defensively, looking far too snooty for a woman wearing muddy hiking boots, cutoff jean shorts, and a concert T-shirt two sizes too big. On the fishing ticket day, she'd worn one too. Tina Turner, then. Today, Bruce Springsteen, the Boss.

He shrugged off the distracting thought.

The young mother shook her head quickly and scooped her daughter up onto her hip. "Nothing, we're fine."

Libby jabbed her cane against the ground for balance. "Wait, don't go. You needed assistance, and I've found it for you in the shape of this fine-looking young conservation officer. Officer Perez, this lady needs your assistance."

"Is something wrong, ma'am?"

The young woman looked back and forth between them, tucking her daughter closer to her side. "We're fine. Just asking for directions. I'll just be going."

Bailey Rae stepped closer and touched the woman's elbow with only a fingertip. "Hold on, Gia. This is Martin Perez—he's a game warden. The police officer I reached out to assured me you can trust him."

Was that a hint of resignation about the "trust" part? She must still be holding a grudge over the ticket. Rules mattered, though. He'd learned that lesson the hard way right before he'd left the army.

Then her words registered deeper. Why would it matter that the young mother could trust him? He reassessed the stranger's tear-streaked face and found . . . fear. Not just the afraid-of-bugs kind. More of a terrified-of-snakes sort.

Libby inched back into her wheelchair, cane across her knees. "She needs our help relocating."

Relocating?

The fear in her—Gia's—eyes shouted as loudly as the faint bruise he could now see blooming on her cheek. He measured his words, not wanting to alert the child. "Ma'am, is what Mrs. Libby's saying true? Are you in need of emergency lodgings?"

Gia chewed her bottom lip, nodding. "For my daughter and me. Just somewhere to stay tonight, until things, um, settle down at home."

His gaze skated to the little girl as well, and while he saw no sign of outward injury, her expression was another story. Withdrawn. Nervous.

Libby tugged her cell phone from a quilted pouch on the side of her chair. "I can call the Lodge-Inn to see about a vacancy. You'll want to use a different name, preferably pay cash—for the sake of getting that cooling-down time." Her face creased with confusion for a moment before she said, "I watch a lot of true crime and 'most wanted' shows."

Not exactly the television lineup he would have expected from sweet little Libby.

Gia clutched her purse in a white-knuckled grip. "How much does a room at the Lodge-Inn cost?"

Since he'd heard that the Lodge-Inn had closed five years ago due to unpaid back taxes, Martin opted for a more affordable answer. "There's a women's shelter in the next county. They'll be better equipped to steer you in the right direction. I can call ahead and see if there's a room available."

Gia exhaled. Hard. "Thank you."

Mrs. Libby tapped the table for attention. "Be sure to park your car somewhere else so he can't find you."

Libby was one of a kind. Martin smothered a wry smile and looked back at Gia. "Have you filed a police report? If not, I can give you a ride to the station first—"

"Martin," Bailey Rae interrupted, "I think we're overwhelming Mrs. Abernathy."

Abernathy? The same surname as the missing fisherman he'd been wading through swamps trying to locate. His instincts ramped into overdrive. "Any relation to Owen Abernathy?"

Her tear-streaked face paled.

The little girl popped her thumb out of her mouth. "Uncle Owen?"

"Ma'am?" Martin asked.

"He's my husband's brother," Gia answered softly. Defensively.

He wanted to wrangle a police officer over here ASAP to help but worried the woman might bolt if he left. "Did you know he went missing a few days back while fishing?"

"Owen's probably just on a camping trip," Gia answered with a smile that didn't come close to reaching her eyes. "He always turns up after a few days."

Logical. But also coincidental. He wondered what more she might share if given the time. All the more reason to personally escort her to the shelter. They might have more luck persuading her to speak with the authorities.

At the very least, he could pass along her location to the police in case they had questions—or concerns. "Sounds like your family's been going through a lot lately. Maybe you and your husband would benefit from a breather."

"Ian and I could use a break, that's for sure," Gia said with a weak smile, her eyes darting to Bailey Rae and Libby. "It's so hard loving the wrong man."

Silently, Libby clasped her hand.

Martin wasn't much good when it came to comfort, but he could tackle logistics.

"How about I call that shelter. I'll even show you where it is. You can follow me." He glanced at Libby, then back to Gia Abernathy again. "And if you need to shuffle where you park, I'll be on hand."

Gia nodded fast, her throat moving in a long swallow. "Thank you. Yes, please."

As he pulled out his phone to place the call, Bailey Rae mouthed *thank you.*

He believed she meant it. But he doubted it softened her grudge.

༄

Three hours later, after dropping off her trailer and Skeeter back at the farm, Bailey Rae knew she should rest easy now that she'd passed over Gia Abernathy to Martin Perez's care.

But she had never been good at putting things out of her mind and moving on. She had worn out that mental hamster wheel far too often to believe otherwise.

Her only defense? Run faster until she found the answers she sought—or she crashed.

Her odds today were pretty even on the outcome.

So here she stood outside the Fill 'Er Up Café in search of answers from Thea and June, who—according to Thea's husband—had come here a half hour ago. Bailey Rae pushed through the front door, bell chiming her arrival to a packed clientele, dining on the supper specials.

Chicken-fried steak or chicken pot pie. Healthy-heart meals were tough to come by in Bent Oak, where deep-frying, homemade biscuits, and real butter reigned supreme. As an employee, she knew the menu by heart, both from waitressing and working as a backup short-order cook.

The old gas station had been renovated into a restaurant. People in Bent Oak were thrifty, the ultimate in upcycling. Offices in back had been converted into a restaurant-grade kitchen, with the former garage transformed into a dining space with soaring ceilings.

During the fair-weather days, the garage door opened to let a fresh river breeze sweep through as if celebrating the remnants of spring before summer sealed the space for air-conditioning. Ceiling fans swirled overhead. Rusty hubcaps and custom license plates that filled in the bare spots showcased the local who's who.

This was more than just a restaurant to her, more than just a place to earn a buck. The eatery had once been the town's only gas station, owned by Uncle Russell's grandparents. They'd both died before she arrived in Bent Oak, but she'd spent hours here on Saturdays passing tools while Russell rebuilt his latest vehicle for dirt track racing. He would give her change for a cold Coke from the bright-red machine while he made use of the garage's lift. She remembered most, though, how he talked to her, drawing out more than a yes or no answer from her, like her opinions mattered on everything from the best fishing currents to the upcoming town council election to her favorite boy band crush.

For a girl who'd been in survival mode for too long, it had felt indulgent to discuss something other than how to make it to the next day.

About twelve years ago, the place had been sold when a chain gas station with automatic card readers put old-school establishments out of business. Aunt Winnie had told Uncle Russell that only people mattered, not places. Still, her steely eyes carried a sadness when passing over the keys, maybe even a hint of tears—quickly gone, of course. Aunt Winnie hadn't been a crier.

To this day, the scent of motor oil made her think of Uncle Russell and self-respect.

Scanning the dining space, she finally located Thea and June in the far back corner. Not their normal table in the center. Their heads were bent close together as they talked, their food uneaten in front of them.

Bailey Rae made a beeline toward them. The familiar faces provided an obstacle course of greetings from a community where chatting without rushing was considered a commandment Moses must have forgotten to haul down from Mount Sinai. Right up there along with *Thou shalt not leave the saltshaker off the table.*

"Mrs. Thea and Miss June," Bailey Rae said, gripping the back of a chair, "do you mind if I join you?"

The two women bolted apart like they'd been discussing state secrets—or the ingredients to Thea's lemon bars, something she shared with no one but her closest friends. Even Bailey Rae hadn't been privy to the recipe.

"Please do." Thea moved her purse from the chair to hang on the back of her own seat. "How did the rest of the day go at the market?"

June patted the empty chair. "You'll have to forgive me if I hope the sale was a bust and you have to stay in Bent Oak." She raised her hands. "I'm just telling it like it is."

"So when you mis-tagged things with an extra digit in the price, it wasn't an accident?" Bailey Rae asked wryly and received a teasing wink from June. "Thankfully, I corrected them after a customer questioned why a Mason jar full of peaches cost fifty dollars."

Thea covered her hand. "Just know we love you and only want the best for you. I'll be sure to keep a closer watch over June when we help you get ready for next Saturday's sale."

"Speaking of the inventory . . ." Moving on to the real reason for seeking them out, Bailey Rae reached into her leather backpack and fished around for the cookbook she'd tucked away earlier. "What's the deal with this?"

Their silence lasted a beat too long.

"Mrs. Thea? I know your hearing works just fine."

"I'm not sure what you mean. It's just local recipes." Thea pressed her fingers to her chest. "All but my lemon bars, of course. Perhaps it's time I shared it with you."

Bailey Rae wasn't diverted that easily. "But Aunt Winnie has so very many copies. Isn't that strange?"

June smirked, tucking a strand of pink hair behind her ear. "Maybe they weren't very popular. Or she over-ordered. You know how Winnie could be with her collections."

Reasonable explanations. Any other day she wouldn't have thought twice. Something had changed, though, when that woman approached her booth at the market, followed by Libby's stranger-than-usual responses.

Now Thea and June's evasiveness made her all the more suspicious. "There was a ruckus at the market earlier. A young mother showed up with a vintage version insisting there was some kind of hidden message directing her here for help."

Both women across from her went silent. Longer than the silence over the cookbooks. Thea wiped a water spot on the table. June fidgeted with a fork, scraping the white gravy off her chicken-fried steak.

Bailey Rae leaned on her elbows, dropping her voice. "Do you have any idea what she's talking about?"

Thea returned her napkin to her lap. "Maybe she just needed some of Winnie's special canned goods before they're sold out. The cookbook does promote them."

A logical assumption, except there was tension sprinkled as heavily as salt at a potluck. "She's leaving her husband, and she is clearly afraid."

An understatement.

June rested her fork on the edge of her plate. "That must have been so upsetting for you after all you and your mother went through."

Bailey Rae would have applauded June's pivot if it had been directed at anyone else. But neither woman had answered the question. "I'm fine. Thank you. Just curious. Libby seemed to understand what the woman meant, and I would have asked questions to clarify, but Keith rushed Libby away when he arrived to pick her up."

Which was just as well, given Libby's memory issues. Thea and June were the better choices to ask.

"Libby's confused," Thea said, shaking her head as she stabbed a fork into the middle of her chicken pot pie, pushing the crust into the soft insides. "That's a sad reality of her Alzheimer's disease."

June pressed her fingers to the edges of her eyes and cleared her throat. "Um, what happened to the young woman? The one with the cookbook?"

A waitress angled in, placing a glass of sweet tea in front of Bailey Rae. Kinsley was a new hire, a teenager working evenings and weekends who hadn't mastered the art of discerning when not to interrupt patrons. "Hey there, anybody need refills? Bailey Rae, can I get your order? We're running low on the pot pie, but I can snag one for you if you want."

"Nothing to eat," Bailey Rae said. "Just the sweet tea."

"Or napkins?" Kinsley pressed. "Does your dinner taste okay—"

Thea cut in. "We're fine, dear."

The teen also hadn't found the balance of how too much attention could be just as bad as not enough. Bailey Rae remembered well from her own early days waitressing here at the Fill 'Er Up Café.

"Thank you, Kinsley," Bailey Rae said, waiting for the girl to leave before turning back. "Martin Perez is escorting her and her daughter to a women's shelter. He's going to text me once they're settled."

Thea frowned. "Not the police?"

"The woman was nervous about the authorities." Bailey Rae squeezed a lemon slice into the glass before sliding in the straw and stirring through the ice. "And regardless, they were otherwise occupied with fallout from the wild pig incident."

"Hmmm," Thea said. "Good, good. So, how did you do on your sales today?"

"The inventory sold better than I'd hoped, but still a ways from my goal. I'll get there, though, thanks to all your help sorting. Before you know it, there will be nothing left keeping me in Bent Oak."

Bailey Rae leaned to sip her tea, the cool drink washing away grit, if not the tension. The tea wasn't as good as Aunt Winnie's and it wasn't in a Mason jar, but it made Bailey Rae think of her all the same—conversation and wisdom shared over a scarred table.

What would her aunt have done this morning to help Gia Abernathy and her daughter? Would Winnie have understood what the woman meant about the cookbook?

As Bailey Rae looked at two of her aunt's best friends across the table, she wished she could ask them and trust that they would give her an honest answer. But sure as she was sitting here sipping sweet tea through a soggy paper straw, Bailey Rae knew they were hiding something.

And no one could make either of these two women say or do something unless they chose. Best to let them keep their secrets and focus on tidying up the remains of her life in Bent Oak.

Her phone buzzed from inside her backpack with an incoming text. She abandoned her tea and snatched up her bag. "That must be Officer Perez with an update."

Thea quirked a perfectly penciled eyebrow. "Nothing at all holding you in Bent Oak, eh?"

CHAPTER FOUR

1971

I'd attended private schools and an elite liberal arts college as Eloise.

Those elocution and etiquette classes, the art history and chemistry of glassblowing courses—well, they sure hadn't prepared me for scrubbing toilets and mopping concrete floors for eight to ten hours a day. But that was my world now as Winnie, working in janitorial services at the paper mill.

For the first time in my life, I was paying my own bills, tougher than I'd been led to believe in Home Economics. I consoled myself with reassurances things would improve.

Surely, they would?

Standing in the abandoned break room in my ugly brown uniform, I peeled off my yellow rubber gloves, wincing at the sting to my cracked fingertips. During my first week, I'd bypassed using the gloves. Out of ignorance? Or an overloaded brain? I wasn't certain, but the error had been self-critiquing.

And another thing I'd learned? Lotion made my raw skin sting worse. Worse than even the burns I'd suffered during my career with glassblowing . . . Although could it be called a career when I gave away most of my work as gifts to friends and for charity auctions?

I threw the gloves into the murky water, where they filled before gurgling to the bottom. When Annette told me I would have a job in the paper mill, I'd envisioned mastering a machine with a massive roll of freshly pressed vellum. Or a device that created pulp from the tree, scents filling the air with the earthy promise of the stories those sheets would hold. Perhaps I could even sketch on scraps to express my art instead of via glass.

Not my lucky day.

Gripping the wooden mop handle that gave me splinters, I pushed the bucket across the cracked linoleum.

Libby lounged in the open door to the break room, a strand of limp brown hair escaping her bun. "You've never been poor before, have you."

"Pardon me?" Then, understanding, I held up my hands. "Oh. Because I should have worn the rubber gloves?"

"In part." Libby leaned toward the bucket, pointing. "Here's the wringer. You don't have to shove your hands into the solution."

"That makes sense." My parents had bragged about my talent, even my intelligence. Clearly, they'd been delusional.

Libby edged in front of me and demonstrated the handle system for squeezing excess water from the mop. "That doesn't make this easy. But it helps."

Nodding, I gathered up two dirty napkins and a half-full Styrofoam cup of coffee off the table and pitched them into the corner trash can. Then grabbed the bottled cleaner and spritzed down a tabletop before swiping a rag over the remaining evidence of the second-shift crowd. A splatter of ketchup. A thin pickle that had calcified to the Formica.

As a child, I'd prided myself on always saying thank you and cleaning up after myself. Like I was doing others some kind of favor rather than just pulling my own weight. Stepping into the bright glare of enlightenment burned as much as that cleanser that I'd grown to dread.

I didn't want to go back to my old life. Yet as far as making a plan to move beyond my current state? I couldn't envision more than the beauty of my lumpy mattress at the end of the day. "Any other tips?"

"Don't mix bleach and ammonia." Libby tapped the cleaners on my cart. "The fumes can make you pass out. Or even kill you."

"I'll keep that in mind." Although passing out didn't sound like a bad idea, I was far from suicidal, in spite of what Phillip would have others think. "Where does your son stay while you work?"

The question had seemed natural, but the moment I spoke I regretted the intrusive words. Would she answer? I'd never been a part of secrets that had such serious implications. But she was my only "friend," and so far as I could tell, I was her only one too. "Sorry if that was nosy. My mother always said the best way to have a good friend was to be one."

"Not nosy at all." Libby emptied a small trash can into the larger bag attached to the cart, helping me finish my list even though she had to be exhausted from her own. "Keith will be in school for a few more days finishing up first grade. I'm still figuring out what to do with him for the summer. He's been having a tough-enough time adjusting."

I didn't have a clue what to suggest. Most of my friends never held a job, and the few who did were teachers who'd usually dropped off their children with their mothers. "I'll help however I can."

"Thank you. Annette has information on some babysitters that I pray I can afford." She crossed her arms, hugging herself. "It's hard leaving him. His dad used to say that I . . . Never mind."

And just that quickly, questions could lead to slipups. I grabbed the handle of my cart. "It's time to clock out."

Smiling, Libby raised her hands. "Praise the Lord and pass the gravy."

We put away our supplies in the janitors' closet, hung up our uniform smocks, and stepped into the factory still in full swing. The facility operated on three shifts, never silent. The whine and grind of the machinery reverberated in my ear, but I was growing accustomed to the point where I could hold a brief conversation.

The factory felt like a beast that swallowed people whole, then spit them back out at the end of a shift, sweaty and wrung out. Except with an excitement to be free that reanimated them by the time they cleared the parking lot.

I pitched the garbage bag into a dumpster by the loading dock. The thud launched a swarm of flies. "What are you going to do with the rest of your afternoon?"

"Pick up Keith from school," she said as we paused for a slow-moving forklift heading toward the line of trucks. "Then we'll head down to the riverbank to do his homework and eat peanut butter and jelly sandwiches."

"I love the water." The beach, specifically. But I couldn't afford the bus fare to Myrtle Beach, even if I'd felt ready to leave the security of my new hometown. I pulled a floppy hat from my sack to ward off sunburn. Although, more than just following old cautions from my mother about preventing freckles, the hat also offered a hint of disguise I welcomed.

"You should join us sometime."

"Thanks. Someday." I needed more time to trust that I wouldn't let something slip.

Halfway across the lot, Libby hefted her satchel higher on her shoulder, fat folds of discarded paper scraps sticking out. She pressed her elbow against them to keep them from slipping free. "I'm not a thief. I made sure it's okay to take the scraps. I use the throwaways for Keith to practice his alphabet, and Annette gave us a used Spirograph. This way he doesn't waste his school notebook."

"Smart and thrifty idea, Mama Libby."

I'd written countless letters, invitations, and thank-you notes over the years, never once giving thought to how that paper came into being. Sure, I understood it came from trees. But I'd missed the intricacy of the process, the intensity of the labor for something so whispery thin. Like glassblowing, there was an art to making paper with the synchronicity of the workers choreographed to perfection inside that building.

Yet for most, without the joy of art. That emotion had been smashed out like waste squeezed from the pulp.

As the ringing in my ears faded, shouts swelled just past a line of trucks near the gate. An altercation of some kind. Men getting heated. Libby stepped back, clutching her bag, her eyes darting as if scrambling for an escape route. Except there wasn't one other than returning into the paper mill, then taking another exit on the far side of the labyrinth. Libby lurched toward the building.

My aching feet protested over the extra steps. I clasped her elbow. "Come on. We'll just walk fast along the edge of the fence. Whatever's going on over there is none of our business."

Libby chewed her bottom lip before nodding. Over the past week I'd figured out that Libby was a follower by nature.

Her wariness made me wonder, though, and worry. What danger had made her run with a child in tow? She claimed to be a widow. Except she never mentioned friends or family to help with Keith, and I didn't ask since I didn't want her prying too deeply into my past. No doubt she felt the same about her secrets. I needed more time to practice this new way of communicating.

Later, though, because things were escalating in the parking lot shouting match.

The barked taunts grew louder, a mixture of "she's mine" and "not anymore," followed by "keep your hands off my girl or I'll . . ." Each sentence was punctuated by a shove. My nerves burned from a cocktail of anxiety and adrenaline.

A half dozen others egged on the pair with an array of "you tell him" and "kick his ass." Figured the argument was about a woman.

And then the fists flew.

Full-on violence hadn't been a part of my world before. Battles were waged through the power of money, social influence, and as a last resort, the court. My only experience with physical fights—beyond playground scrapping—occurred when my cousin got pregnant in the eleventh grade and Uncle Cecil punched her bony boyfriend.

The Carlisle family reunion probably hadn't been the wisest time to announce their impending parenthood.

Carlisle.

Just that fast my maiden name popped into my head when I needed to erase it for good. No mistakes allowed or I could end up back in that institution. My cousin had been sent to "boarding school" in California. Not the first of our set to disappear for around nine months.

How had I missed the pattern of women being shuttled away when they became a problem?

I clutched Libby's arm harder and walked faster along the pavement, past an eighteen-wheeler and the forklift.

"Ladies, you'd best stand back," a deep voice echoed from inside the eighteen-wheeler's cargo hold as his steps thundered along the metal truck bed.

Another man called to us from the forklift as he leaped down. "Stay right there while we calm those fellas down."

The first guy emerged from the cargo hold and the two men converged, advancing toward the fight like the lead cops in *The Mod Squad*, except without Peggy Lipton. While I wasn't at all interested in auditioning for that Peggy role, I couldn't help but admire the view.

Both were around my age and wore paper mill uniform shirts with reflective vests. Forklift Guy had a head full of loose blond curls and looked like something straight out of a college fraternity. Truck Fellow, with his short Afro, had a long-legged stride that broadcast calm and confidence.

How long had it been since I'd allowed myself to look at a man other than Phillip? The Eloise part of me shouted a warning not to notice anyone who wasn't my husband. In spite of the whole "free love movement," married women weren't supposed to gawk at other men.

The Winnie part of me, however, insisted there was no harm in looking. Only looking. The last thing I needed or wanted was a man in my life. Experience told me the outcome would be worse than mixing bleach and ammonia.

Distance would protect me from the fumes.

Libby and I skirted the eighteen-wheeler, continuing our trek toward the exit gate leading to Main Street, me half dragging her as she cowered at every shout. With my peripheral vision, I kept track of the altercation being broken up by the *Mod Squad* duo talking everyone down.

Forklift Guy's voice rode the muggy breeze. "If you two intend to start this up again, you need to wait until you're off my father's property."

The owner of the paper mill had his son working on the loading dock? Surprising. And intriguing. Making me curious to know more about these two guys.

But now *Libby* was dragging *me*. Eager to leave work? Or the argument? Either way, she wanted no part of taking in how the two men calmed and dispersed the crowd with just their words. That kind of energy was mesmerizing after so long living a life full of tension and walking on eggshells.

As I reached the gate, a lean brown hand pushed it open for us. Libby clutched my elbow tighter.

I turned to say thanks and found the truck guy working the latch.

"It sticks sometimes," he said, his deep voice even warmer up close. "You may want to clear out of here quickly in case they resume their disagreement over a lady friend."

"Thank you." I read the last name stitched on his shirt. Mr. Davis. Related to Annette? Although Davis was a common surname around here. "That was an impressive job of crowd control, Mr. Davis."

His smile creased dimples into his cheeks. "Mr. Davis was my daddy and grandpa. Just call me Russell."

2025

Bailey Rae lined jars of fresh spices along the counter, separating the unopened ones from the others. The sealed containers she could sell. The others would go with her to Myrtle Beach for cooking in the food truck.

The dark walls of the farmhouse-cabin were closing in on her, and she looked forward to the open skies of a seaside home. Sorting and pricing went slower today without help. According to Keith, Libby had been even more disoriented than usual since the episode with Gia and her daughter at the market. He was keeping his mother close to home for a while, with Thea and June's assistance.

Reaching into a cabinet, she pulled down jars of canned green beans, checking the dates on each. Maybe she should donate some to the local food bank, let it feed those who needed it more, like with the wild pig—

Skeeter bolted to his feet seconds before a knock sounded outside the mudroom, and she scratched the hound behind the ears. He made a fine security system.

His nails clicked along the hardwood floors as he walked beside her through the kitchen and into the living room. Already the space looked sparser without all the clutter, each sale at the market and trip to the dump ridding her of another tie to the town.

Opening the cabin door, Bailey Rae found . . .

"Good morning, Officer Perez. Are you here to give me another ticket for harming Mother Nature?"

He didn't smile. "Not unless you've started a personal compost pile in the woods for all the clutter on this porch."

The implied criticism stung. She'd been up until two in the morning boxing linens to donate and placing them outside to load in the truck later.

"That would be so noticeable, even a satellite could register the pile. But no worries, Officer, they're all going to charity, not illegal dumping in the forest." She waved Skeeter outside to stretch his legs, joining Martin on the planked porch. An old ceiling fan wobbled overhead, barely stirring the muggy morning air. "So what *does* bring you out this way?"

"I'm afraid I have some bad news." He tugged the brim of his uniform ball-cap. "It's about Mrs. Abernathy."

The air rushed from her lungs, from worry *and* guilt. She hadn't thought of the woman and her child much at all once Martin texted that they were settled at the shelter.

"Come sit and tell me, please." She motioned to the two rockers, quickly moving aside a crate of old towels. "What happened?"

Sitting, he swiped off his hat and rested it on his knee. "The police notified me this morning. I'm afraid Ian Abernathy located the shelter and waited outside for his wife. He attacked her"—he lifted a hand quickly—"but she's alive."

"And Cricket?" She sank into the rocker, thinking of the way the child had clutched the rag doll. The rush of the river in the distance echoed the roaring in her ears.

"The little girl was inside the shelter with the other children, so thankfully he wasn't able to get to her," he said, fidgeting with the cap on his knee. "It appears Abernathy had been staking out the place, and when Gia stepped outside for a breath of fresh air, he made his move."

More of that guilt twisted her gut, along with a hefty dose of fear. "How bad is it? I know you said she's alive, but you wouldn't be here unless it was really bad."

"Gia's in the hospital. Broken ribs. Fractured eye socket. Extensive bruising," he detailed, his voice low and professional. Only the tic in the corner of one eye hinted at a deeper frustration. "There were two witnesses, but Abernathy got away before the police arrived."

Bile burned her throat. She understood all too well what the kid must be feeling, the confusion of being displaced from everything familiar, even if the familiar had been dangerous.

"Where's Cricket?"

"For now, Cricket is with the shelter's childcare. A social worker will be taking over soon, though."

The relief lasted for only one long exhale. She couldn't shake the sense this was her fault. Her problem to fix. "I have to do something. She came to me for help, and I just . . ."

"And you offered her more than her own family managed."

At any other time she might have appreciated the praise from someone who'd judged her rule breaking with his ticket book. Not today, though.

"Except what I did wasn't enough." She gripped the arms of the rocker. Clearly, Gia had expected Winnie to help. "I know Aunt Winnie would have found a way to do more."

"It's in the hands of the authorities now." He slid his hat from his knee back onto his head.

"That doesn't mean I can just look away. Wait here." She bolted to her feet and into the house.

"What are you doing?" He trailed, hovering in the doorway.

"Putting together some things for her to have at the hospital." She grabbed an oversize canvas tote from a hook by the door, one of Winnie's bags, then continued on to the kitchen, opening cabinets for snacks. Granola bars. A jar of nuts. "She needs to know someone cares, even a stranger. Maybe there's something more I can do after all. I'll never know if I don't try."

Next, she dug through a box marked DONATE on the sofa, sifting and sorting. Socks. Slippers. A gently used jogging suit. A zipper pouch with hotel toiletries.

"Bailey Rae, hold on." Martin rested a gentle but firm hand on her arm. "I'm sure the hospital's counseling staff will connect Gia with services for her and her daughter once she's released—"

"Yet look where she is now." Standing, she hitched the stuffed bag onto her shoulder and met him nose to nose. The woman's words about the pain of loving the wrong man haunted her. "I know they did their best and this isn't the shelter's fault. But something different has to be done or who knows what will happen next?"

Would Winnie be disappointed in her for not doing more at the outset?

"Inserting yourself into a domestic-violence situation can be dangerous." He planted his feet as if blocking the doorway would make a difference.

"I'm well aware." She wasn't backing down. This was too personal.

Their standoff lasted for at least a half dozen heartbeats. Long enough for her to catch a whiff of his earthy scent. She tightened her grip on the bag. Skeeter nosed open the screened door, which closed after him with a slam that broke the spell.

"Fine. But I'm driving you," Martin said, sighing in exasperation. "While you finish with whatever you're packing, I'll get the air conditioner running in the truck."

CHAPTER FIVE

2025

Window down, Bailey Rae drew in deep breaths scented with evergreens and marsh as Martin drove. Yet she was still shaking inside, for both Gia and Cricket. She hated thinking about what that woman and her daughter had been through in the past twenty-four hours.

Except the nerves ran deeper. Because her own past was still dogging her today with memories she'd pushed to the far corners of her mind. She hadn't even bothered arguing with Martin about going on her own. She wasn't a fool.

Some of her mother's boyfriends had been better than others. Like Darren, who brought different board games for them all to play together. And George, who planned picnics with fast food at the park.

But the others? She didn't even want to think of their names. The ones who threw furniture, fists, and words that had the power to break her mother as much as the violence. She could still hear the shouts that echoed even with her hands over ears while she hid under a table, in a closet, or on a perch in a tree.

Clutching one of Winnie's old canvas bags in her lap, Bailey Rae traced the stitching with one finger. Had she shied away from helping Gia initially because of those memories? Unwilling to get involved in a spiral of hurt she understood all too well? Not much of a tribute to all that Aunt Winnie had done for her.

Even now, she could almost hear her aunt's voice nudging her to mind her manners. "Hey, uh, Martin? Thank you for coming to tell me about Gia, and for driving me over to see her. I'm sorry if I came off a bit . . . brusque back at the cabin."

"No need to thank me," he said with a quick dip of his beard-stubbled chin. "I'll rest better knowing you're not out there running around half-cocked, putting yourself in danger."

"I retract my apology."

He half smiled, staying silent as the pickup powered along the two-lane county road, lined with dense pines, trunks skinny as they crowded each other reaching for sunlight.

Hugging the bag tighter, she looked around the truck cab, never very comfortable with lengthy silences. The unknown rarely boded well. She turned up the radio just as a Chris Stapleton tune blended into a Kane Brown number.

She tapped her toe in time until finally she couldn't stand the silence between them any longer. She turned down the radio. "I know this bag may seem kind of silly to you. But when I was a kid, something like this would have meant the world. My mom was in a similar situation to Gia's, except because my mother was an addict, it kept happening."

"I'm sorry to hear that," he said with genuine sympathy.

"It's how I ended up with Aunt Winnie. She's not my biological relative. She just helped my mom out a few times, and somehow I ended up sticking around."

"Where's your mother now?" he asked, easing off the gas as a cow crossed the road, taking its sweet time while the rest of the herd bellowed from the pasture.

"She's dead." Her gut knotted with the familiar mix of sadness and anger. "About eighteen months after the last time she dropped me off. She was addicted to drugs, alcohol, and men."

"I didn't know that about your past. That's rough."

Grieving the loss of someone who'd already disappeared had been strange, and she hadn't been adept at regulating her emotions in those days. She hadn't cried like expected—instead she'd raged at the simplest of perceived injustices. Like taking her plate to the sink. Extra homework. A cross word from the Watson twins.

Until one day, while canning squash, Winnie talked about missing her own parents. She'd shared a simple memory of being mad at her father over where to go to school and how difficult it had been to forgive him, even though she loved him. Winnie had never spoken much about her past before that, so the impact hit hard. Her own memories—the good ones—had bubbled to the surface that day, allowing her to begin grieving her mom.

"I'm not looking for sympathy, Martin." Then or now. "Just relaying facts. I don't know how much you've heard about my aunt, but she helped a lot of women and kids over the years, people who were down on their luck."

"I've heard some stories. No doubt, her passing left a hole in the community."

Her gaze tracked the four-rail fence alongside the road as they sped into the next town. "More than you can imagine. I remember this one time a mom and her two sons came to stay with us, food was disappearing, and Aunt Winnie couldn't figure out where it was going." She tapped the box of granola bars sticking out of the top of the canvas sack. "For the longest while, she thought it was me. She kept telling me that even if I'd taken the food, it would be okay."

Bailey Rae shifted the canvas bag to the seat, wishing the knot in her gut could be as easily shuffled away. "Then when they left, we found all the food wrappers under the bunk beds—Pop-Tarts, crackers, granola bars. Aunt Winnie said kids who've been starved have food issues. I had a lot of struggles in those times I lived with my mom, and while we certainly didn't have lots of money, I wasn't starved."

She pushed aside thoughts of the nights she'd gone to bed hungry. She didn't want to think about what her mother may have done to provide what she did. The thought alone lent dimensions to her mom she hadn't considered before. Had Yvonne been a prostitute as well as an addict who happened to provide for her kid? Or had providing for her kid pushed her into prostitution, leading her to addiction to cope?

Martin glanced over at her fast before returning his attention to the road. "Sounds like a lot for a kid. For an adult, even. That explains your tough exterior."

Was that what he saw when he looked at her?

She almost asked him to expand on the idea, but that felt self-indulgent, or even compliment seeking. So instead, she touched a military patch of some sort Velcroed to the visor. "What's the deal with this? Do you have a family member or friend in the service?"

Or a girlfriend?

He flipped the visor, hiding the patch. "I used to serve in the army, as an MP—military police."

"And now you're a conservation officer? Why not a cop? Seems like a more logical transition."

"I like the peace out here."

"That's it?" After all she'd shared? "There are plenty of other careers that offer silence—with fewer mosquito bites."

He quirked a dark eyebrow. "I got bit by far worse overseas."

"Compared to mosquitoes in the South?" She jabbed a thumb toward the swampy marsh just beyond the ditch. "That's saying a lot."

"Try shaking your boot out every morning to check for scorpions."

She shuddered but then stayed quiet rather than pushing to keep the conversation alive. Sharing had eased some of the tension inside her, like a slow release from a pressure cooker, a little bit at a time to keep from getting burned. Still, she knew that digging up the past didn't necessarily serve the same purpose for other people.

The truck jostled in a pothole just before a bridge spanning a narrow channel of the river. A small johnboat with a lone fisherman drifted below.

Martin draped a wrist over the steering wheel. "I took the job because I want the chance to clean things up rather than tear them down."

Some of the old anger at him faded. "Aunt Winnie liked you. She defended you when the town was griping about all their illegal dumping citations. Which is saying a lot since she wasn't known for being much of a rule follower."

"Your aunt was a fierce individual with a big heart." Turning, he looked at her over the top of his sunglasses, his brown eyes full of sympathy. "If I haven't said so before now, I'm sorry for your loss."

"Thank you." She looked away, the intensity of his gaze amping the pressure inside her. "I owe her . . . everything."

"Yet you're leaving behind the town and home she loved."

His words got her back up, but she pushed down the urge to explain how moving to Myrtle Beach had always been Winnie's dream.

Plans would be made. Only to be canceled. There'd been no missing the whisper of fear in Aunt Winnie's eyes once the time drew close to leave the city limits, as if doing so would burst a magic spell.

The truth was likely far simpler. Aunt Winnie had suffered from some level of agoraphobia. Sure, she could leave her farmhouse, barreling down Main Street and county roads in her old Ford truck with confidence. No farther.

But sharing that with Martin would feel like a betrayal of Winnie's memory. "I learned long ago not to care about other people's opinions of me."

"You mean you don't care about *my* opinion," he said with a wink, stopping the truck at a blinking red light at a crossroads.

"To think I was starting to like you. Don't you have someone to rescue from a rampaging pig?" Bailey Rae slumped in her seat, but some of the sting had left her words now. Something had shifted between them with those few hints into the man inside.

"I'm sure I do, but none as interesting as you."

Her mouth dried right up.

A honking horn sent them both sitting upright, and he eased his foot off the brake.

Twenty minutes later, they pulled into the hospital parking lot. She couldn't bolt out of the truck and into the elevator fast enough. Each squeak of her shoes on the tile floors took her one step closer to finishing up business and heading out for the coast. Martin was a distraction. Simple as that. And she wasn't like her mother, to be swept about by the changing winds of attraction to a new handsome man. Especially not one who had far too many secrets lurking in his deep brown eyes.

Mind and purpose back in focus, she knocked on the door to Gia's hospital room. "Gia, it's me. Bailey Rae from the market. And the game warden, Martin Perez."

"Come in," a soft voice called from inside. Weak. But alive.

Could Bailey Rae have lived with herself if the woman weren't? Thankfully she didn't have to go through that emotional minefield.

Bag in hand, she drew in a bracing breath of antiseptic air and pushed through the door.

After a single look at Gia Abernathy's battered face, Bailey Rae knew. The woman needed a lot more than a bag of granola bars or hand-me-downs, and her mission for her final weeks in Bent Oak had just expanded.

∞

1971

Libby and I began walking home together after that fight in the paper mill lot. Last week's altercation had spooked us both. Even though we hadn't shared about our pasts, an unspoken bond existed between us, an understanding that we'd both faced something dangerous and survived.

We were warier now. There was comfort in numbers. So we walked down the narrow sidewalk along Main Street toward the towering brick elementary school. Today was their last day of the school year, and I wondered if our work schedules would stay the same.

Libby swiped her forehead. "Slow down, please."

I hadn't realized I was double-timing along the sidewalk. Most likely stomping out my frustration. I punished the pavement because I couldn't punish Phillip.

It was my wedding anniversary today.

I hated the memories that one word—anniversary—evoked. Hated the state of being married but not. Most of all, hated that Phillip still crept into my thoughts.

Did he miss me even a little? Did he have any regrets about how low he'd sunk to cut me out of his life? And on this awful day, I had to admit that I missed the man he'd pretended to be.

However, I didn't miss the woman I'd been—the one who embraced that shell of a life we'd shared. I would hold on to that knowledge as I scraped out a new, braver life for myself.

Libby plucked an azalea bloom off a bush as we passed the gas station. "Did you know that one of the men who broke up that fight is Annette's grandson?"

I chewed my lip, because yes, I had asked around about Russell Davis after meeting him, discovering that he'd just returned from Vietnam, where he'd driven a supply truck. Now, he drove a truck for the paper mill. His connection to Annette made any draw to him all the more complicated. "I think I may have heard something."

"I wonder why Annette didn't mention having a grandson who worked with the mill."

"Why would she?"

"She told us about the gas station she and her husband own." Libby tucked the flower behind one ear, her brown hair still up in a bun for work.

"That wasn't personal. She just let us know so we could get discounts. Which would be nice if either of us owned a car."

"Thank heavens we don't live in Maine or somewhere else snowy." Libby strolled a few more steps, but I could tell she wasn't done talking. She rarely said anything impulsive, instead waiting and choosing her words for fear of saying the wrong thing. "I just wondered if Annette told him about us."

"Does it matter?" I asked, sidestepping a buckled patch in the concrete. "I can't imagine Annette would do anything to risk our safety."

"Russell gave Keith an old Matchbox truck last time we stopped by the gas station for a Tootsie Roll." Libby pressed a chapped hand to her chest. "Wasn't that the sweetest thing?"

She couldn't possibly mean . . .

"Are you interested in Russell Davis?" Now wouldn't be the right time to admit I'd begun scanning magazines at the library for articles about *The Mod Squad*. "This seems rather fast, considering you, uh, just arrived in Bent Oak."

"I'm not interested romantically in him or any man in this town." Libby shook her head vehemently. "I'm only getting my bearings by learning as much as I can about everyone."

Her pitiful expression made me feel like I'd kicked a puppy. There was no sense inflicting my bad mood on her.

"How about after we pick up Keith, we come back here to the park and feed the fish?" I motioned toward the little oasis smack dab in the middle of Main Street, complete with brick fish pond, benches, and lush landscaping, compliments of the garden club currently gathered at the large gazebo. All those pastel pantsuits and dresses made them look like a big polyester bouquet, which brought on another of those anniversary memories. One of me at my mother's garden club, where they'd hosted my bridal shower.

My wedding had been a bona fide circus. Ten bridesmaids, with groomsmen plus ushers. Plus two flower girls and ring bearers. A string quartet played in the cathedral. The reception, held at our country club, featured a full sit-down dinner with prime rib and shrimp. It probably cost more than I made in a year now.

Libby pressed her hand to her chest again, breathless. "Do you think we could stop and sit for a moment? We're running ahead of schedule to get Keith."

I didn't want to hang out near the memory generators, but Libby did look pale. The shifts at the mill seemed to hit her harder than they did me. I assumed it was because she had a child to look after as well.

How tragically ironic all those miscarriages had turned out to be a blessing in disguise. It would have been so much tougher to leave with a baby. "Sure. Are you all right?"

"I was just up late mending one of Keith's shirts he ripped in a playground tussle." Libby sagged down onto a wooden bench, dedication plate in memory of some Watson relative.

Lord, I hoped there weren't a bunch of honorarium benches back in Mobile with my name on them, since I was very much alive. Not that my husband would have bothered. But maybe the old garden club would have purchased one.

Or perhaps I'd left no imprint at all on my previous life.

I stretched my legs out in front of me toward the low brick wall encircling the little pond, only to realize it was empty. "What happened to the fish?"

"Yoo-hoo," a voice called from the gazebo—a woman in lemon yellow. "Someone put dish soap in the water fountain." She glanced sharply over at another lady in lilac. "It's not funny. It killed off the koi. Thank heavens I was able to scoop them out before morning. Can you imagine if a child came by to feed them and saw them all floating with bloated bellies?"

An older woman with a silver-blond bouffant sniffed. "There's no need to be so graphic."

There was so much polyester and hair spray over there, a single spark would send them and the gazebo up in smoke.

Lilac Lady called out, "Would you two like to join us?"

"Shhhh," Bouffant Woman said in a theatrical whisper that wasn't fooling me for a minute. "They're on their way home from work. They must be worn slap out."

I glanced at Libby and rolled my eyes at the implication we were not garden club worthy.

Lilac Lady stood up anyway. "Come on over and introduce yourselves. I insist."

Apparently, she carried some sway since the others backed down. Libby leaned her head toward mine. "We shouldn't be rude."

Heaven forbid.

But since Libby never asked for anything, I followed along the walkway, bordered with monkey grass. I climbed the white steps into their world, my old one. Even the menu could have been transported straight from Mobile. Cucumber sandwiches. Ham salad. Tomato aspic. And slices of pound cake.

My mouth watered, and I missed my mother in that moment. I didn't understand missing my mom and resenting her at the same time, wishing she'd prepared me better for the world. Wondering if her seeming happiness with my father had been real or if I'd imagined it.

Libby thrust out her chapped hand. "I'm Libby Farrell. I have a little boy named Keith." She spun the thin gold band with her thumb. "His father passed away."

"I'm Winnie Ballard and I'm divorced." Divorced in my heart, which was what really mattered. Sure, it wasn't a part of my paperwork or backstory. Worse yet, it was so far from the truth I shouldn't have thought it, much less said it aloud. But the anniversary was much on my mind today and the bad mood along with it. So the words were already out there now.

One by one, they introduced themselves in a flurry of names I wouldn't remember. My brain was packed fuller than Annette's card catalog thanks to this new beginning.

Lilac Lady motioned to the picnic basket with a hand towel draped over the top. "Would you like to sit and have something to eat? We have plenty of sandwiches and pound cake."

Charity? I think not. Poverty hadn't fully stamped my pride out of me yet. "No, thank you. I'm still full as a tick from lunch."

Libby rested a hand on the crook of my arm, stopping me before saying, "If you don't mind, my boy Keith would enjoy a piece of that cake."

"Of course, take two. It's lemon and a secret family recipe." Lilac sliced off three generous servings and wrapped each in a napkin before passing them all to Libby before I could insist again that my rumbling stomach wasn't interested.

Even as I hungered for the familiar foods, I needed to escape. Fast. Before I let down my guard and unwittingly disclosed something that could reveal my past wasn't too different from theirs except with one big asterisk. "Nice to meet y'all, but we need to hurry on our way to pick up little Keith."

This time, I didn't give Libby time to stop me. We made our way back out of the town square, past the drained site of the great koi bubble bath, and onto the sidewalk.

Libby passed over the extra slice. Turning it down would be childish, and I didn't want to hurt her feelings.

I peeled back the napkin. "Doesn't it bother you to accept their charity?"

Libby broke her slice in half before putting the rest in her purse. "Why should it when I've already had to take so much more from Annette and her friends?"

Now that caught me off guard. I looked down at the cake in my hand and thought of how Libby had tucked away extra for her son. Upon a closer look, she appeared to have lost weight since our arrival.

Pride had driven me to turn down those sandwiches. What would push me to the point that pride no longer mattered? I felt mighty close right this minute as I realized my quick refusal had cost my friend a much-needed meal. That Lilac Lady—I couldn't remember her name—who I'd made fun of in my head had shown more awareness and compassion for Libby today than I had. "What was her name again? The one who offered us sandwiches. She was wearing a lilac dress."

"Sylvie Tyler," she said without hesitation. Libby remembered everything. "Her son was the one driving the forklift the other day when he and Russell broke up the fight."

The forklift guy? As in "Pete" from *The Mod Squad*? The son of the mill owner? Which meant Sylvie's husband owned the factory.

Now that gave me food for thought. It had been easier when I could vilify everyone in my previous world.

And speaking of food, I took a bite of the lemon pound cake. It was good. Really good. Although mine was better.

I'd spent countless hours of my life perfecting the recipe and could show them up in an instant. If I had the extra money to buy the ingredients. But my time would be better spent learning from Libby how best not to kill myself in a tragic mop bucket accident.

My life wasn't about garden clubs or competitive baking anymore. Phillip's betrayal had ensured that.

I needed to forget about the past if I ever hoped to build a good future for myself. One that didn't consume me with memories of all I'd lost. Maybe instead of thinking bitter thoughts, I should be keeping an open heart and mind when it came to helping people like Libby who deserved a break.

But first, I planned to ask Annette how long it would take for me to ditch this half-alive feeling and be declared legally dead.

CHAPTER SIX

2025

Martin had serious reservations about Gia Abernathy and Cricket staying with Bailey Rae even for a night or two, but there'd been no deterring her once her mind was set. At least he could give her home and property a once-over to make sure Gia's husband wasn't lurking in a closet or behind a tree.

Although there were sure enough boxes around for someone to hide behind. He carried the woman's small suitcase, just the basics donated by the shelter. Bailey Rae had offered to outfit them with more from her stockpile and even donate furniture from the farmhouse—if the woman didn't mind brown-and-orange plaids from the 1970s. Whatever it took to help keep Gia safe until her husband was located by authorities. Not that they'd had much success finding him—or the man's brother either, just his empty fishing boat.

And Martin wasn't overly confident they would anytime soon. Portions of the river were deep and treacherous, used in the past for log driving to the paper mill. Other stretches were narrow and marshy, populated with gators and snakes.

Minutes later, a thorough clearing of each room assured Martin that no one lurked in the farm cabin other than Skeeter, who'd had no sense of personal space and kept bumping into his legs. Standing in the open doorway, Martin waved to the two cars out front—his truck and

Keith Farrell's van. At least Thea and June had convinced Bailey Rae to let Keith stay in the Airstream out back for protection, and they would keep watch over Libby. Keith appeared to be relieved for the break from caregiving for his mom.

Gia stood at the open truck door with her arms wide for her child. The little girl leaped out and wrapped herself around her mother like a spider monkey. Gia flinched but didn't let go in spite of her cracked ribs and battered face.

Martin's gaze shifted to Bailey Rae, protective urges thrumming a steady cadence in his brain. Bailey Rae had to be exhausted from working in the restaurant, clearing out the house to sell, and now taking in temporary pseudo-boarders.

Bailey Rae motioned toward the hall, a cluster of thin bead bracelets sliding along her wrist. "You can set that down just in there. I'll show them to their room in a bit."

"And you're certain no one had access to the security system while you were away?" he asked, nudging the suitcase farther in a corner by a box of children's books. A Little Golden Book rested on top, yellowed with age. *The Little Engine That Could*.

"Absolutely." She waggled her phone at him. "I have an app."

He would still feel better once he'd swept the property beyond the yard as well. Keith and a lazy hound dog felt like pitiful defense against a man who beat his own wife.

Back in the living room, Bailey Rae knelt in front of Cricket, who hadn't pulled her thumb from her mouth since they'd picked her up from the social worker at child services. "Gia, I'm sorry I don't have more toys for her to play with. I sold most of them last weekend."

Keith opened a hall closet—still full of jackets—and reached up on the top shelf. "There may be a few things left. Let me look around. Aunt Winnie and Uncle Russell used to keep a few special toys here for when I came over to play. Aha. Here we go."

Smiling, Keith pulled down a shoebox with childish handwriting on the outside: KEEP OUT. THIS BELONGS TO KEITH FARRELL. He pivoted back to Cricket, who wore a pink shorts set a size too large. "Matchbox trucks were my favorite. I used to sit on that same braided rug. My good friend Russell taught me how to use the grooves as guides on a racetrack."

Lowering himself to the rug, Keith lifted the lid from the box. He ran the cars along the curves and transformed the floor covering into their own Formula 1 tournament, while Bailey Rae persuaded Gia to put her feet up in the recliner. Close to her daughter, of course. Although she would likely drift off before long, with Skeeter keeping vigil beside the chair.

Martin shuffled from foot to foot, eager to get started scouring the grounds around the cabin.

Bailey Rae smoothed her hands along the floral sundress she'd changed into during the scramble to get to the hospital today, explaining on the ride over that she'd wanted to make a good impression on the hospital staff when they released Cricket and Gia into her care. "Do you have time to stay for supper? It won't be anything fancy. I'm working to clear out the freezer before I go. Tonight's menu is gumbo stew served over grits."

Grits.

As if he needed more motivation to head outside. He stifled a wince. "I can't, but thank you."

She laughed softly. "Your disrespect for grits is showing. If you can't stay, at least let me make a to-go dish for you, and you can let me know what you think of grits made properly, by a Southerner."

"I imagine you will use this gift of a meal to make a believer out of this Arizona boy."

"That I will." She held up a hand as she walked toward the kitchen, hips swaying gently. "It's all about the consistency, salt, and butter."

She multitasked with smooth efficiency and confidence. Setting a pot of water on the stove to boil. Placing a container of gumbo on the counter. Carrying a mug of hot tea and an ice pack for Gia, whose face looked even worse today. But what alarmed him even more? That the child didn't seem in the least concerned about her mom's injuries, as if this were a normal occurrence.

While Bailey Rae stirred the grits, adding a surprising amount of butter and salt, she nodded toward the living room, where Keith and Cricket moved trucks along the circles in the braided rug. "Uncle Russell didn't just show Keith how to use the rug as a racetrack, he also bought cars for Keith when he was a kid with no father. They're probably worth a fortune now. Not that I would ever sell them. Too much sentimental value. Also, as you saw by the very official labeling on the box, I am not even sure they belong to me."

"That was kind of him," Martin said, leaning against the archway between the two rooms. He wasn't letting anyone out of his sight. He understood that the past and present were melding in his mind. The threat of the random shooter in the hangar then. The threat of Gia's husband now.

"My aunt and uncle never had children of their own, so they enjoyed spoiling other people's kids." She turned the stovetop to low and began pulling bowls from the cabinet, along with a disposable plastic container. "Russell was part of a NASCAR pit crew. He even raced a bit, before his health failed and he took on more long hauls as a truck driver at the mill."

Cricket nudged a toy vehicle with her toe, sending it off the rug and toward the kitchen. "Dirt track? Daddy do that."

At the mention of Gia's husband, Bailey Rae stepped back from the stove. "I think I may have some blocks. Would you like to build towers?" She patted Martin on the chest on her way past. "Stir the grits so they don't get lumpy. Hopefully the blocks will distract her from mentioning her father again."

Her touch lingered. "Grits aren't supposed to be lumpy? I haven't tasted them any other way."

Her laugh carried as she dumped a tub full of colorful blocks onto the rug, effectively distracting the child from discussions of her father.

Together, they stacked, then toppled, then repeated the process over again. Each time, Cricket giggled in surprise like it was the first.

Martin couldn't draw his eyes from Bailey Rae.

Then he heard a *pop, pop, pop* behind him and nearly hit the floor. Only to realize it was just the grits bubbling in the pot. The grits he'd forgotten to stir. His mind still full of wartime gunfire, he sprinted back to resume his post at the stove.

Stirring, he let the even movement slow his heart rate and took in the sound of voices drifting from the other room to will away the echoes of the past in his head.

"Keith," Gia said, softly. From fear? Or because of the ache in her jaw? "It's kind of your mother's friends to look after her while you're here."

"They insisted it's no trouble at all," Keith answered. "We're a tight-knit group. Those women helped raise me after my dad died. Now they're there for her as she would be for them."

Libby had seemed so disoriented at the market sale, no wonder they were keeping a close watch on her. A hand on his shoulder made him jolt, only to find Bailey Rae had come up behind him undetected. He needed to get his head together. He would be no good to these women in need of protection if he let the past smother the present.

Bailey Rae closed her fingers around his and took over stirring again. He slid his hand away slowly and turned to face her. Her green eyes held his, her aloe scent mingling with the spiciness of the gumbo. His guard down, he couldn't deny that she tempted him as he stood beside her, both of them unmoving other than her slow stirring of the grits, while voices from the other room filled the silence.

"I'm curious." Gia resumed her talk with Keith. "You're good with Cricket. Do you have children?"

"No, just stepkids and divorces."

Gia gasped. "I'm so sorry."

"Well, I guess you could say I've mastered the art of knowing when to call it quits—" Keith stopped short. "That came out wrong. Please don't take offense."

Martin cleared his throat, stepping away to resume his post in the doorway connecting the kitchen to the living room. The sensitivity from Keith surprised him. But then Martin hadn't learned much about the man in the past few months.

His instincts from days as an army cop resurfaced. A part of him that he'd hoped to leave behind after he'd ended his time in the military. But he was learning the past couldn't be so easily buried. "Bailey Rae"—he lowered his voice—"are you sure you're comfortable with Keith staying here?"

"He's like family," she answered without hesitation, ladling food into the to-go container. "Libby, Thea, and June too. A couple of those ex-wives of Keith's had trouble with how close we all are. Then the last one left when his mama began showing symptoms of Alzheimer's. The woman kept insisting on correcting Libby. Keith finally told the wife that if his mama insisted a sandy field looked like snow, then wet it down and build a snowman. Because saying different wouldn't erase her confusion."

"It's admirable the way he takes care of her." Martin walked to the counter as she sealed the lid on the plastic container. "Okay then, if you're sure about him staying in the Airstream. I'll do a sweep of the grounds before I leave. Promise me you'll keep the doors locked and your cell phone close by at all times."

"Of course." An impish light glinted in her eyes an instant before she scooped a spoon through the remainder of the grits. Cupping her hand underneath, she lifted the spoon to his mouth. "I'm curious about the verdict."

He looked at the unappetizing glob, but then he'd never been one to turn down a dare. He stepped closer, cradling his hand under hers as he angled forward to taste . . .

Once again, she'd surprised him.

The buttery smoothness melted along his taste buds. "It's good."

"Told ya so," she said with more of that sass that drew him. Easing back, she dropped the spoon in the sink with a clank. "I'll set the alarm system, and we have Skeeter as a backup."

Her words returned him to reality. That state-of-the-art security system seemed pricier than he would have expected since Mrs. Winnie had been so frugal. Still, would it be enough so far out in the country? "I can stay over too."

She thrust the container into his hands, holding on for a moment, the two of them connected by that tub of grits and gumbo. "Thank you. But we've imposed enough, and you mentioned needing to get to the office to finish some paperwork."

Rather than argue, he decided to take the evening off and eat his supper in the truck, parked at the end of the driveway where he could keep watch.

Because both of his jobs had taught him all too well. The worst creatures came out at night.

༄

1971

I wondered how long it would take for the fall weather to cool down. The walk from the factory to the gas station to pick up Keith from Annette felt twice as long. Even when fanning my face with a church bulletin the mill had misprinted.

Back in Mobile, I hadn't realized how much the breeze blowing off the Gulf blunted the heat. I'd lived in a house on the coast with a pool growing up, and near the ocean with Phillip before moving to the country. Here, the river was beautiful, but the marsh gave the air a pervasive mugginess that no breeze could alleviate.

This summer adapting had been rough for Libby. For me too since we didn't see as much of each other, but her difficulties were rooted more in the logistics of caring for her young son.

I volunteered to help with Keith when I could, if she wanted to pick up a swing shift. The offer just fell out of my mouth. Maybe from some latent grief over not having a child and from a sense of guilt over having it easier than she did. She'd agreed, but only if I would let her teach me how to cook something other than desserts.

Two weeks after school resumed, Keith landed in the principal's office for fighting. Libby had to clock out early for the resulting parent-teacher conference about his behavior. Then Keith caught chicken pox, and she'd needed the extra money again to pay the doctor bill and make up for lost work time with her sick child. She was worn down.

I felt small for missing her. At least I wasn't tired *and* lonely.

Although maybe Russell would be there when I collected Keith. I spent far too much time avoiding him while trying to catch a glimpse of him without being noticed.

I stepped off the sidewalk onto the drive leading to the only gas station on Main Street. The other two were on the outskirts of town, the self-service kind of pumps. Whereas this place? Full service, compliments of Annette's husband, the owner. Complete with the *ding ding* announcing the arrival of a new customer driving under the porte cochere.

Except that was a word I didn't use anymore. Porte cochere. That was my grandmother's word for a covered area in front of the entry.

As I waited for a vehicle to back out of the two-bay garage, Russell rolled out from under a Chevy Chevelle with a racing number five painted on the side.

He tugged his work gloves off and tucked them into a pocket of his coveralls. "What can I help you with, Winnie?"

"I'm here to pick up Keith for Libby."

"Right, he's inside with Granny in the back office."

I should have thanked him and moved forward. But I didn't. I just kept fanning my face, the heat growing inside me. "It was kind of your grandmother to watch him. Libby will want to know if he behaved."

"He's no trouble as long as you keep him busy." Russell leaned a hip against the front quarter panel. "Granny had him work on his ABCs with the card catalog."

As that heat built, I could no longer ignore the truth. I was totally turned on by this man. And that was dangerous to building my new life, especially so soon into the process. What if I let something slip?

"Thank you," I said crisply and started through the garage toward the office in back. Just as I reached for the doorknob, an arm stretched in front of me, briefly landing his hand on mine. *Russell.*

I huffed my hair off my brow. It didn't help.

Russell pulled his hand back. "Have I done something to offend you?"

Had I given him the impression I was avoiding him out of racism? I wasn't even sure how to voice that thought but desperately wanted to make sure he knew that wasn't the case.

So I turned to face him and rested my fingers lightly on his wrist. "Of course you haven't offended me. I'm sorry if I gave that impression. I, uh, I want . . ."

Again, I struggled with words to discuss a subject that had gone woefully unaddressed in my upbringing.

"Good. I'm glad." He nodded with a slight smile that broadcast understanding and relief. "I wanted to clear the air since we'll be living in the same town."

"You've been absolutely mannerly," I said, needing to be sure he truly heard me. "And the way you and your grandmother have helped Libby has been generous."

Russell hung his head, a pulse throbbing in his forehead that echoed my racing heart. It was one of those precipice moments of life, where the air feels different, charged, just before everything changes.

Throwing back his shoulders, he met my gaze full on. "I've been helping her because it's the only way I could find to see more of you."

My jaw dropped, and my stomach did the same flip that happened on a roller coaster.

He held up a hand. "Not that I'm using her or her boy. Granny is the one watching him. I've just stuck around when he's here."

A half smile pushed through my confusion and, yes, the excitement because he'd noticed me. I'd been unseen for so very long. Even when screaming from the rooftops, nothing. Now, when hidden, he had noticed me. "That's still using them a little bit."

"Am I forgiven?"

There was something in his golden-brown eyes that hinted he understood that his grandmother was doing more than shelving books at the library. Maybe he even helped in some way. But those words stayed unspoken. It was a sacred part of the network. No link broken. Nothing discussed without Annette's approval. Even Libby and I hadn't shared our stories. The one time I'd hinted to Annette . . . she'd cut me off.

So I didn't press him on that expression, but I took a sort of comfort in it all the same. If he understood my journey on some level, then that lessened the pressure of this attraction I felt. I wouldn't have to explain the obstacles to him.

I allowed myself a little latitude. "What would you have done if I hadn't shown up? Keith's been looking forward to passing you tools. It's all he talks about."

"If you didn't show, then I would still pitch in where needed," he said without hesitation. "I'm not so heartless as to let down a little kid. Especially one who's lost as much as Keith."

My heart softened. All signs indicated he was a good man. "Then you're forgiven." I touched the hood of the car. "Tell me about this vehicle you're working on."

"It's mine."

Now that surprised me. "But . . . it's a race car."

"It sure is," he said with more love than I'd heard in most men's voices when they spoke of their spouse. "Grandpa kept her stored in the garage for me while I was in Vietnam. Now that I'm back, I'm giving her a tune-up. I don't just drive trucks for the paper mill. I do a little dirt track racing as well. And in between long hauls, I fill in when needed on pit crews for NASCAR. I'm hoping for a permanent spot as a gateway to getting behind the wheel one day."

"NASCAR?"

"You look surprised."

I didn't know how to say what I was thinking. "It's not an answer a person hears that often."

"You mean it's not an expected answer from a *Black* person," he said in a matter-of-fact tone. "It's true there aren't many Black NASCAR drivers. But it's not unheard of. Elias Bowie back in 1955. Wendell Scott began in 1961 and has had hundreds of starts in the Grand National Series."

"I'm sorry to have assumed." And I meant the apology this time.

"You don't know if you don't ask." Russell stroked the hood of the car with reverence, his hand skimming close to mine. "I'm following my dream."

"I'd like to watch you race sometime." The impulsive words fell out before I thought them through.

His eyebrows lifted in surprise. "How about Saturday? There's a dirt track racing event. I can make sure you get the best seat in the house."

Did I dare accept? I wanted to, and not just because the whole event sounded exciting. But because I was drawn to Russell. From his handsome face to his calm, kind voice. Not that I was by any means in a good place to act on the attraction, even if I had somehow managed to extricate myself from Phillip in a divorce. I was still too . . . broken. I needed time to heal.

And what then? How could I consider a relationship when I was still married? Annette's attorney friend had told me the answer wasn't clear-cut as to how long it would take to be declared legally dead. If I'd made the evidence appear overwhelming enough that I'd drowned and if Phillip pursued it aggressively, the process could be fairly quick. However, the issue of my inheritance could slow it down.

All a nonanswer.

Annette had assured me she would do her best to find the information for whenever I might need it. Although the unspoken addendum to that? As long as finding out didn't put the network at risk. It went without saying that she needed to ask questions with caution.

Which meant I was still in limbo. And if I never got the answer, I knew one thing for certain. I could take on that guilt for myself, but to let Russell become closer while unaware of my past . . . That was a sin I wasn't willing to commit.

"Russell, if you're inviting me as a friend, then I accept."

"Good. Very good." He didn't seem in the least deterred by the friend reference. "I'll let Granny know you're here for Keith."

My head swirled with the implication of the discussion with Russell long after I'd walked away from the station, Keith's little hand tucked in mine. In his other fist, he clutched a toy truck.

What did the world see as they watched us stroll past? Did we look just like the mothers and their children shopping on Main Street, others playing together in the front yard with a white picket fence?

I understood Keith wasn't mine, but I felt like a very special aunt, closer than that even because of the way we'd come to Bent Oak. They say secrets don't make friends, but in my opinion that wasn't the case. Sometimes they make best friends, the necessary sort.

Keith looked like a regular kid with a Batman backpack. His brown hair was mussed like he needed it to be wet and combed back into place. He had a splatter of ketchup on his striped shirt.

Except he didn't chatter like other children. Had his life experience robbed him of the chance to be a child?

I gave his sticky hand a squeeze. "What are you learning about in school?"

"Dinosaurs." He kicked a stone along the sidewalk.

"Ah, I can see that now." I pointed to a paper sticking out of his half-zipped bag. "That's a very good drawing. Maybe I can help you finish coloring it when we get to the apartment?"

He shook his head. "I don't need crayons. We don't know what color they are. All they found was bones."

"That's a great point." I wanted to keep him talking, to be a part of helping him open up. "I guess I just assumed they looked like green alligators and lizards."

"What about chameleon lizards?"

"You're a smart kid."

"Not really. I just like learning about dinosaurs because it's important."

"We all have subjects in school that we enjoy more than others. That's about finding your talent. I loved art. Maybe you're going to be a scientist one day."

"That's not why I want to learn all I can about dinosaurs."

"Why is that?" I asked as we turned off Main and onto Fourth Street.

"Because," he said in a secretive voice, "I think that pterodactyls and dragons are the same thing."

I thought it was a cute premise. "But dragons aren't real, silly boy."

He looked up at me with eyes so like his mother's it stole the oxygen from the air. "Sure they are. Just sometimes the dragons pretend to be people."

CHAPTER SEVEN

2025

Bailey Rae pulled the last of the dishes from the drying rack, the silence of the cabin heavy in spite of her houseguests, the first people to sleep under the roof since Winnie had drowned. She'd been spending as little time as possible in the house, afraid it would trigger her grief. But being here now had the opposite effect. She took comfort from straightening the milk-white glassware on the display shelves, recalling the stories behind the collection of items found at flea markets and garage sales. Working at the farmhouse sink brought happy memories of helping Winnie with spring cleaning. The kitchen had been the heart of the home, and spending time in it reminded Bailey Rae of how places had the power to heal.

Would the cabin offer the same to her guests?

Not too long after Martin had left with his supper, Keith retired to the Airstream, while Gia and Cricket sealed themselves in the guest room. Because of exhaustion or avoiding questions? Either way, they'd holed up with their pain and secrets behind the door.

Leaving Bailey Rae alone, with only Skeeter for company while she boxed away more of the keepsakes. She wouldn't have room for them in the camper but could tuck them away in a storage unit for someday when she had a house.

Sitting on the braided rug in the living room, she pulled a stack of photo albums from the shelf. There weren't many pictures around Winnie's house, but those weren't the days of cell phones and unlimited selfies. Just a few Polaroids were tucked in an album with sticky pages, cellophane sealing them in. Faded images without the artfulness of how to extend a leg just so, or how to tip the face to the most flattering light. No perfectly adjusted filters to hide behind, just truth in the lines on their faces and the emotions behind their eyes.

Still, there was an authenticity to those imperfect moments. She paused at one of Libby smiling even with the dark circles stamped under her eyes, all the more apparent with the wind lifting her long hair. Keith clung to her hand. Bailey Rae felt a gut punch at the similarity to Gia and Cricket. To herself and her mother.

She flipped the page to a newspaper clipping of Russell beside his race car, Winnie sitting proudly on the hood wearing bell-bottom jeans and a floral halter top. Her hair shielded most of her face, all layered and curly, still blond and so different from the graying braid or messy bun Winnie had worn for as long as Bailey Rae knew her.

Under the photo, Winnie had written: *Us. 1978.*

Her aunt had never been clear about the starting point for their relationship. She'd insisted the present mattered most. So Bailey Rae had come up with ways to trick Winnie into giving a timeline for different things. Since jars of canned fruit and vegetables had dates on them, Bailey Rae would ask who helped with those. Or she would thumb through old magazines and search for the address sticker to pinpoint who dropped it off and when.

For the longest while, she'd wondered why it mattered to her so much. But then in a psychology magazine, she had stumbled on an article about memory disruption and sequencing in trauma survivors. Gaps in her memory frustrated her, but more than anything, they scared her. What did those holes contain?

How unfortunate she'd already tossed the old magazines or she would have hunted for some of those articles to give Gia—

A knock at the front door startled her into dropping the photo album. Her stomach lurched and her eyes darted to the corridor leading to Gia's room, then back to the cabin's main entrance. Skeeter scrambled to his feet and sniffed along the bottom of the door. But he stayed quiet. The dog only barked when strangers came around.

Bailey Rae parted the lace curtains to peek outside, then breathed a sigh of relief. Keith stood on the porch with a couple of Coke cans in hand. The shirttails of his button-down flapped loose from his jeans, scruffy but scrappy. As always. Except with much less hair these days.

She slid the chain off, then unlocked the dead bolt. "Is everything okay? Or is this a DoorDash delivery?"

Chuckling, he passed her one of the cans. "I saw the spare-room lights go out and thought you might want some company."

"That's thoughtful of you. Thanks." She popped the tab and joined him on the porch. "And thanks for staying over too."

"I love my mother," he said, leaning against the railing with his drink, "but I have to admit, I don't mind the quiet night's rest."

"You've taken on a lot with her care." People around town whispered about Keith not being able to hold down a job—or a relationship—but his devotion to his mother made up for a host of flaws.

"I'm all she has." He shrugged, shirt rippling on his wiry shoulders. Some people gained pounds with years, while Keith seemed to shrink. "She's all I have, for that matter."

Bullfrogs croaked from the river, interrupted only by a screech owl and tinkling wind chimes. The sounds of home. Soon enough to be replaced by the lulling whoosh of waves echoing through the wide-open spaces with fewer places to hide. Or so she imagined her future life near the water. "That was a nice story about Uncle Russell and the grooves in the rug. I forget sometimes that he was like an uncle to you as well."

Winnie and Russell had been old enough to be her grandparents, but they'd always seemed so much younger. Their deaths had caught her unaware.

Some people had to come to the realization that their parents were imperfect humans who were doing life for the first time too. She always knew that about her mom. It was Winnie and Russell who seemed like superheroes, unmovable and steady forces who she thought would always be there to save the day. "Didn't you arrive in town about the same time Winnie did?"

"I was little then." He tipped back his drink, taking his time while avoiding her gaze. "I don't remember much about my life before coming to Bent Oak."

Did no one else understand her need for timelines? "Do you have any idea what Gia meant about the cookbook having a code?"

"Not a clue."

"Your mother seemed to know something," she pressed, frustrated.

"Mom is confused." He rolled the can between his palms. "Maybe Gia just heard how kindhearted Winnie was."

"Possibly, but the recipe book she held was old, and she seemed so . . . convinced." She shook her head, staring into the woods at the fat oak trees cloaked in Spanish moss. The dense forest kept its secrets hidden from prying eyes. "I should just ask Gia tomorrow."

"Sorry I can't help you." He crushed his can with his bootheel. "Well, I'm gonna head on back to the Airstream. Call me if you need anything, and I'll be here in a heartbeat."

And he would be. Keith might have been a troubled teen. While he might not be the best husband or employee, he was loyal to those he considered family. Family by choice rather than by blood, he would say.

She hadn't thought about how she would miss Keith too, even though he'd been a part of her life for decades, always there to help. The realization of how she'd overlooked him left her feeling guilty and small. He came in second for so many people he considered family. Bailey Rae had Winnie and Russell. Thea had her husband and two children. He just had his mother, who would soon forget he even existed.

"Hey Keith? Hold on just a second. I have something I want to give you." She took his empty can and tossed it in the recycling before grabbing the photo album. Back outside, she thrust the worn book toward him. "I thought you might want some pictures of you and your mom. Maybe one of Winnie and Russell too."

He opened the fat album, flipping pages slowly. Nostalgia spilled out of pages touched with dust. Shades of happiness and heartache wove together to make the fabric of memories.

"Wow, I haven't seen some of these." He skimmed a finger over a photo of him swinging from a rope into the river. "Back when I was a kid, we had more freedom to explore. Especially once I was in junior high. Mama would go to work, and I would meet up with friends. We would float on an old inner tube. We didn't have cell phones to check in and take a million selfies. No live streaming. Just us, getting to exist in the moment and make choices. Good ones and bad ones."

"I can't imagine what it must have been like. No cell phones or chasing social media perfection." Less pressure. "It was a different time."

"Easier to hide what we were up to." He plucked a photo from the album, the one she'd noticed earlier of him as a child clinging to his mother's hand. He slid it into the front pocket of his button-down shirt. "I'll check the yard once more before heading off to bed. Don't worry. I'm a light sleeper."

Clutching the album against the dull ache in her chest, Bailey Rae stayed on the porch long after Keith had slammed the Airstream door closed. She chalked up the twinge to change, not that it lessened the discomfort.

Back inside the cabin, she placed the photo album in a box marked KEEP/STORAGE, full of files and important papers. Newspaper clippings. Letters. She'd felt guilty and emotional reading them, although some were more benign, like the ones from some guy asking for more information about paper mill employees back in the 1970s. She grabbed an unused cookbook and added it to the box for good measure since hers would be covered in cooking splatters. She thumbed through the pages. What about this simple publication had drawn Gia?

Bailey Rae scanned the recipes from everyone in the town, from Uncle Russell's catfish stew to his grandmother Annette's skillet cornbread. Women from the factory had contributed, as well as ladies from the garden club. Some of the recipes were accompanied by a picture of the "chef," while others included photos of Bent Oak, the factory, the town hall, the river.

Quite the homage to local flavors on so many levels.

Flipping a couple of pages, she lingered on one of Winnie's recipes. No image of Winnie stared back, though. Just a snapshot of canned preserves with a pound cake on a picnic blanket with a large satchel and floppy hat resting beside. Signature Winnie. The sight of the jam recipe stirred tears in her eyes and flavors on her taste buds.

Sleep wasn't even remotely on the horizon with her mind racing and her heart missing Winnie. So one by one, she pulled out the ingredients and lined them up on the counter. She would take solace in the kitchen for a little while.

She had a pantry to clear and memories to pack away.

Ninety minutes later, Bailey Rae washed the bowl, beaters, and spatula while the cake cooled on a rack. The warm scent of vanilla lingered in the air. Her pantry and fridge were now shy a pound each of flour, sugar, butter, and eggs, but her mind was full of the memories associated with this recipe. She'd stood at this counter the day she'd realized her mother wasn't coming back.

After Winnie had dried all the tears, she'd offered to share a secret recipe that would be known only to the two of them, the connection coming at a time when Bailey Rae felt so adrift. Somewhere between sifting the flour and scraping the last bit of batter from the bowl, her chest eased enough that she could breathe without hiccups.

Now, as Bailey Rae dried her hands on the skirt of her dress, a flicker of light in the woods caught her attention. Her breath hitched.

She checked in with Skeeter, but the hound snoozed on the rag rug by the mudroom door. She looked back at the window, pushing the curtain open farther away from the pane that needed a good cleaning. The faint glow still shone through the trees. In the distance. Like a car parked at the top of the lengthy dirt driveway.

Her stomach knotted even as she told herself there were a thousand benign reasons. A couple parking to have sex. Teens out drinking.

Or an angry, abusive husband stalking his wife.

She snatched her cell phone off the counter and didn't question why she bypassed calling Keith to phone Martin instead.

He picked up after one ring. "What's wrong?"

"I'm sorry to bother you." Her voice trembled. "But I think I see a vehicle parked at the end of the drive. I noticed the light . . . It may be nothing . . ."

"That's me." His deep tones rumbled from the speaker. "I'm at the top of the drive. I have the dome light on inside my truck to finish up paperwork."

Relief sucked the adrenaline from her, and she slumped against the counter. "You stayed anyway? Don't you have to get up early for work?"

"I got someone to cover my shift. Leaving you out here with only Keith Farrell for protection didn't sit right." He paused, then admitted, "I wouldn't have slept anyway, worrying about you."

She didn't even hesitate asking, "Do you want to come inside? The light's better in here, and I have food."

"I'm already at your door. I just didn't want to ring the bell and wake your guests."

"I'll be right there." More excited than she wanted to ponder, she disabled the security system and flipped the lock, waving him inside.

Martin hung his game warden ball cap on the hook by the door. "Why are you still awake?"

"I'm too spun up from all that happened today, so I decided to bake." Waving him deeper into the cabin, she plucked a clean knife from the drawer.

"Smells good, sweet. Not at all like grits, although I confess to being a convert, as long as you're the one cooking them."

"Well, I've been doing more than emptying the freezer of gumbo. I've also been on a quest to use up opened staples, like the flour and sugar." She slid the blade around the edges of the tube cake pan, then loosened along the center hole. Lifting carefully, she tried to ignore Winnie's voice in her head insisting she hadn't let it cool long enough.

Breathing a sigh of relief as the cake held together, she eased the finished product to a dish. "This is Aunt Winnie's secret recipe for pound cake. She didn't share it with just anybody."

He hitched up to sit on a stool at the kitchen island. "I haven't been in the South long, but even I know how some of these ladies hold their recipes as close as state secrets."

"Would you like a slice?"

"If it's half as good as the grits and gumbo, I would be a fool to pass it up."

"You should see what I can do with a fish fry. Well, if I was allowed to fish, which of course I would never do illegally." Grinning, she cut a generous slice.

He forked off a bite and tasted. His eyes slid closed in ecstasy. "Man, that tastes even better than it smells."

The praise warmed the corner of her heart that still felt like a homeless six-year-old who had crummy grades in school because she fell asleep on her desk. "When I open my restaurant, it will be like having Winnie with me every time I cook one of her specialties."

"Restaurant?" He swiped a napkin along a crumb at the corner of his mouth.

"A food truck, actually." She'd only told Winnie's friends, no one else, half-afraid that people would laugh at her. "That's what I plan to do with the money from selling this place."

"I heard from Thea and June that you were leaving, but nothing detailed."

Winnie and her friends always had been able to keep a secret. Or maybe they were hoping if they didn't vocalize her move, it wouldn't happen. "I'm relocating to Myrtle Beach. I'll live in the Airstream by the ocean and support myself with the food truck business."

"Why Myrtle Beach? Why not Charleston or Edisto?" he asked, already halfway through his hunk of cake.

She bit her lip to hold back a smile that he hadn't questioned her dream, only the location. "Aunt Winnie talked about going to Myrtle Beach all the time but never made it there. She seemed to be a bit agoraphobic about crossing the county line."

Once the words were out of her mouth, she wished she'd labeled her aunt as a homebody or even a hermit rather than agoraphobic.

"So she lived in Bent Oak all her life?"

"Actually, no." She wished more of those photos in the album carried dates. "She came here as an adult . . . I'm not sure exactly where she grew up. She was an orphan, and she said it hurt too much to discuss her childhood."

Looking back, it felt self-centered or uncaring not to have delved deeper. Would he judge her for that?

"What foods will you serve?"

She breathed a sigh of relief. "Southern specialties, like barbecue, cornbread, slaw. The pound cake, of course. Then I'll rotate other dishes like chicken bog."

"All right, I have a question." He held up a hand to stop her as he continued with a wry grin, "What in the hell is chicken bog? I'm not gonna lie. The name does not make it sound appealing."

His good-natured teasing caught her so off guard she burst out laughing. A much-needed tension release for the pressure cooker of the past few days.

Finally, she quieted and caught her breath. "You've been here for months and you don't know what chicken bog is? Not very observant, are you."

His grin kicked up higher on one side, pushing a dimple into his tanned cheek. "I guess you'll have to teach me—"

Skeeter cut the rest of his answer short, leaping up onto all fours and barking his fool head off. The hackles along his spine rose, and he took off running for the front door, ears flapping.

Bailey Rae gripped Martin's arm. "He only barks at strangers."

Martin's shoulders braced, like a soldier on alert, poised for action. "Stay here. Bolt the lock. Call the police."

He charged across the living room and grabbed his cap. Skeeter raced past her to catch up. The dog threaded the narrow space between Martin and the doorframe before leaping off the porch. The door slammed closed behind them.

She wanted to argue that she wasn't completely defenseless, but he'd already disappeared into the dark and she really should call 9-1-1. Except once she did the line rang and rang, only to throw her on hold. The department was small and understaffed, with a high turnover as people either quit or moved to a bigger city with better pay.

The recording assured her that if she had to hang up, her number would stay on file and the first available operator would respond. She ground her teeth and peeked out the windowpane, watching the bobbing illumination from Martin's flashlight move farther away.

Then swing around and bobble closer again.

She yanked open the door, cell still clutched in her hand with the inane recording cycling through for the fourth time. "What did you find?"

"Some tire tracks," he said, his tone tight with frustration, "but whoever it was is long gone."

The light flipped on inside the Airstream a moment before the door swung wide. Keith poked his head out, his hair sticking up. He jogged down the two steps, shirttails loose. "What's going on?"

"We heard a noise outside, and Skeeter about lost his mind over whatever it was." *Breathe in the flowers. Blow out the candles. Breathe in the swamp fumes. Blow away the mosquitoes.* "Martin found some tracks . . ."

Keith scratched a hand along his neck. "Could be a deer . . . or one of those wild pigs."

Martin shook his head, aiming the flashlight beam past the sprawling oaks and toward the path leading into the pines. "Those tracks weren't made by an animal."

Bailey Rae walked alongside Martin, with Keith trailing them until she was close enough to see outlines in the soft earth. Footprints, one set of which appeared to be made by work boots, disappeared into the dense pine woods.

Night sounds mocked her overhead—yes, just birds and bugs, but their high pitch jarred the senses—joined by the sound of an engine cranking. Not a car. But the machinery was distinguishable all the same. A four-wheeler. The engine caught and revved, then grew softer as someone drove it farther and farther away in the direction of the river.

Keith cursed softly under his breath. "Whoever it was appears to have left."

For now.

The unspoken two words hung in the air like mosquitoes making their presence known one bloodsucking bite at a time. In the silence that followed, Skeeter returned, panting heavily but calmer now that he'd chased off whoever had been lurking outside.

Martin adjusted his hat. "The best we can do is sit tight and wait for the police to come out so we can file a report."

Like the reports that had been so beneficial to Gia and Cricket in the past? His words didn't bring any more reassurance than the recorded message droning through Bailey Rae's cell phone. And now she had two people depending on her to find answers in her short time remaining in Bent Oak.

CHAPTER EIGHT

1978

In many ways, Alabama and South Carolina were like identical twin sisters, making it easier to slide into life here in Bent Oak. Almost too much so, in ways that could lead to complacency. Over the years, I forced myself to concentrate on the differences. Mardi Gras was a big deal in Alabama. Not so much in South Carolina.

And of course, there was the coastline. Alabama only had that tiny portion around Mobile, which made my city a sort of Mecca for the region. Yes, a person could hop across the border to Florida and enjoy their sunny beaches. But that snippet of the Gulf Coast? It belonged to the people of Alabama in a way that made Mobile special. South Carolinians loved their beaches as well, but with so many more coastal miles, they didn't treasure it the same way I did.

My father doubled his family portfolio by recognizing the worth of the Florida Panhandle's coast so close to Mobile. He invested. Big.

Growing up with such wealth, I never imagined the satisfaction I would gain from opening my own stall at the farmers' market to supplement my income at the paper mill. I certainly never imagined working two jobs. But I was proud of my booth, with the checkered cloth on my table rippling in the sultry breeze.

"Thank you for your business," I said to a young shopper with a baby on her hip. I passed her three jars of canned goods—peaches, green beans, and pickles—along with a small bag of freshly shelled pecans, thanks to Annette's generosity in letting me gather pecans from the library grounds.

Sweat beaded down my spine as I slid the money into the cashbox and served the next customer. Summer in Bent Oak was hotter than hot, but I no longer passed up an opportunity to be outside.

Moving from the cleaning crew to the assembly line had brought a pay raise, but not much. So I needed to think of low-profile ways to increase my income. The logical choice would have been to create art. But I didn't dare risk showcasing my glasswork for fear of a piece—my style—being recognized.

There were weeks that my hands ached to create. Back in Mobile, I'd focused on beach-themed items . . . sea creatures, shells, coral. Now I envisioned creating the regional flowers and creatures. A bowl shaped like an overlarge azalea blossom. Or a Carolina wren trapped in an orb.

And my pièce de résistance would be a twisted oak tree with the finest Spanish moss draped from the branches. I'd seen it in my mind so many times I felt like I could have created it with my eyes closed. Those projects had to stay locked away in my brain, however. I turned my artistic side to other creative ventures.

Like baking. I started by selling pound cakes and baked goods like my mother had taught me. Instead of donating them for charity events, now I sold them to put food on my own table.

Then canning. Libby showed me how to can my own preserves after we spent a day strawberry picking, Keith in tow eating more than he saved. I even made my own jars, as close as I could come to indulging in glassblowing. Those were big sellers.

I took pride in how often the ladies of the garden club showed up at my booth. Soon they began to place last-minute orders for times they just plumb ran out of time to bake. Even if it meant I stayed up past midnight, I filled those orders, desperate to pack the hours in my day and increase the money I'd hidden away in my tampon box under the bathroom sink. I'd yet to meet a man who would touch a container of feminine products.

How ironic, now that I could open my own checking account and even apply for a credit card, I didn't dare risk the paper trail. Not even with my forged documents.

Especially with my forged documents.

Although one thing was certain. I was finding my way in the world. Not just at work and taking help, I was now in a position to give back, to assist others, and it felt good. Really good. Far better than any fundraiser I'd organized for the hospital where Phillip practiced medicine.

Libby and I had been assisting Annette in small ways. Bringing food. Picking up extra clothes from the thrift store for new folks on their way through. No one else stayed in Bent Oak, though, as Libby, Keith, and I had done seven years earlier.

And it turned out that seven was a magic number of sorts for me. The point at which Phillip declared me legally dead.

I stumbled on the answer while helping Annette scan back issues of magazines into microfiche. The monotony of it was mind numbing, but I owed Annette. I never said no.

Then I saw it.

In the society section of *Brides* magazine. A small article covered the wedding of the year—that of Phillip Curtis to a wealthy debutante. There had even been a short mention of the tragic death of his first wife in a drowning accident and how after seven years, she—I—had been declared legally dead.

Phillip had truly moved on.

My hands trembled then and now at the magnitude of that moment. Of knowing I was free. But also trapped, because now, there was no going back. While wonderful, there was so much unknown that came with freedom. That freedom also meant no more excuses to live in limbo.

I cleared my throat to thank Sylvie Tyler for her business. "I appreciate you. I'll be sure to have those extra tomatoes for your husband."

"Honey, I appreciate *you*. He does love tomato sandwiches, just like our son." She gathered up her three bags of honey-roasted pecans with a smile, stepping away for the last in line for the afternoon . . .

Russell.

So handsome I couldn't help but let my eyes linger, especially given my newfound freedom. We'd been friends for years. I'd cheered on his dirt track races and his wins. Any events within the safety of the county lines, of course.

But never more than that with Russell as time marched, fashions changing like the seasonal leaves on the trees. His bell-bottom jeans then, slimmed down now. His tie-dyed T-shirts now replaced with polyester button-downs with wide collars that showcased his strong neck. Most importantly, the ways that we were different didn't turn as many heads as before.

Russell's smile, though, stayed constant, radiating kindness and affection. "I hear you have the best preserves in the state of South Carolina."

I reached under my table and pulled out a jar of strawberry jam. "I saved an extra for you as a thanks for fixing my car the other day."

Yes, I had purchased my own vehicle. With cash. A ten-year-old green Dodge Dart that I had affectionately named Olive.

He scooped up the jar. "She still has plenty of life left in her."

"Would you like to go on a picnic sometime?" I blurted, but I didn't regret the impulsive invitation one bit.

For seven years I'd held back, not daring to take a single step beyond friendship. And to be fair, the time had given me a chance to heal. All the while, I kept thinking my infatuation with him would pass with a sharpened perspective. I treasured his friendship—and his grandmother's—too much to risk it.

Except my attraction to Russell had grown with every day, month, year. Over time I learned all those nuances that too often got lost when relationships progressed at a fast pace, rushing to connect rather than savoring each layer of the person.

To reveal their character. Or discover red flags.

Russell was all character and charisma.

Had I—out of necessity—waited too long?

Then a slow smile spread across his face. "Yes, I would very much like to join you on a picnic. Under one condition."

"What would that be?" I asked, enjoying the new flirty nature to our exchange.

"Let me pick you up."

My breath hitched. This was it. Something I'd fantasized about but barely dared dream could happen.

"It's a deal." I extended my hand and he clasped it in his, his calloused palm warm against my own work-roughened hands. Seven years of anticipation flowed between us, back and forth. Exciting, and frightening as well after all I'd been through. But I wanted to try. With him. Later, I would figure out what that might look like. I'd learned these past years about caution. Finally, I was ready to take a risk. "Saturday at one o'clock."

His smile widened. "It's a date."

2025

Bailey Rae stifled a yawn, and it wasn't even suppertime.

Radio blasting, she steered her pickup into the lot behind the library, where staff parked. The habit had begun when Winnie brought Bailey Rae with her, and it seemed natural to continue even when driving on her own. No one questioned.

She'd just picked up her last paycheck from the Fill 'Er Up Café while Gia and Cricket attended story hour at the library under the combined watchful eyes of Thea and June. Soon, Bailey Rae would be her own boss. She would have control over her life, thanks once again to Winnie and Russell.

But first, she needed to tie up loose ends with Gia and Cricket, plus finish her market days.

Another yawn caught her by surprise, her jaw popping at the stretch. Sleep had been tough to come by even after the cops finally arrived and came to the same conclusion as Martin. Someone had been snooping around the yard, but no way to tell who. Gia's husband? A Peeping Tom? Or even the missing fisherman . . . except he wouldn't have a four-wheeler.

The gravel crunched as she crossed the lot, then climbed the concrete steps, a smaller staircase than the sprawling one out front made to accommodate larger groups entering and exiting, such as class field trips. Gripping the metal railing, she could almost imagine she held Winnie's hand again, coming to story time led by Libby while Winnie volunteered reshelving books.

The place felt like a second home. She'd spent countless hours deep in one of the fat beanbag chairs, escaping between the pages. Winnie would say that art had a transformative power that couldn't be found anywhere else.

Well, her aunt had said it in easier-to-understand language back then. But coming from such a nuts-and-bolts, practical person, it surprised Bailey Rae enough to make her sit up and take notice.

A familiar voice drifted past the rows of shelves, Libby leading story time, thanks to the "chauffeuring" help of June and Thea. Libby might not always remember her own name, but she could still read books to children. The doctor had told them Alzheimer's looked different for each person diagnosed. He had a patient who no longer recognized any of his family members but could keep track of sports scores.

Very little had changed at the library over the years. The scarred tables had been refinished. The card catalog had been traded out for a long line of computers, each with its own privacy cubby. Above the fireplace, a framed and matted fourteen-by-eighteen photo of Russell's grandmother Annette stared down at them with eyes so like Russell's.

Careful not to distract, Bailey Rae allowed herself a moment to breathe and tugged a chair from one of those cubbies.

As Libby continued to read *The Three Billy Goats Gruff*, she drew interactive responses from her young audience filling the rug.

"Who's that stomp, stomp, stomping across my bridge?"

Tiny feet hammered the floor.

Most of the faces were familiar but welcoming, since it seemed there was often someone's cousin, brother, or sister visiting. Except for the police officer sitting by the front door thumbing through a *Field & Stream*.

Smack dab in the center, Gia sat cross-legged with her arms wrapped around her daughter in her lap. Cricket had stayed even closer to her mother since the brief stint with child services while her mother was in the hospital.

This evening, Martin would be picking her up to ride along when taking Gia and Cricket to a new shelter. One with tighter security. So far, they hadn't been able to persuade Gia to file a police report. She insisted that it wouldn't work and if her husband found her, he would only be angrier.

No doubt, the woman spoke out of fear for her life and her child's.

Bailey Rae didn't remember her own mother being that terrified—or that concerned for her child's well-being. Yvonne had rarely grieved for the last guy, always focused on the next man and his potential drug stash.

Bailey Rae shoved the memories aside like reshelving a one-star book she'd finished and hoped never to read again.

Story time concluded, with the head librarian directing the children to tables for crafts—making paper-bag puppets of the story characters. Thea pushed Libby's wheelchair toward a lounge area in back. June followed, waving for Bailey Rae to join them in the same spot where Aunt Winnie used to have bagged lunches with her friends while Bailey Rae finished her homework.

June pulled over an extra chair. "What's this I hear about the police being called to your place last night?"

Bailey Rae slung her leather backpack onto the table. "Turned out to be a great big nothing burger. Skeeter barked up a storm. There were some footprints, but no one around. We heard a four-wheeler crank to life in the distance, but that could have been any number of people."

June shook her head, a newly purple streak of hair sliding forward. "I'm just glad you're all right."

Bailey Rae squeezed Libby's gnarled hand. "Thank you for loaning Keith to us."

Sniffing, Thea mumbled under her breath, "Not much of a sacrifice, if you ask me. Skeeter would be more help than that man."

Libby just smiled, not appearing to take offense, which was the best way to deal with Thea. "Well, Gia's husband wouldn't know that."

Bailey Rae nodded. "You're right, Mrs. Libby. Martin Perez stuck around too. He parked his truck at the top of the road."

Thea asked, "What happens now?"

"Martin located another shelter. I'm not clear on the details, but we'll drive them over together this evening."

Libby's face furrowed. "I hope Gia doesn't go back to her husband. It's harder to leave than people think." The fog cleared from her gray eyes. "I had a cousin in a similar situation. She barely escaped with her life."

The result of that outcome weighed heavy on Bailey Rae's conscience. "I'm not sure what else I can do."

June slid an arm around her shoulders in a familiar half hug. "Honey, you have done as much as possible. Just reach out to her when you can. She'll need support."

Libby leaned forward, elbows on the table. "But use a burner so he can't track you down if he takes her phone."

Suddenly, Libby's advice for Gia to hide her car made more sense. "I'm sorry about your cousin." Libby's face creased in confusion, but Bailey Rae knew better than to press her. "Thank you again for pitching in. I know I'm the one who volunteered to help Gia and Cricket, which makes them my responsibility."

Thea tugged her ever-present white gloves more securely in place before stepping behind Libby's wheelchair again. "We ladies need to stick together." She leaned over Libby's shoulder. "Let's go find that son of yours."

June bustled alongside, her sassy purple streak glowing under the fluorescent lights. "Bailey Rae, now you call us if you need anything. Anything at all."

Clustered together, the three moved almost as one on their way toward the entrance and its wheelchair ramp. An image of them from the past superimposed itself in her mind, the three of them walking arm in arm with Winnie, all of them with straight spines and fire in their steps.

Winnie's death had hit them hard, adding fresh gray to their hair and stooping their shoulders. But the fire was still there, even when diluted by cataracts. These ladies were badass, and she loved that about them.

Whatever it took, she would make them proud by helping Gia, then launching her new life.

⁓

Windshield wipers slapped the rain away, lightning slicing the sky. Bailey Rae winced, counting down seconds in her head until thunder rumbled outside Martin's truck. *One . . . two . . .* Another bolt shot down, the quick crack so close she couldn't tell if it was thunder or a split tree.

Storm clouds darkened the sky, bringing nightfall early. Thankfully, the game warden vehicle came equipped with a laptop computer he'd opened and set to a weather radar. The screen bathed the truck's cab in a marshy glow.

Bailey Rae squinted from the passenger seat, helping Martin keep watch for deer crossing the country road. She definitely didn't want to peer too far into the woods, where the river current swept higher, fast, the narrow channel swollen with rain. She couldn't let herself think of Winnie's body submerged there or further, trapped by tangled roots.

Better to focus on searching for vulnerable Bambis along the edge of the back road. Some deer would bed down to ride out the weather, but others could still spook and bolt. Difficult enough to see in advance in even the best of weather.

At least they had dropped off Gia and Cricket at the new shelter before the skies really opened up. Bailey Rae scanned the brush just beyond the passenger window. "I'm sorry this drive turned into such a hassle."

"No need to apologize. I wanted to help. I'll rest easier knowing all of you are safe," Martin said, gripping the steering wheel, his forehead furrowed in concentration. "Not just Gia and Cricket."

The security at the new shelter appeared top notch, with a locked gate around the little community. There was even counseling available on-site that would—hopefully—allay Libby's concern that Gia would return to her husband. Bailey Rae wished hers were as easily settled, because she was struggling to trust people after how badly the last attempt played out, landing Gia in the hospital.

Bailey Rae leaned forward to swipe her arm along the fogged windshield. "How did you find the new shelter? I've never heard of it before."

"It's legit." He switched on the defogger, blasting air upward. "With a tax ID number. It's just smaller and less known, but that makes for tighter security. I have every reason to believe he won't find her, as long as . . ."

"As long as she doesn't reach out to him." She swallowed down bile. "We've done all we can, haven't we?"

He answered with a tight nod, never looking away from the two-lane road.

Bailey Rae tapped the edge of the computer, the radar covered in bands of the downpour. "The weatherman really let us down with the forecast earlier."

"Agreed," he said, his grip on the steering wheel turning whiter. "It's just as risky to turn back as to forge ahead. Or we could pull over and wait it out."

Since Skeeter had a dog door to get in and out, she had nothing else pressuring her to return home. No one to worry if she didn't arrive on time . . . Depressing. "We should probably—"

Lightning split the sky, the crack of thunder so close the storm must have been right over them.

Martin winced. "Right. I'm pulling over."

He put the truck into reverse, arm across the seat until they reached the top of the hill, where he shifted into park. The hammering rain on the roof and hazy interior seemed to shrink the space, leaving her fidgety from adrenaline letdown and needing to fill the awkward silence between them.

"We have a healthy respect for thunderstorms around here. Did you know that lightning struck Winnie's barn years ago and burned it to the ground?" she babbled. "The red barn that's there now is a rebuild. Folks say lightning doesn't strike twice, but I'm not sure I believe that. I think there are places in the world that have these negative gravitational pulls that attract bad luck. Is that silly?"

"Not at all." He shifted sideways, toward her, his elbow resting on the back of the seat. "Back home in Arizona, there are vortexes—or the more proper term is vortices. Anyway, these sites are believed to have healing energy. So it only makes sense that if there are these positive vibes, there would be places with negative ones as well."

She hadn't expected an answer like that from him, but then perhaps she'd been so busy paying attention to the rule-following military side of him, she'd missed the nature-loving warden side. "Do you miss Arizona?"

"Not particularly," he said, taking off his hat and placing it on the dash. "I was a military brat, so I grew up all around the world. Dad's last station was in Arizona while I was in high school. He and Mom decided to stay."

"Any siblings?" she asked, pressing for more from him. Curious if he had any more surprises locked behind that handsome face.

"One sister. She's in the air force, married with two boys. They get Mom and Dad at holidays since I'm childless. The grandkids are a big draw."

How . . . sad. "I'm sorry."

"I could always buy a plane ticket and join them," he said practically, without a hint of hurt or anger. "Maybe if I'd lived in Arizona longer, I would have felt differently."

"I've been in Bent Oak since I was six, and I can't wait to leave." The beach was calling her name. Less forest. Fewer negative force fields of memories to flatten her.

Martin stretched his arm ever so slightly and brushed back a lock of her hair. "No high school beau holding you back?"

"A beau?" She laughed, lightly punching him on the arm. "Who says beau anymore?"

He grinned, rubbing the top of his arm. "I thought it sounded Southern. I guess I missed the mark."

"Well, bless your heart," she said with a wink.

The air crackled in the minuscule space between them. Maybe it was all the talk about a positive vortex. "I didn't have a boyfriend until the twelfth grade."

His eyebrows shot up in surprise. "Were the boys at your school idiots?"

"You sound like Aunt Winnie." The highest compliment she could pay anyone. "Anyhow, my new *beau* seemed so nice, almost too nice. I figured there had to be a catch."

"Ah, man, I get the feeling I'm going to have to kick some ass after this story is finished."

"Actually," she said, angling to face him more fully, her knee hitched on the seat, "he turned out to be every bit as nice as he seemed the first time he sat beside me at lunch. I thought he felt sorry for me because I was alone that day, thanks to the resident mean girls, Sissy and Missy."

He shook his head. "Some people don't change."

She laughed and he joined in, their sounds twining. The rain on the roof softened until she could hear only the two of them. A month ago, she wouldn't have expected to find an ally in Martin, but then he'd surprised her these past couple of weeks.

"My 'beau' was one of those super-religious guys who walked the talk. I hadn't met many of those sorts." In her early days in Bent Oak, she hadn't been able to envision what a "good guy" would even look like. "Beau—for the life of me I can't recall his name now... Anyhow, Beau and I had been dating for about six months when he invited me to his youth group at church. I was so nervous. I put on my best jeans—no holes in the knees—and I buttoned up my shirt all the way to my neck."

Martin laughed softly with her, not at her.

Encouraged, Bailey Rae leaned closer. "By the time I got there, my nerves were chewing me up alive. It didn't help that Sissy and Missy belonged to the same youth group. But this was important to Beau, and he was important to me. So I decided to bite my lip and stay quiet."

"How long did that last?" he asked, grinning while the rain continued to drum the roof in a steady downpour.

"Not long. The youth leader was telling about how if your hand offends you, cut it off, if your eye offends you... and so forth. Then he said something about being careful who you keep company with, and I could have sworn Sissy or Missy—I never could tell them apart—was staring a hole in my back—"

"Remind me to write them a ticket."

Bailey Rae clapped a hand over her mouth for a moment before continuing, "The next thing I knew, I blurted, 'Poor guy. Who does that? Because if he looks at the wrong woman, I wonder what they'll cut off him next.' Needless to say, that was the end of my budding romance with Beau."

"Now I would pay good money to have seen Missy and Sissy's faces." His sense of humor was surprising. "Did you tell Winnie?"

"Oh, I didn't have to. She'd already heard about it from three different sources by the time Beau dropped me off." The rest of the story unfolded in her memory, how Winnie told her she didn't have to go back anywhere she didn't feel welcome—which pretty much left nowhere to go except Winnie and Russell's. But that part of the tale sounded too sad, and she wanted more of Martin's smiles.

"Aunt Winnie located a nondenominational church with a youth group where I could wear my ripped jeans and favorite rock band T-shirts. I never sat alone at school again."

When had his arm stretched farther along the back of the seat, until her shoulder brushed his bicep? She'd had enough dates—real boyfriends—since Beau to know that the draw between them was a moment away from leading to a kiss. A great big complication at a time when she needed her life streamlined.

Except she wanted that kiss from him. She wished she could ask Winnie for advice, which was a ridiculous thought. If Winnie were still alive, Bailey Rae wouldn't be leaving. So she was on her own with this decision.

A squawk blared from the computer, startling them apart and saving her from deciding anything. The lights on his laptop flickered with a weather update full of warnings, but for the next county over.

Martin scrolled along the screen. "Seems like there's a break in the storm long enough that I can get you home if we leave now."

Was he asking her if she wanted to stay here and explore that attraction? Or testing the water to see if she would invite him over?

Before she could finish thinking that possibility through, much less draw a conclusion, he turned away and put the truck into drive again.

Pulling back onto the road, he said, "After I drop you off, I need to head into the office and catch up on paperwork. Let me know if you hear anything from Gia."

Just that fast, he'd dismissed her and whatever they'd almost shared. For the best. Because she didn't need anything interfering with her plans to leave. Still, she couldn't shake the feeling of being that high schooler in her buttoned-up shirt who'd been judged as lacking.

Her mama had it all wrong expecting a man to fix the emptiness, but Yvonne had been right about one thing. The importance of knowing when to pull up stakes and move on to the next town. Preferably one without the opaque river that served as Winnie's final resting place.

CHAPTER NINE

_1978_

Russell's Chevy Chevelle ate up the back road that ran parallel to the river. As I tipped my head out the open window, the wind swept my hair across my face and tunneled through my crocheted top. The scarf around my head trailed like a kite tail. I indulged my artist's eye. From the ancient oaks that learned to twist into hugs as they grew. To the river's current creating crystal peaks that glinted in the afternoon sun like freshly blown glass.

Excitement and nerves tangled inside me like those tree branches, two parts of a beautiful adventure in my new life. I told myself this outing with Russell was just a picnic. Yes, a date, but a simple date.

A date with *seven years* of anticipation.

Which made it far from simple.

Once we cleared the city limit, he floored the accelerator, the engine growling in celebration. When watching him compete, I'd heard the echo of the finely tuned racing machines, but never from inside the vehicle. The sound amplified until the entire car vibrated with life.

I tucked my head inside again and combed my fingers through my hair until it settled into place. "Where are we going?"

Since I'd packed the food, I told him to surprise me with the location—as long as we stayed within the county. Thankfully, he hadn't asked about my aversion to leaving the area.

"We're almost there." Slowing, he took the turn with precision, guiding his souped-up sedan over a narrow bridge with sides so low they provided precious little protection. "It'll be obvious in a moment."

I didn't want to think about the irony of how I trusted Russell more than Phillip, a man I'd chosen to marry. Instead, I tipped my head back and let myself savor this day. I could taste freedom on the wind.

Time passed in a comfortable silence born from our long friendship. Miles later, he eased his foot off the gas, the car coasting as our destination came into view.

A dirt racetrack waited by the riverbank. Not the one he used for competition, but grooves in the earth testified to the loop's age and use.

He put the car in park by a wooden picnic table, a woodpecker tapping in the quiet. "Don't worry. It's not some illegal racing operation. The land belongs to my grandparents. Grandpa cleared this loop for me to practice."

"Your grandfather was a thoughtful man."

He'd died two years earlier. Annette had struggled with the loss, so much so she'd begun asking Libby and me for more help with small tasks in the rescue operation. To start, we'd hand carried documents—new birth certificates, diplomas, and driver's licenses—from the paralegal to the library.

"Yes, he was. I miss him." Russell's throat moved in a long swallow, and he dried his palms along his jeans. "When I first got back from 'Nam, this was the best place to blow off steam and help me return to my old self."

He didn't talk about his time in Vietnam often, and I knew well that a person was entitled to secrets. So I just let him choose his own words and pace now.

Russell scratched his collarbone, his sepia-hued skin glistening with a light perspiration. "These days, I come out here sometimes to practice and test out tweaks to the Chevy. What do you say? Would you like to go for a spin?"

Lightning in a Mason Jar

"Are you sure? You might take that offer back when you hear I got ill on a Ferris wheel." Only once since I'd never tried again. Looking back, it could have been the cotton candy and caramel apple I'd begged my father to buy since Mama restricted my desserts. In hindsight, that seemed ironic, given all the sweets she'd taught me to bake.

Russell tucked a lock of hair behind my shoulder. "I won't go any faster than you're comfortable with."

We both knew he wasn't just referring to the car.

I leaned my cheek against his wrist. "How about we take it one lap at a time and see how it goes?"

Again, we were talking about more than this afternoon. I trusted this man with my safety.

"I think that's a mighty fine plan."

He passed me a shiny silver helmet, which gave me a moment's pause as I envisioned wrecks from races. But this wasn't a competition, and I wasn't living my life on the sidelines anymore. Besides, if I wanted to know more about Russell, this was an important facet of him. I longed to experience what he did when he raced.

Dropping his own helmet into place with one hand, he shifted the car out of park with the other. He kept his foot on the brake, revving the engine, once, twice, fueling the RPMs. Then peeling rubber, off we went. The Chevelle sure had a lot more giddy-up-and-go than my Dodge Dart.

Cautiously, I watched the speedometer as we took the first lap around the track at fifty miles per hour. Nothing more than a highway speed, but it felt faster without slowing for the turns. My nerves tensed and I braced myself, but at the same time, the motion of the vehicle gave me a thrill. Russell cast quick glances my way as if to check my comfort level, and each time I gave him a nod.

I'd attended Russell's races countless times over the years, cheering him on alongside his grandparents and my friends. But sitting inside the vehicle with him offered new insights to the sport. And to Russell. I'd seen his calm control over the years, but there was an edge to him now.

A fire in his eyes. An energy that had begun building from the moment he put on his helmet. His passion behind the wheel mirrored what I'd experienced firing up a torch to create works of art.

Again, he turned to look at me, and I offered a thumbs-up. Faster. By the fifth loop, we were almost flying. This time, he pressed the pedal to the floor and my heart leaped in my chest. Squealing, I grabbed the roll bar and braced my feet against the floorboards.

He guided the vehicle around a hairpin turn, the back end of the car fishtailing. Dirt spewed behind us in a cloud, and for an instant I thought we would spin out. Then he righted our world, powering straight on again, shifting gears. My squeal turned to a shout of exhilaration.

To think I could have missed this.

Missed him.

Somehow, Russell milked even more power from the Chevy, sending it soaring across the finish line, then sliding sideways to a stop. The dust created a cloud around us, the grit settling faster than my heart rate.

Ears ringing, I sagged back against the seat, the world spinning in front of me. Breath by breath, I let the experience sink inside me as I inhaled the scent of earth and Russell. A heady perfume. I turned my head to smile at him. He smiled back. The world stopped spinning, his dear, familiar face coming fully into focus.

Memories drifted around me like leaves falling from the trees. Of him replacing the bald tires on Olive and refusing to charge me. But more than just helping me. How he cleared limbs from old Mr. Underwood's front lawn after a storm. When he anonymously placed a sack of school supplies on Libby's front stoop, something I wouldn't have known except I'd run into him at the Thrifty Nickel and recognized the Evel Knievel lunch box he'd tossed on top of a buggy full of paper, crayons, pencils, and glue. Russell was a good man.

And mighty easy on the eyes.

I unbuckled my helmet and shook out my hair. "That was incredible. A little scary, but so exciting. Although I can't imagine what it's like with other vehicles crowding the track."

My heart rate had almost returned to normal. But not quite. With Russell's voice in my ear, I had the feeling that my pulse wasn't thrumming just because of the car ride anymore.

"It's a lot like navigating that channel over there in a johnboat during the height of fishing season." He motioned toward the riverbank, where another picnic table waited with a Mason jar of flowers in the middle. He'd planned. "I thought we could have our picnic over yonder. Best view in the county."

When he said the last part, he was staring at me.

Butterflies swirled in my stomach. "I brought a blanket too. Maybe we can sit by the shore and feed crumbs to the fish."

"Great idea. Next time, I can bring fishing poles."

Next time. The flutter increased, and my toes curled in my sneakers.

He hefted the picnic basket from the back seat while I lifted out the blanket, a soft quilt I slept under each night. I hadn't thought that part through, because now every time I drew the cover over me in bed, I would think of him.

Even more than I already did.

Hugging the quilt, I picked my way toward the table, sidestepping roots and crunching spikes from the sweet gum tree. "What got you started racing?"

"My bicycle didn't go near fast enough for me, so I built a dirt bike from scraps at the junkyard. Since my grandparents owned the garage, I had the perfect mentor whenever I ran into a problem with the design." He set the picnic basket on the sturdy plank table, the benches lightly shaded by oak tree branches. "It took me months, but I succeeded. She was a sweet ride. After I tore up Granny's garden one too many times, Grandpa made this track for me."

I touched the Mason jar full of dahlias and daisies, a delicate—and thoughtful—addition to the wooded picnic spot. "Are these from your grandmother's garden?"

"Guilty as charged. I was careful only to pick the ones from the back." He winked before continuing, "My grandfather took me to a race over in Darlington. You probably don't know, but they have this egg-shaped track with brutal turns. I could calculate in my head how the drivers should navigate . . . Sometime during that trip I realized I'd heard the calling, and now I'm chasing my dream."

A whisper of unease teased through me to hear him speak about his ambitions. For the first time, I realized his dream was big enough that it could very well take him away from Bent Oak. I dropped the quilt onto the planked seat and refused to let the day be tainted by what-ifs.

One container at a time, I set out our lunch of pimento cheese sandwiches cut into triangles. Corn fritters. Deviled eggs. And of course, pound cake with sweet tea.

He whistled his appreciation. "That's quite a feast."

"I'm a fan of picnics after my shift. Libby and I come swimming down this way sometimes, when Keith's in school." I pointed north. "Not too far that way, actually."

His forehead furrowed. "Winnie, I don't want to be inappropriate or forward, but is that safe out here, swimming alone?"

I bristled at that, ghosts of days with Phillip reminding me of all the times he censured me under the guise of being protective. "Are you worried we're skinny-dipping? If so, why does that matter? Men skinny-dip."

We actually hadn't. Instead, we'd stopped short of stripping completely, leaving on our cotton underwear and support bras. Probably not wise to include that part since the picnic was spiraling.

"I worry for your safety. Not just the current, but being out here unprotected," he said simply. "Do you have any fear?"

An odd statement coming from a man who'd just taken on a racetrack at a hundred miles per hour. Then I reminded myself this was

Russell, my friend, a man who'd shown himself to be honorable time and time again.

Could his comment about pursuing his dream, even if it meant leaving town, have driven a knee-jerk reaction from me to push him away? "I have all sorts of fears," I admitted, resting a hand on top of his. "So many that every now and again I decide on the easiest one to face to give myself a break from the weight of it all."

Today, I would dismiss my fear of rejection.

"Well, to ease *my* fear"—he flipped his hand to clasp mine—"next time you ladies decide to take a swim, let me know. I'll just sit with my back against the tree—facing away, of course—and make sure no one else walks up on you."

"What a noble and selfless deed," I said with a smirk, drawing a laugh from him as we shook hands on the deal. Then I shifted my attention back to pulling out plates and setting the table. "I enjoyed watching your race last weekend. Congratulations on your win."

"Why didn't you stick around afterward?" he asked, pouring tea from the gallon jug into two glasses.

"I had a busy week coming up at the mill." An excuse. I'd made a hasty retreat, too tempted to stay.

"Maybe after the next race, we could go out for drinks and dancing at the Tipsy Cow. Do you like to dance?"

Like to dance? I *loved* to dance. All kinds. Even disco. But most of all, doing the shag to beach music.

"I can hold my own." The warm sun on my skin relaxed me as we filled our plates and sat across from each other. My fingers itched to trace the checkered pattern of his plaid shirt, to feel the heat of his skin through the fabric. "My mother signed me up for lessons at a local studio the day I turned five. Tap. Ballet. Jazz. Three times a week. Even baton lessons. She had plans for me to be a pageant girl."

Sharing even a benign part of my past felt strange after closely guarding my secrets for so long. But this memory was generic enough, not particularly traceable, and I wanted to offer at least some part of my history to him.

He quirked a dark eyebrow. "From your tone, I take it that you didn't agree."

The day before the pageant, I stood up to my mother for the first time. I was only seven. Knees knocking, because I wanted to take a pottery class that afternoon instead. My father told me if I made my mother happy by participating in the pageant, then he would pay for private pottery lessons. We struck a deal.

Daddy forgot to stipulate that I should try to win.

I was fifth runner-up. There were seven contestants. My mother was so embarrassed she never asked me again. I expected my father to be angry—Mama was his world, after all. But he congratulated me on being a tough negotiator. He was proud of me.

Even then, I'd known that wasn't an invitation to join the family business. If I'd been a boy . . .

I shook my head. "I wasn't a pageant queen."

"You're more beautiful than any of them."

His gaze held me and I believed it, even as I sat there in cutoff jean shorts and a crocheted shirt that Libby had made for me as a thank-you for helping Keith with his homework. Because his compliment had more to do with me as a person than the external. I wasn't sure how I knew, but I did.

"Thank you."

I wanted to compliment him in return but didn't want it to sound obligatory after his remark. So I let my eyes speak, in the same way his had.

He smiled.

I heard him.

Russell stroked a thumb across the inside of my wrist. "How's the first date going for you so far? Do you think you might be ready for another?"

Well, he'd certainly waited long enough for me. His few relationships over the past seven years had been fleeting, although each one had filled me with jealousy as green and ugly as the slime coating the swampy waters. I'd no one to blame but myself, and my only consolation came from my patience. My feelings for him were affirmed by my determination to do everything in my power to make sure he didn't get hurt.

I'd been so focused on freeing myself, I hadn't given much thought to how my decisions would affect others. Now I couldn't think of anything other than that. I'd rejoined the world, and even with my knees shaking like the day I'd asked for pottery classes, I wanted more.

Wordlessly, I stood and leaned across the picnic table to graze my mouth over his, lingering just long enough for my answer to be clear. Then I sat down again, enjoying the stunned look on his face.

I unfolded my napkin and draped it across my lap. "Are you ready for lunch? I'm starved."

2025

Bailey Rae hadn't expected a pit stop with Martin to check out a report of illegal dumping near the river would lead her on a trip down memory lane.

Aunt Winnie had adored this stretch of the river. She'd told me more than once how she and Uncle Russell fell in love there. No doubt, though, Winnie would weep to see the area now, a scrapyard for someone's broken-down furniture, mattresses, and trash.

Bailey Rae eyed the overgrown path ahead of them as Martin parked his work truck. He'd driven her to the shelter to drop off more supplies for Gia and Cricket, detouring afterward when the call came over his radio. He'd offered to take her home first and circle back, but she'd insisted she didn't want to add the extra driving to his day after all he'd already done for her.

The answer had sounded logical to her ears, and far preferable to admitting how much she didn't want the day with him to end. "Thank you for taking me to see Gia and Cricket. I felt better knowing they hadn't returned to . . ."

"Right. Me too, honestly." He adjusted the brim of his game warden ball cap, his sunglasses shading his eyes. He reached under the front seat and pulled out two pairs of protective gloves, passing one over to her. She hopped out of the truck and tugged the gloves on, eyeing the mess in front of her.

"I think our checking in on her helped," she said, stopping by a dilapidated picnic table and slapping a mosquito on her neck, "letting her know that people care."

Hands on his hips, Martin kicked at a moldy mattress, a long exhale puffing his cheeks. "Are you sure you don't mind the detour? This won't take long. I just need to get an idea of how much manpower will be needed to clear it up."

She wouldn't have minded in the least if the river hadn't brought back memories of Winnie's death. As it was, she tried to focus solely on the task at hand so she didn't get lost in the past. In the grief that could still take her by surprise sometimes.

Instead, she focused on the closest pile of debris—a broken end table, an old television, stained mattresses, and a mountain of big green garbage bags containing heaven only knew what. That didn't even take into account the stray soda cans, beer bottles, and empty fast-food containers littering the shore. Was that a rolled-up carpet in the shallow end? "Sounds like a pricey proposition."

"I found a couple of teens needing volunteer hours for their Eagle Scout badge and a church youth group to help out."

The closer they walked, the worse it looked and smelled, rotting waste defiling this sacred space. Anger flared inside, a much easier default emotion than grief.

Winnie had always talked about the water like it was a living, breathing thing. If that were true, Bailey Rae didn't need to be a doctor to know what happened when blood turned to poison.

Martin cursed under his breath. "Whoever did this only had to drive two miles further down the road to the dump."

"I never thought about this being part of the game warden's job."

Kneeling, he snagged a couple of empty cans half submerged in the river and emptied them before tossing them onto the mattress. "If this aquatic trash contains something as simple as cleaners, pesticides, even a flea collar, it could contaminate the water supply. Preventing illegal dumping is just another aspect of conservation and preservation, keeping the ecosystem in balance." He shot a wry grin. "Rules are there for a reason."

She plucked three large pieces of broken glass from the mud and added them to the rest on the mattress. "I guess now isn't the time to say that fishing without a license pales in comparison to this . . ."

"While I see your point," he said, looking at her over the top of his glasses, "the top end of the fine is the same for both."

"Really?" She froze, feeling the blood drain from her face as worry for her bank balance blindsided her. "Do I owe a fine? I thought it was a warning."

"It was."

She sagged back against an oak tree, disturbing a mockingbird from a low branch so that it fluttered past her in a blur of wings and chirps. "Thank you."

"Just doing my job," he said. "Make sure you get that license before moving to Myrtle Beach. They're a lot stricter over that way."

"I've never given much thought to where game wardens worked or moved." Bent Oak was such a small town, might he want to transfer to a more prime spot later on? Like Myrtle Beach? "Do you choose your region, or is it like the military, where they move you where they decide you're needed?"

"I applied for this opening," he said simply. "My top pick."

She pushed aside the hint of disappointment and returned to shifting cans and bottles from the shallows over to the mattress. "Uncle Russell's family used to own land in this area. Winnie had held on to as much of the Davis property as possible, but Russell had insisted on selling off parcels to ensure her care after he was gone." The loss of both of them was too much to bear sometimes, overwhelming her in the quiet of night or in moments like this. "The three acres with the cabin and barn are all that's left."

"I didn't know that."

"Aunt Winnie used to say this river was the lifeblood of the community. That seemed such a beautiful image. But now? All I can see is the day I found her bag snagged on a rotting tree by the shore." More of that anger burned inside her, making her feel like the six-year-old who'd wanted to lash out at the world. "She saved me, and I couldn't do anything to rescue her."

Martin peeled off his glove and rested a comforting hand on her shoulder. "You're making her final resting place beautiful. That's something."

It didn't feel like nearly enough. She pointed to the knotty roots protruding from the water.

"Uncle Russell used to cut off the cypress trees' knees. He would strip the bark, refinish them, and gift them as doorstops." The memory helped give her something positive to think about while the shadow of Winnie's death hung heavy over her.

"I'll have to try that sometime."

She sat on a fat tree stump, feeling like someone had plucked the stuffing clean out of her. "I still don't understand how it happened. She was a great swimmer. Some whispered around town that she'd killed herself, but Winnie would never do that."

Kneeling in front of her, he said gently, "These waters can be unpredictable for even strong swimmers."

"She wasn't suicidal," Bailey Rae insisted again, shooting to her feet as the anger in her grew into a fiery blanket covering a grief that could well swallow her whole.

She channeled all that fury at the filth dishonoring her aunt's memory as she fished debris from the water one soggy piece at a time. Hamburger wrapper. Big Gulp cup. Floating water bottle.

"My aunt was eccentric. Not mentally ill."

"Winnie was a wonderful woman. I'm glad I had the chance to meet her." He followed her, picking up cigarette butts and letting her vent.

"There were people in this town who didn't appreciate her the way they should," she said, leaning to tug at a soggy T-shirt barely bubbling along the surface.

Frustrated at life, she yanked harder to dislodge the fabric from the branch, or whatever was underwater leaving a long shadow on the surface. She jerked again, then slipped on the muck. She plopped into the shallow water. Bubbles gurgled ahead of her as a mass under the T-shirt began to ease upward.

Not the shape of a fat branch at all.

More like a body.

Bile burned the back of her throat, and every cell inside her screamed in denial. This couldn't be her final memory of Winnie. Not this way.

Screaming, she scrambled up onto the bank, desperate to escape but unable to leave Winnie. If this was her.

Martin held up a hand for her to stay back, everything about him shifting into a calm professionalism she envied.

Shaking and wet, Bailey Rae lowered herself to the ground, unable to pull her eyes from the murky water. Taking deep breaths, she clutched fists full of grass to anchor herself as Martin waded into the river.

CHAPTER TEN

Martin had seen dead bodies in both his military and game warden careers. Difficult. Haunting. But there was something especially disturbing about a corpse that had been in the water for an extended time.

Steeling himself, he secured his grip on the shirt, ankle deep in the water. His boots sank into the muck, making each step a slog. Carefully, he eased the body over just to make sure the person wasn't still alive, even though his gut told him otherwise. The face came into view, covered in mud and algae. The gaping wound on the temple left no doubt. The individual was dead.

First order of business? Preserve the crime scene. Protect evidence as best he could while ensuring the current didn't reclaim the body. Or risk the body coming apart if he pulled it to the shore. Stretching, he grasped a fat stick. He maneuvered it through the neck of the T-shirt and into the mucky water, effectively staking the body in place.

One task at a time, he let training override all else. His brain felt like a warehouse full of boxes storing memories and emotions, with him choosing which to unseal and when. Compartmentalizing, some would call it. Not the healthiest of coping strategies, but the best he'd been able to manage to date in spite of all the sessions with a military shrink before he'd opted not to renew his army contract.

He sealed up the horror of securing the bloated body, tucking away the memory to be dealt with another time. On autopilot, he tugged out his cell phone to call the police department, then his boss, since the job description included assisting law enforcement in a rural setting such as this. Backup should arrive within a half hour. Until then, he could only stay with the body.

Which meant he couldn't drive Bailey Rae home yet.

How had he forgotten her? He glanced over his shoulder to search for her. She sat farther up the embankment, her head between her knees. Her shoulders shook, hard and fast. She must be either crying or hyperventilating. He stalked past the mattress pile, startling a foraging squirrel.

"Bailey Rae?" He knelt in front of her and started to reach for her, then remembered his hands were still covered in filth and death. He clenched his hands into fists to will away the feel of the soggy shirt.

"Is it Winnie?" Her voice trembled, and she didn't look up. "The body. Is it Winnie?"

Winnie? His gut sank that it had never occurred to him she might think so.

"No. Oh my God, no," he rushed to assure her. The face had been obscured, battered, but the body was obviously male. He should have guessed her mind would go there. His compartmentalizing had blinded him to her fears. "No. It's a man. Not Winnie, I promise."

"Thank God." She folded into herself, hugging her legs and pressing her face to her knees. Weeping harder, she rocked back and forth. He wanted more than anything to haul her against his chest and hold her until she'd cried herself dry, but he couldn't do a thing until he cleaned his hands and cleared his mind.

Martin climbed the slope past the picnic table to his truck and tugged his rucksack from the toolbox. He strode back to Bailey Rae and dropped it onto the ground beside her. He unzipped the canvas bag and gave his hands a once-over with an alcohol wipe even though they'd worn gloves. Wordlessly, he nudged her arm gently with the pack. She glanced at him with tearstained eyes and nodded.

Plucking three wipes, she scrubbed her hands and then her face. Mundane tasks could go a long way toward restoring equilibrium. Next, he smeared vapor rub under his nose before passing the small jar to her.

She drew the container to her nose and inhaled deeply before dabbing the menthol just over her top lip. "You must think I'm a wimp. Since Winnie passed without being found, I've lived in fear of the day I'd get word that she's been discovered."

"You were upset, and understandably so." Even as a trained professional, he was struggling to keep his mental boxes from overflowing. "I should have realized you would assume it was Winnie. I'm sorry for not speaking up right away."

"You had your hands full, and I wasn't any help." She wadded up the wipes.

"You helped in the most important way. You found him."

She started to turn to look toward the river.

Dipping his head into her line of sight, Martin drew her attention back to him. "Can you imagine if one of the Boy Scouts had stumbled on him during their Eagle Scout cleanup?"

People drowned annually in this river, some found, others never recovered. A sad reality.

"That would have been so bad," Bailey Rae whispered.

"Yes, ma'am, it would have." He stuffed the wipes and menthol back into the backpack, restoring a little order to this place of chaos. "I've called the police, but it may take them a while to get out here. After they arrive, I'll still need to stay even after you've given a statement. Is there someone you can ask to pick you up?"

"I'll text June." Nodding, she pulled her phone from her back pocket. Her fingers tapped across the keyboard, an answer swooping in seconds later. "All set. She'll be here in about twenty minutes."

That was a long time to sit vigil. "Do you want to wait in the truck?"

"I would rather stay here with you." Her green eyes held a vulnerability he'd already learned she didn't show often. "Is that all right?"

"Of course." He draped an arm around her shoulders and tucked her against his side, a comfortable fit.

"I'm tougher than this. I always have been. Ask anyone who knew me as a kid." She melted a little closer against him. "But this... hit me. The violence and imagining what happened to my aunt..." Her words trailed off, her eyes squeezing shut.

"Death is upsetting, no matter how accustomed a person may be." Living with PTSD was its own special kind of hell, and he'd had a long time to experience the toll it took. "Doctors. Cops. Firefighters. Military members. We get shaken by the senseless loss of life."

"But you held it together just now."

"On the outside. Inside?" He thumped himself on the chest. "My run tonight will be twice as long."

"Because of what you saw here?" She waved toward the gurgling river.

"Of course," he said simply.

She angled back to study his face as the wind rustled the branches overhead, releasing a shower of pine needles. "I've mentioned my crummy childhood before. But one of the positive side effects from that time? I learned young how to read people. If an adult wasn't going to protect me, I had to do that for myself. All of those instincts tell me there's something more going on in that handsome head of yours."

"Handsome, huh," he said, deflecting.

She tapped a finger along his forehead. "Don't hold back because I was hyperventilating a few minutes ago. Sometimes the best way to pull yourself back together is to help somebody else."

He mulled over her words, not sure if she was right or not, but knowing that at the very least she needed a distraction. If opening up one of his more painful boxes would help her get through the next twenty minutes, then so be it. "Remember when I told you I served in the army, as a military police officer?"

"The scorpions in the boots," she said with a snort of disgust. "How could I forget that?"

"Fair point," he said, appreciating her dark humor. Although he suspected she used it as a defense mechanism, like with reading the room. Still, there was no defense against the pain of his most harrowing memory. "My last year in the military, I was guarding a group of incoming refugees in a hangar. A random shooter opened fire. Seven people died, two of them children."

Relating the facts in news-headline style didn't begin to mitigate the horror of what he'd experienced. But it was the only way he knew how to share a scene that would haunt him forever.

"Martin, how horrible." She rested a comforting palm on his stomach, and he quickly clasped his hand over hers.

"It was. I know that I did everything I could." The official reports on the incident had said as much. His superior officer had underscored that fact, as had two other MPs who'd been there with him. "That doesn't stop me from hating myself for not being able to do more. Do you understand what I mean?"

"Absolutely," she said. "Like how I blame myself for Winnie's death. Because I fear it wasn't an accident but that she killed herself over losing Uncle Russell. Every day I wonder what I could have done to stop her."

He turned to look at her, seeing the loss and guilt in her eyes. Logical or not, that emotional burden was real. "Very much like that."

A flurry of doves took flight from the trees, drawing her gaze skyward. "It's just so tough when everywhere I look there are so many memories."

Silence settled between them, weighted down by grief with nowhere to go. He'd come to this town to give himself distance from his nightmares, but for her, that meant leaving Bent Oak. What a time to realize he would miss her, more than he could have imagined when he'd torn off that warning ticket for illegal fishing.

She rubbed her finger just above her lips, where she'd smudged the menthol. "Do you think the body is Gia's brother-in-law?"

"Yeah," he said heavily. "I do."

If so, he needed to know if the damage to his skull had been caused by rocks or by a human.

※

1978

Attending Russell's races had taken on a different flavor for me now that I'd ridden in the passenger seat of his Chevelle. As he fishtailed around a curve, I felt the momentum in my stomach. The excitement in my veins.

And an awakened desire that, before meeting Russell, I had thought I'd lost.

Then my breath hitched until I grew dizzy as one car after another came within inches of scraping his. My hands clenched in fists until my dime-store mood ring cut into my finger, until finally he powered past another vehicle to cross the finish line. The checkered flag swooped through the air to declare his victory.

Attending the race this evening marked another first, in that I'd come alone. Libby and Keith had an end-of-the-school-year function—I'd loaned her my car since she'd baked two dozen cupcakes. Not even Russell's grandmother had shown up for the race, which was unusual for her, but then Annette had been burning the candle at both ends lately. This past week, I'd even manned the library's front desk for her while she drove across the state to help launch a new women's shelter. I envied her energy and her passion that seemed undimmed by age as she approached eighty years old.

I also admired her. Her opinion mattered to me. Annette hadn't acknowledged the shift in my friendship with Russell to something more, and I wondered what she thought. Or had she been too busy to notice?

There was no denying, the picnic last week marked a change for us, a freedom to stop tiptoeing around the fact that we wanted to spend more time together. No more making up excuses to attend the same events.

A roar from the track drew my attention back as Russell finished his victory lap and slid the car into a showboating stop in front of the stands. The Chevelle sported a hefty amount of mud and a fresh dent on the right quarter panel, but Russell's face shone with pure joy.

Hands in the air, I waved and cheered, my mood ring turning an excited yellow. I dodged through the crowd, past the Tyler family and others from the paper mill on my way toward the winner's circle. Breaking through the last layer—who knew Bent Oak boasted this many citizens?—I landed a prime spot to see Russell hold his trophy over his head.

Sweat streaked his temples, and his golden-brown eyes glowed. He made a slow spin to face everyone shouting their congratulations, only to pause when his gaze landed on me. I lifted my arms again, waving and whooping it up like I'd never done before. Unladylike, right? I didn't care.

He extended a hand.

I pointed to my chest, mouthing *Who me?*

He wriggled his fingers, nodding.

A little drunk on exhilaration, I closed the gap between us in a half dozen strides. Hugging the trophy against his chest with one arm, Russell clasped my hand in his and raised our arms up to a fresh round of cheers from the crowd.

I arched up on my toes to shout, "You've had quite a winning streak lately."

He leaned down to speak into my ear, his breath warm. "Just winning one for my biggest fan."

"Aw, I'm flattered."

He winked. "I meant my grandmother."

"Oh, now I'm embarrassed." Had I misread? Was he just glad to see a familiar face? I hated old insecurities that I'd thought were long gone.

"Don't be embarrassed." He set the trophy on the hood of his car. "I was joking. You're my girl."

He looped his arms around my waist and lifted me into a spin. Squealing, I rested my hands on his shoulders, seeing only him. The rest of the world blurred in comparison.

Slowly, he lowered me until we were face-to-face, and I planted a quick kiss on his mouth. His eyes flashed with surprise—and more.

He eased me down onto the hood of his car just as someone shouted, "Smile."

I turned to the voice—the photographer for the *Bent Oak Weekly*. My skin tingled with anxiety, for fear of detection. I tipped my head as quickly as I could to shield my face with my hair. The *Bent Oak Weekly* had a readership smaller than most high school enrollments, but I wasn't taking unnecessary chances, not when happiness was finally within my grasp.

Russell's hands tightened around my waist. "Are you ready to go dancing?"

Yes. Yes. Yes. I wanted to squeal in abandon but settled for a more dignified response. I stretched out my legs, wriggling my toes in my ballet flats. "I have my dancing shoes on."

"All righty, then. Just give me a minute to head over to the restrooms for a quick shower and change—"

"Winnie? Winnie," Libby's voice called out from a distance, insistent and drawing closer.

I glanced at my watch. Keith's end-of-school party wasn't due to finish for another hour. I clenched Russell's arm. Libby and I counted on each other for so much more than friendship.

"Over here," I hollered back, raising a hand.

Libby angled past the reporter, tugging Keith behind her. She ran the last few feet, still wearing the jean dress and white sneakers I'd helped her choose for the school event. Her expression worried me.

"Winnie, Russell, I'm so sorry to interrupt. I know it's a time to celebrate." She paused, catching her breath. "But Annette collapsed at the school's book fair. She's on her way to the hospital."

Russell swayed, bracing a hand on the hood of his car. "What's wrong?"

I'd never seen him flustered before, and somehow that shook me all the more. The world started spinning again, but in the very worst way. I managed to hold it together enough to slide a comforting arm around Russell's waist. I should have paid closer attention to Annette this week, should have noticed she'd stretched herself too thin.

Libby continued, "It looks like she's had a heart attack. She was conscious and talking when they loaded her in the ambulance. But she wanted me to give you a message."

"Yes?" Russell asked.

Wincing, Libby shook her head. "A message for Winnie. She needs you to come to the hospital right away. She said it's urgent."

༄

Waiting room chairs weren't any more comfortable here than back in Mobile, where I'd sat with Phillip after my father's stroke and my mom's cancer treatments. Then, the latest diagnosis on my fertility issues. Between all my lost pregnancies and my stay in the institution, I dreaded setting foot in a hospital, because every time I entered these sterile halls, I lost a little more control over my life. Even the word launched a well of nausea that reminded me of miscarried children and the loss of my parents.

In my world, hospitals rarely had a positive outcome.

Russell, still in his racing gear, clutched my hand. Or I gripped his. Either way, we clung to each other as time ticked by until we received further news from the emergency room physician about Annette's condition. Because yes, she'd suffered a heart attack.

And so we waited. And waited. Silence was broken only by the occasional rattling cart, voices over the PA system, and the television mounted in the corner broadcasting a football game.

A nurse rounded the corner, her shoes squeaking on the linoleum. Her name tag read VICKI TYLER. The paper mill owner's daughter, newly back in town after completing college.

"The doctor says Mrs. Davis can have visitors now, one at a time, but to keep it brief. Ma'am, she wants to talk to you first," Vicki said, clearly not recognizing me or Russell from the mill. "Then you can come on in, sir."

I didn't have the emotional energy to ponder the ironies of Vicki not having a clue who we were even though Russell and I had worked for her father for years. I'd probably behaved the same oblivious way countless times in the past, and it shamed me to think about now. Silently, I followed her down the sanitized corridor to a private exam room in the emergency department.

While I'd believed I'd prepared myself, I was sadly mistaken. Annette lay on a gurney hooked up to a heart monitor, with an IV taped to her hand. Her ashen skin and weary eyes shattered me. "Annette, I'm so sorry this happened."

"Wipe that scared look off your face. I'm not fixin' to leave this earth yet." Annette patted the bedrail for me to come closer. "But the doctor says I'll need to put my feet up for a little while. I'll need some more help from you until I can get my sea legs back under me."

I was relieved to hear her stern voice, stronger than I'd expected from her pallor. Although I was confused to think she'd turn to me first for help.

"You know I'm happy to pitch in with more volunteer hours anytime. Or run additional, uh, errands." No great hardship at all. I had always supported the library, but in my prior life, I'd purchased whatever I wanted to read. Those days had changed.

At first, my frequent stops at the Bent Oak Public Library were to meet Annette, and each time I checked out a book or two as a cover.

Over time, my choices changed from whatever I could grab fast, to escapism reading, to novels I'd read in school and wanted to reread with fresh eyes.

Annette adjusted the white sheet covering her. "This is about more than reshelving books and picking up mail." She motioned for me to move closer. "I wouldn't ask unless it was an emergency. We have a newcomer arriving in the morning."

All my rambling thoughts of reading the classics scattered as I focused on what I thought she meant. The kind of "help" she provided to other women in need. Women like I'd once been. But while I'd contributed to those efforts in a peripheral manner, I'd never imagined I would be trusted with a more active role.

"A newcomer?" I needed her to confirm she meant what I thought. "Like you. Like Libby. Someone who will be staying."

The *beep, beep, beep* of the heart monitor filled the silence, chirping as her words sank in one at a time like the drip through the IV.

While I realized others had passed through, I didn't know of anyone else who'd stayed. Or maybe their cover was rock solid. None of which mattered right now. "Tomorrow morning? Of course I'll do whatever you need, but I don't know how. What if I mess it all up? There are so many more . . ."

"You will be just fine. I'll walk you through it. But first, there are a few details that won't—can't—be written down." Annette motioned me even nearer, until my ear was close to her mouth and she whispered, "She has two master's degrees in math and accounting. She's brilliant."

"And she's coming here because?" Would Annette answer? I'd helped in bringing her paperwork from the paralegal and post office but never opened the envelopes.

"She saw something she shouldn't have," Annette said, each whispered word an increasing effort as she adjusted the oxygen tube at her nose, "and the police won't protect her."

Talking was taking a toll. "You should rest now. Let me get the doctor—"

"No, just one more minute." After two deep breaths, she continued, "She did nothing illegal. She was only guilty of being in the wrong place at the wrong time, with nowhere to hide."

"Annette, what about that new Witness Protection Program?" Created earlier this decade, I'd watched news stories about how it had revolutionized criminal investigations.

"The police will assume she's involved. That's just how things work sometimes." Annette gripped my hand. "Please, I know I can trust you. She's my cousin's grandchild."

I understood how dangerous a powerful man could be. My experience with my husband had given me a front row seat. After being locked away, I was never allowed to even discuss my own diagnosis with my physicians. Back in Alabama there had been rumors of our governor keeping potentially fatal medical information from his wife. I'd dismissed those rumors as impossible. Now? From my own experience, I found that the unimaginable was all too possible.

I didn't have to think twice. I was all in. "Whatever you need."

CHAPTER ELEVEN

Present and Past

Bailey Rae flipped from her back to her stomach, then to her side, struggling to get comfortable in a bed so much softer than the places she'd slept for the first six years of her life. The sheets were clean. She didn't have to share. She had a pillow and a rag doll she'd pretended not to want, but when no one was looking, she'd hugged it until her arms went numb.

Maybe if she stayed really still and quiet, her mama would forget about her, and Bailey Rae could stay here. It wouldn't be the first time she'd kept so quiet her mother had forgotten all about her. Once, Bailey Rae had spent almost a whole day in a motel after her mom and her boyfriend skipped the bill. Each of them thought the other had stashed her in the back of the station wagon.

Bailey Rae had hidden in the shower until they peeled out of the parking lot. She'd enjoyed the best day watching television and feeding herself by snaking her arm up into the vending machine like she'd been taught. She'd taken a nap on a pool lounger, full of Cheetos and two Snickers bars until her mom woke her up madder than a wet hen.

Yvonne's number one rule: Don't upset the latest boyfriend. And apparently, the boyfriend had been livid at backtracking for a snot-nosed kid.

This bed, though, was better than even the motel one because it came with a house owned by a grandparent-like couple. Everything inside her wanted to stay in Bent Oak, not that she would ever say the words out loud.

Asking for stuff that couldn't happen just hurt worse. Sometimes she thought her mom denied her those things just to be mean. Soon enough, Bailey Rae stopped asking for anything.

Meanwhile, might as well make the most of one good night's sleep. In the morning she would stuff the doll and nightie in the back of the station wagon faster than she'd jammed those stolen Cheetos in her mouth.

Twitching, she burrowed deeper into the dream world, trying to block out the swampy night sounds. Scary-loud bullfrogs. Screech owls. The knock, knock, knock of branches against the window.

Except it wasn't a branch. The rapping grew louder, along with shouts. "Yvonne, get your ass out here. I know you're in there." Then the shift to fake apologies. "Baby, I'm sorry. Come on. I love you . . ."

On and on it went from Yvonne's boyfriend. The worst one, with the biggest fists and a quick trigger. Hunting for her and smacking aside anyone in the way. Bailey Rae had learned that smaller targets were harder to hit, so she curled into a ball under the covers with her hands against her ears. Still, she heard the muffled sounds of Yvonne and her "man" yelling in a worn-out repeat of so many fights before.

Then the calm voice of the grandpa-like man—Russell—slid underneath it all, settling the storm. She'd never had a grandpa, but in her deepest of dreams, the ones she knew better than to speak aloud, her grandpa sounded like Russell. Bringing peace and calm. For now. Because it never lasted. Then she was left with nothing but hurt that somehow made her do bad things.

The bedroom door creaked open, and Bailey Rae held her breath, peeking from under the quilt. Then shook with relief. The grandma-like lady—Winnie—dragged the chair out from the dressing table and sat. She didn't say a word. She just waited, letting Bailey Rae know that she wasn't alone and defenseless in a world with dangerous adults spinning out of control.

For a moment she almost believed this could last. Until water began trickling in through the window. Dripping, flowing, pouring, more and more covering the floor. Bailey Rae scooted back in her bed, flush against the headboard as a river grew deeper in her room.

Which way should she turn? Try to escape through the window? Or reach for Winnie? Because she couldn't swim. Choosing wrong meant death.

Surely opening the window to run away would be worse. Decision made, she extended her arms for Winnie, only to find she'd disappeared without even a goodbye.

The waters grew darker, bubbling up the contents of the barn . . . quilts, cookbooks, rag dolls, even a photo album with pictures sliding out of her longtime friends as well as Yvonne and Martin.

Parting it all as it floated by . . . a body.

Floating through her childhood bedroom.

Closer. And closer until it seemed near enough to nudge . . .

Bailey Rae bolted upright in her bed, heart slugging, the grip of her nightmare working to haul her back. Another nudge made her shriek, only to find Skeeter. He nose-bumped her leg again before putting one paw, then the other on the edge of the bed.

For the second night in a row, Bailey Rae had woken from a night terror, sheets soaked with sweat. She'd expected it right after finding the body with Martin. But this evening's repeat left her wrung out.

And alone, since she'd sent her friends home.

Once June had brought her back to the cabin, Thea and Libby had already been waiting in the drive. The ladies had tucked her in with a glass of sweet tea—spiked with Southern Comfort. Skeeter even kept vigil from the foot of her bed, while Keith had slept in the Airstream again. She'd welcomed the collective presence of their makeshift family and sensed they needed her too.

None of them had slept well that evening.

However, she'd hoped for better tonight. No such luck.

She flung aside the quilt, averting her eyes from the rag doll tucked away in the corner curio cabinet. "Come on, Skeeter. Keep me company while I finish up in the barn for this weekend."

Skeeter had been her companion, but tonight? She needed him to alert her of any unwanted company, because her quiet little town of Bent Oak wasn't feeling so sleepy anymore.

∽

2025

Between yawns, Bailey Rae had sold out most of her truckload at the farmers' market, an uneventful day in comparison to two weeks ago, when she ended up helping a young mother and child. She should have been relieved over the quietly successful day. Instead, she couldn't shake the jittery sensation, waiting for what could go wrong next.

No amount of smelling the flowers and blowing out candles seemed to help.

Loading her truck with the leftovers, she hefted a box with only three cookbooks, two quilts, and two jars of canned okra. No takers on the okra. Not surprising.

She suspected the high traffic at her table had more to do with the incident at the river. The market had always been a hot spot for gossip, but chatter was buzzing overtime with rumors about the man who'd drowned.

Nausea roiled all over again, and she shoved the box to the back before grabbing her water bottle off the table. How much longer until she recovered her emotional footing after the horror from that moment when she'd assumed she'd found Winnie's body? No matter how many times she showered, she couldn't rid herself of the feel of that shirt in her fist.

At least the police department had confirmed that the body was, in fact, the lost fisherman. The drowned man's brother—Gia's husband—was wanted for questioning. But he'd been lying low since landing his wife in the hospital. The police chief insisted the rest of the information would be sealed, as the investigation was still ongoing.

That should have shut down the whispers. It hadn't. This was Bent Oak, after all, with a small police department and low crime. Nothing worse than the occasional poachers . . . and illegal fishing. Finding that dead body in the river, with a bashed-in skull, had rocked the town to its core.

She was definitely locking her doors, the same as everyone else. Something she'd been sure to tell Martin when texting him after he left three voicemails.

Thankfully, June had shown up to help her pack away the market stand, which meant less chance of running into Martin. June folded her chair and tucked it into the truck. "Are you feeling better today? I've been worried about you. You were pretty shaken when I picked you up after you gave your statement to the police."

The purple streak in June's frequently colored hair was beginning to fade out, the natural gray taking over. Bailey Rae suspected the added stress of the week had kept the woman from her regular salon visit. Were all of Winnie's friends having nightmares too?

"I'm better," Bailey Rae lied. She'd been afraid to close her eyes again last night for fear of replay of the nightmare. "Thank you for staying over the other night and for checking on me today."

"No thanks necessary." June yanked the checkered tablecloth off and folded it. She fast-stepped to the side of the truck bed, reaching over to drop the fabric into the box. "I think we were *all* more than a little shaken by the news of that poor fisherman. It was almost like losing Winnie all over again." Her voice cracked on the last words.

"I hear you," Bailey Rae said softly. Every day felt like losing Winnie anew.

Kneeling to unhook Skeeter's leash from the table leg, she saw one last painted rock with a weeping willow stenciled on the smooth, flat surface. She started to toss it into the box, then hesitated. Surely she had room for one tiny memento in her Airstream, in honor of all the times she and Winnie had stenciled patterns on stones. Bailey Rae clenched her fist around the treasure.

Winnie was a collector of rocks, each one representing a memory. Once the Mason jars on her kitchen windowsill were filled, Winnie painted a few and shared them with others to make space for new rocks. New memories. While passing Bailey Rae a palette of oils and a brush, Winnie allowed silences to stretch between them as they looked for the latest, smoothest stones to decorate. A patient woman, proving she wasn't going anywhere, she'd given Bailey Rae as much quiet space as she needed. After a few art sessions, Winnie commented how the overflowing rocks were like stockpiled emotions, and when they overflowed, sometimes a person had to find a way to showcase the most important ones.

June tapped the edge of the market table with her knuckle. "Bailey Rae? Earth calling Bailey Rae?"

"Oh, sorry." Bailey Rae jolted, shifting her focus to June and tucking the rock into the pocket of her jean shorts. "What were you saying?"

"I was chatting up Officer Underwood earlier, the fella who took your statement by the river." June leaned closer. "I slid in some questions about Gia—an easy-enough segue since she's the drowned man's sister-in-law. Anyway, I'm sad to say she never did file a report for an order of protection against her husband."

"That's disappointing." To say the least. She was keenly aware that Aunt Winnie wouldn't have failed. "I'm worried about her but running out of ideas to help."

Bailey Rae wanted to race down to the police station and shout for justice. Except Winnie had lectured her more than once about catching more flies with honey. All a part of Winnie's ongoing crusade to teach Bailey Rae about overcoming her anger-management problem.

She slammed the tailgate closed just as Libby's voice carried on the wind. Keith pushed her wheelchair while Thea and her husband walked arm in arm alongside. Bailey Rae wanted to climb into the cab of her truck with her dog, go home, and crawl under the covers until the grief and frustration eased inside her.

No sooner had the thought formed than a memory blindsided her of hiding under a blanket in the back of her mother's old station wagon, with the paneled siding and squealing brakes.

Bailey Rae dug deep and plastered a smile on her face, waving to her approaching friends. "I'm all out of the peaches. Sorry."

Thea tucked her gloved hand deeper in the crook of her husband's arm. "Looks like you sold most *everything*. Congratulations, dear."

"One step closer to moving." Why did she feel like there was unfinished business for her here, no matter how much of the old barn she cleared out?

"In the meantime, you know you're welcome to stay with us. We have all those empty rooms since the kids moved away."

Smiling, Bailey Rae shook her head. "Mr. Councilman, do you offer those spare rooms to everyone in town?"

"Only family," Howard Tyler said, ever the politician. Polished and affable. The winning combination. Along with his family's money from their paper mill.

Bailey Rae scratched her tightening throat. "Maybe I'll take y'all up on that when I come to visit."

Thea rubbed her elbow. "I'm going to hold you to that—"

Libby interrupted, waggling her cane from the wheelchair. "Thea, see that young lady over there? Doesn't she look just like that teenager Winnie and I helped from North Carolina? She wouldn't leave her dog behind, because how could she abandon her to the hands of—"

"Howard, honey," Thea interrupted, hugging her hubby's arm tighter. "If we hurry, we can get some fresh fruit before that last truck pulls away. Libby, would you like some too?"

"Oh yes, I've got a hankering for blueberry pancakes." Libby grabbed the arms of her wheelchair and began to push upward, only to sag back. "I seem to be feeling a little weak today. I must have put in too much overtime at the paper mill. The assembly line is easier than when I worked custodial. But still. Maybe I'll just sit here for a spell. Where's Keith?"

Their close group went silent, the sorrow heavy as Libby inched even further away, retreating to a time when she and her friend had been able to help others. It hurt Bailey Rae to see, so she could only imagine how the woman's decline pained the friends who'd known her for decades.

June squeezed Bailey Rae's elbow, whispering, "I should help Keith. When Libby starts like this, she goes downhill fast. Are you okay with loading the rest?"

"I've got everything under control," Bailey Rae said, understanding how much June would want to be with her friend right now. "Keith needs you far more than I do right now."

When she was a kid, she'd thought that Keith and June were a couple. After all, they were about the same age. Later, as Keith married and divorced again and again, Bailey Rae realized they weren't an item. Their connection was more of a brother and sister sort. They were a part of this strange family that went out of its way to help each other and just about anyone else who blew through town.

What would it have been like to add Gia and Cricket to the community? They would have fit right in. And she really didn't want to think about how the only thing she looked forward to involved time spent with Martin. Because she tried so hard not to be like Yvonne.

Sure, Martin wasn't like the men her mother had chosen, but that didn't stop the fear of lowering her guard and losing control of her life. Better to focus on things she could fix, like checking in on Gia and readying for her final market on the Fourth of July.

Her hand went to the painted stone she'd pocketed earlier, the memory of Winnie ever present. The only answer for the anxiety churning inside her was to focus on her future and add pages to a photo album of her own making.

༄

1978

I'd walked into the Bent Oak Public Library more times than I could count over the past seven years, but I'd never envisioned myself becoming an official part of the network that helped women find new lives away from abuse. Yes, I'd promised to pay it forward, but more like being asked to donate a coat or give someone a ride. As for the scary parts? I had planned to keep my head down. Those other aspects of the operation could be handled by those more seasoned in the process.

For at least the fifth time in the past five minutes, I adjusted the paperwork on the table in the back room, in between running to peer outside the library's massive stone-silled window overlooking the back parking lot. Still no powder-blue Ford Maverick. The transport was only eleven minutes late, but each second felt like hours.

When I'd spoken to Annette at the hospital, the prospect of managing an intake had felt like an exciting adventure. Now I couldn't lie to myself. I was scared to the roots of my hair. Not for myself. I'd already survived some of the worst heartaches life could throw at a person. My fear stemmed from worry I would fall short, and this woman's safety would be at risk.

Or that in some way I might jeopardize the entire network shielding other vulnerable women and children.

That day, though, when Thea had finally pulled into the parking lot in the blue compact car, I had no choice but to set my fear aside and step up. Thankfully, Libby was manning the library's front desk while I handled the rest. Initially, I'd worried that Libby might be jealous or hurt because Annette had put her trust in me for the riskier part of helping Thea take the next steps in assuming her new identity. Outwardly at least, Libby seemed relieved to take her post, date-stamping books. I suspected Annette had chosen me because I didn't have a child depending on me if I got caught in the crosshairs somehow. I hoped Libby understood the same.

As I peered out the window into the back lot, I was reminded all too fully of how little we really knew about each other, not even our real names.

Finally—thank heaven, finally—the pale-blue sedan slid into a parking spot by the concrete steps. I yanked open the door and threw myself into the distraction of settling this new woman into our community—the newly named Thea Young.

Lightning in a Mason Jar

From the moment I set eyes on her, I forced myself to think of her only as Thea. Her other name no longer existed, just as I had scrubbed my own from the corners of my mind. I certainly didn't want to risk revealing her connection to the Davis family.

I wouldn't have guessed at their kinship if Annette hadn't told me, but that was a good thing. That would make Thea's new identity less complicated. Thea was tall and confident, with the most incredible black hair spiraling past her shoulders. She wore a chic jean jumpsuit, somehow managing to radiate composure and class during what had to be the most terrifying time of her life.

As I waved her into the back room, I wondered if I had ever been that sure of myself. I didn't think so. Although that made me wonder how much harder it might be for her to adapt to a new life when her old one had brought her such self-assurance.

Then Thea's appearance of confidence dimmed a bit as her coal-dark eyes darted around the back room of the library. "Where's Annette?"

"I'm Winnie. I'm sorry to let you know that Annette's in the hospital. She had a heart attack." I rushed to add, "She's going to be all right." I prayed. "She sent me in her place. I've helped her in the past."

That seemed the safest way to lend credence to my assistance, rather than explain I'd once stood in her very shoes. Well, not exactly her shoes. I wore my sneakers, scuffed from shifts at the mill, and she wore high heels with faux wood soles.

Thea fidgeted with her neckline, her pulse throbbing visibly in her throat. "I'm not in a position to argue."

My nerves faded the deeper we sank into the meeting. "Annette sent a note, if that helps." I passed over the folded piece of paper. According to Annette, she hadn't written anything incriminating but shared a message in a code that the young woman would understand. "I hope it makes sense to you. She said something about your grandmother teaching you to understand the special language."

Thea unfolded the lined notepaper, scanned, then breathed a sigh of relief. "My grandmother—Annette's cousin—was a codebreaker during

World War II. Not something many people know. After the war, the men came home and took back their jobs. My grandmother made a game out of sharing her skill with us."

Annette hadn't gone into that much detail, but I treasured the nugget of information about Russell's extended family.

I tapped the manila envelope on the round table. "Here's the information about two job interviews for a bookkeeper position. One for a feed and farm supply store and the other at the paper mill."

"Bookkeeper?" she said, her face a study in disappointment.

On the one hand, I felt sorry for her. On the other? Well, that other hand remembered all too well the sting of bleach from working long janitorial shifts.

"It's a place to begin." I tried to make the transition easier, because all mop buckets aside, I did comprehend the huge shock to the system that came from launching a whole new identity. "I realize you're overqualified, and that none of what has happened to you is fair—"

She gave her head a shake. Resigned. "I understand. It's what has to happen."

As Thea kept rubbing the tissue along the tabletop, I noticed her fingertips were raw, much like mine had been back before I learned not to plunge my hands in a bucket of cleaning solution. What had happened to her on her way here? "Could I get you some lotion? I really wrecked my hands when I started working in the paper mill, with the chemicals and all."

Pulling away, she clenched her fists. "It's not that. I just can't be found. Ever."

The steeliness of her voice was underscored by the way her spine snapped straight. Resolve, yes. But underneath that? A deep-seated fear that helped me understand the reason for her raw fingertips. She'd scrubbed away her fingerprints to reduce the chance of detection. Perhaps also the reason she kept cleaning off the table, just in case.

Annette had briefed me on Thea's past, but I hadn't considered the implications of a wider network, a dangerous one, determined to locate her. Such a different scenario from my own. If anything, Phillip wouldn't have wanted to find me at all.

Any resentment over her pencil-pushing job vanished. My heart ached for her. "Thea, I promise you," I vowed, reaching across the table but stopping shy of touching her. I could see now the confidence was a mask to hide her brittle control. "I will make it my mission to help you find something that puts your education to good use."

I'd experienced how the soul could wither when talents were denied. We'd had to make ourselves smaller in so many ways to escape detection. There had to be someplace to funnel our new sense of selves. A place for us to feel a sense of purpose and meaning.

Pushing the packet of paperwork across the tabletop, I passed on her new identity just as Annette had done for me, and the rush of fulfillment almost drove me to my knees. Was this a part of my purpose? A role in my life that had real meaning?

On some cellular level I'd come into my own, and I knew just what to say next. "Thea, as Annette let you know, I can be trusted. But please understand that stories about your past like that one about your codebreaking grandmother can be as identifiable as fingerprints. You have to be very careful going forward how you spread them about."

As I uttered those words, stepping into Annette's shoes, a complete peace washed away the last vestiges of fear. I could do this. I *would* do this.

Finally, after all those years ago watching and admiring women on my old television set making a difference, I had found my way. Close on the heels of that revelation came the realization that for the past seven years, I'd still been allowing others to take care of me. Now I felt a soul-deep calling that it was my time to look after others.

CHAPTER TWELVE

2025

Kneeling in the dirt, Bailey Rae plucked a plump red tomato from a vine in Winnie's garden even though her basket was almost overflowing with tomatoes, cucumbers, peppers. And of course, okra, okra, okra. Skeeter peered at her with his kind eye from a bed of pine straw, crunching a floppy carrot she'd tossed over from the garden. With some luck, gathering up the last of the harvest before she left would help her sweat out the tension that kept her up half the night.

At least she hadn't dreamed about Winnie again. In fact, the silence inside echoed—no Winnie, no Russell. So much so, the quiet had chased her out of bed early in the morning to the familiar concert of cicadas and rustling of squirrels racing along their deciduous tightropes.

The crunch of gravel alerted her to a car turning from the road onto the drive, the driver tapping the horn twice in greeting. Bailey Rae squinted to see . . . Thea's sleek silver Lexus wove past the twisted oaks and stopped by the garden. Thea slid from behind the wheel, the luxury car otherwise empty. Surprising. Winnie's friends usually traveled in a pack.

Bailey Rae pushed to her feet and dusted her palms on the back of her jean shorts. "What brings you out this way?"

Thea scratched Skeeter on the head, wearing leather driving gloves like an auto racer, a far cry from her job as bookkeeper at the paper mill owned by her husband's family. "I'm only checking in on you. You seemed, um, tired at the market."

"I'm not sleeping well." She settled for the safer explanation rather than risk crying over Winnie. "My to-do list keeps me awake."

"Well, I can help with that." Thea peeled off her driving gloves and tucked them into her purse. "Pass me a pair of gardening gloves if you have them. Winnie always kept extras." She nodded toward the bucket of tools beside the basket.

"You'll get your beautiful clothes dirty. How about you sit on the glider and just keep me company," Bailey Rae said, surrendering.

No doubt Thea had something on her mind, and no one deterred her once she set her course.

"This shirt is ten years out of fashion." Thea smoothed a hand along her trouser jeans and picked her way down the row toward Bailey Rae. "I won't cry if it gets a few stains. That will just give me an excuse to throw it away."

"If you're sure." Bailey Rae squatted beside the basket of vegetables. "But I insist that you take some of the tomatoes and okra home, as my thanks for your help and conversation." A wave of nostalgia hit her as she remembered the many times Winnie had gifted houseguests with a sack of homegrown goods.

"It's nice to see someone keeping Winnie's tradition alive." Thea scooted the basket closer. "Howard loves his tomato sandwiches for lunch. He says mine are even better than the ones his mother makes for her garden club."

Thea's refusal to join the garden club when she married into the Tyler family still circulated through the rumor mill.

"There's no shortage of tomatoes around here."

"But none like Winnie's," Thea said sentimentally.

Tears burned, even closer to the surface than she'd realized. Bailey Rae didn't trust herself to speak, so she continued to pick from the overburdened plants while Skeeter nudged her in comfort.

Had nine years already passed since Skeeter was left at the top of Aunt Winnie's drive? Kinda like the owners figured it didn't matter if the pup got run over or rescued on a remote country road. Teenage Bailey Rae had understood the feeling and deemed the dog hers.

Thea shifted to a line of peppers, her own eyes suspiciously bright. "I don't blame you for wanting to leave Bent Oak."

Surprised, Bailey Rae sat back on her bottom. "I thought you loved it here. At least that's what you always say during your husband's reelection campaigns for town council."

Thea shot her a wry grin. "Those aren't my *exact* words. I tell everyone that this is my home and how welcome Bent Oak made me feel all those years ago." Her gaze slid away, and her hands made fast work of pinching peppers free. "Truth is, when I first arrived, I hated it here."

Bailey Rae hugged an arm around Skeeter, caught up in the revelation. "Why did you stay?"

"My friends and my job," she said simply in that pragmatic Thea fashion. "Then later because of Howard too."

Her job? "I never got the impression you particularly enjoy being a bookkeeper at the paper mill."

Thea stared off in the distance, toward the cabin and maybe even past before returning her gaze to the ground. She picked up a stone from the churned earth and placed the cool weight into Bailey Rae's palm, closing her fingers around it. "It can be surprising where we find fulfillment. Now go find yours. You'll always carry a piece of us with you."

Bailey Rae gripped the rock until the edges cut into her hand even through the glove. Could leaving be that simple? She wanted it to be. But her path to departure seemed littered with nightmares and death, which only served to amplify her concern for Gia and Cricket's safety. Fear of another hospital visit, or worse.

Could that be the real cause of the sleepless nights? Bailey Rae thought back to hearing at the market that Gia still hadn't filed for an order of protection. Maybe one more phone call of support would make the difference, showing Gia she wasn't alone with her own silence.

Bailey Rae pocketed the stone and hugged Thea hard. "What do you say we get some sweet tea before we tackle the rest?"

1978

The hospital elevator smelled as strongly of antiseptic as it had the day before. But I'd come better prepared this time. I'd chewed two antacid tablets just before stepping into the air-conditioned lobby. Just as a precaution. So far, the emotional high of successfully settling Thea in the boardinghouse had me tapping my foot to an ABBA tune piping through the speaker.

The elevator doors slid open in front of the nurses' station, where Russell leaned his elbows on the counter, deep in conversation. Could he be flirting with the young woman? The jealous notion blindsided me. An irrational thought, no doubt fueled by Phillip's incessant flirting with other women.

I needed to remember Russell was nothing like Phillip. And Russell had made his interest in me clear. As I looked closer, his intense expression showed concern rather than playfulness. The green-eyed monster inside me retreated. Such a distracting beast. I hauled my focus back to the task at hand—updating Annette on Thea's arrival.

Had she said anything to Russell? I'd wondered before and was curious all over again about the layers of secrets that made up my life in Bent Oak. How much did he know? Was it okay to ask Annette? Or would even questioning knock me out of the running to help out again?

Or worse yet, what if I was relocated to another town?

About two years ago, I'd picked up paperwork from the paralegal for a woman in her fifties who'd been found by her ex and needed yet another new identity. A horrifying prospect that still sent me reaching for the roll of Tums in my hobo bag. Maybe I'd been too quick to believe I had a better handle on being in a hospital again. My surroundings already seemed to have ignited all my deepest fears.

Russell glanced up, his golden-brown gaze holding mine for a handful of rapid heartbeats before he met me halfway.

I hitched my bag higher on my shoulder and wished I'd had time to change out of my paper mill uniform, which smelled of chemicals even when freshly laundered. "How's Annette doing today? Is she up for more visitors? I just wanted to pop in and give her an update on the errand she needed me to run."

"The doctor just stopped in to see her, but Granny should be ready after that." He shoved his hands in his pockets. "Do you want to grab a quick cup of coffee? There's a machine at the end of the hall."

When I nodded, he palmed my back, guiding me down the corridor to the concessions nook and popping coins into the slot. How did my relationship with Russell fit into the shift in myself that had happened with Thea yesterday? Surely Russell must know *something* about what his grandmother did in that library, but how would he feel if I joined? His NASCAR dreams would do more than take him out of town. They could involve a level of recognition—fame even—that I couldn't be a part of, even more so now than before. I hadn't forgotten about the local paper snapping a photo of us together after his last victory. I couldn't afford to court disaster that way.

"Winnie? Are you okay?" He angled his head into my line of sight, holding two Styrofoam cups. "I can stay with Granny this afternoon. You don't have to be here. I'll let the mill know they'll need to find someone else to drive my haul. You just came off a long shift. Go enjoy some of that fishing you love."

He'd noticed? Of course he had.

I took the warm cup from him, our fingers brushing. "You're sweet to have picked up on that."

"Winnie, I've made a point of learning everything I can about you. Like how you have cooking peach jam down to an art form. And how your eyes turn the color of bottled glass when you make your own jars. I can keep listing if you would like."

His intensity stirred butterfly nerves in my stomach, just a hint. But not enough to scare me off. "Uh, that's plenty. Thanks. I feel bad for not learning more about NASCAR stats."

"You're there cheering on my races. The world would be a boring place if we liked exactly the same things. Now, wouldn't it?"

"Not everyone sees it that way." I breathed in the scent of java and reminded myself that I was no longer a prisoner of the past—no matter what subconscious cues the hospital atmosphere was sending to my brain. "In my, uh, last relationship before I moved here . . . When he would say 'we have nothing in common,' that was code for me to join in with all of his interests, while he ignored mine. I know it sounds like such a small thing."

"Not at all." He waited for me to continue, drinking his coffee, giving me space.

But I didn't say anything more. That was all I dared risk. If I slid down that *Alice in Wonderland* rabbit hole of memories, I might lose myself and let something slip. It was exhausting, keeping so many secrets. But the alternative? Risking landing back in my old life? Unthinkable.

I worked hard not to remember the time in the hospital—not this one. The psychiatric hospital. The calendar insisted I'd been there for nine months. My brain remembered only half as much. At times I questioned my own sanity. Had Phillip been right in committing me? Except why, then, did he never visit after that first week? I'd long wondered. Was my mind clearer because of the treatments or due to the distance from Phillip's influence?

Near the end of my stay, I'd needed an off-campus appointment with a specialist because of uterine cysts. I hadn't seen newspapers in the longest time. As I waited for surgery, I tore into the society section of issue after issue to catch up with my friends. Friends who hadn't come to see me, but then, would I have visited them if the positions were reversed? Likely, I would have told myself they needed rest and I didn't want to disturb them. Excuses to cover the truth of confronting uncomfortable subjects.

Looking back, I'm sure there were people in my Mobile social circle who pushed boundaries, but in those days, I still saw the world in black-and-white terms. All good. All bad. Not a healthy outlook.

Which was why the newspaper articles hit me hard. Photos of Phillip at one society event after another, a beautiful woman on his arm. No mentions of me. Nothing. Not even a comment about my absence. I'd been erased.

The cysts turned out to be worse than expected, and I ended up having a hysterectomy. While tears leaked from my eyes, the nurse had patted my hand, telling me how lucky I was not to have cancer. My husband had sent flowers. Wasn't that nice?

As if a dozen roses made up for his absence.

My anger at Phillip grew, along with my hunger for information. I asked the candy striper for newspapers and magazines, reading material to pass the time. A young hospital aide would be less likely to question what I should and shouldn't access. But I needed to find some mention in one of those articles that I'd existed. That I'd mattered. And at every turn of a glossy page, I came up blank.

With Russell, I felt seen. Such a simple thing. But to me, it was everything after Phillip's brutal dismissal. The way he'd used his connections in the medical world to have me committed against my will. How he'd cut me off from all contact with anyone except him, while making himself sole executor of the inheritance from my parents. Memories of finding all those magazine articles with him out with other women while I stayed locked away. Abandoned. Gaslit. With no legal recourse.

Which made it hurt all the more that I struggled to see a way forward with Russell. Because he deserved to be seen as well, all of him, his hopes and dreams. "Thanks for the coffee. I don't want to keep you from your job."

"Are you sure you don't want me to call out of work?"

"Please, don't do that on my account. I have the rest of the day off to sit with Annette." We had plenty to talk about anyway. "I'll catch up with you later."

I arched up on my toes to kiss him on the cheek. Then froze. What had I just done? How could I think of setting him free one moment, then an instant later bring us closer?

Pivoting away before I did something even more reckless, I raced toward Annette's room, tossing my empty cup in a trash can on my way past. I couldn't afford a misstep. Thea's arrival had reminded me more than ever of my tenuous position in life. Most of all, how isolated this reframed existence could be, unable to open up fully because of secrets. Except with Annette.

Right now, the last thing Annette needed was the stress of my confusion. I should focus first and foremost on the importance of the task she had given me. And my feelings for Russell? How the past shredded my ability to trust my own judgment?

I would sift through those later, in the quiet of my boardinghouse room. Small, but it was my space. Where I controlled my life.

I used the ten minutes waiting outside Annette's door to file away my jumbled emotions and focus on my mentor. Once the doctor ducked back into the hallway, his curt nod offered little indication of her condition. Much how Phillip—the all-powerful physician—so often dismissed me.

Teeth clenched, I reminded myself Phillip wasn't here. He was off making some other poor woman's life miserable.

"Hello," I called through the door, tapping two knuckles on the panel. "It's me."

"Come on in," Annette called out.

I let myself indulge hopeful thoughts that she sounded stronger today. I tucked inside and closed the door behind me so that we could talk freely. Although the sight of her in a hospital gown gave me pause.

She didn't even raise the head of the bed as she motioned me closer. "Catch me up on how things went at the library."

The other bed in the semiprivate room was empty.

Still, I kept my voice low. "All went well yesterday, and our 'guest' is settled. Being on this side of things, seeing the impact, I want to be you when I grow up."

"Now that's a first," Annette said, smiling, fanning laugh lines that seemed deeper than before. Proof of her mortality beeped from the monitor beside her bed. "Well done, my dear. I look forward to hearing all about it."

I dragged a chair as close to the bedrail as I could get to minimize the chance of anyone hearing. Also, to clasp Annette's hand because I needed that connection, to feel the reassurance of her alive and warm.

Sparing no details, I reviewed Thea's intake, including the bit about the secret code and my caution. Annette's nods of approval made me feel like a child winning a parent's endorsement. Better, in fact, than all the first prizes I'd won as a child in art competitions.

Out of breath as I finished my recap, I sagged back in the chair, inordinately proud of myself, almost managing to forget where I was and Annette's health scare. "Is there anything else you need for me to follow up on?"

"Nothing that I can think of right now. Best to keep things low key after a success like this. I knew I could count on you." Annette adjusted the bleached hospital sheets before leveling a somber stare. "Although to be clear, I'm still not okay with you and my grandson being together."

Her words shocked me, like a slap across the face. And also confused me. She didn't approve of me? "Then why did you trust me with . . . what I did yesterday?"

Her weary sigh seemed to deflate her under the sterile covers. "Because I'm getting old, and my work here is too important to let it die with me. I need you to step in."

Again, Annette surprised me silent, even as I stung from her reproof. I must have misheard. "Annette, I'm confused. You've warned me away from Russell in one breath, then suggested this huge responsibility should be mine. May I ask why you disapprove? Is it because . . ."

"Of the color of your skin," she said simply.

I had feared that, even if I hadn't been able to say as much. It was tough finding the right words that wouldn't offend—or more importantly, words that wouldn't hurt. I hadn't grown up in a family that talked about race. We discussed classical literature, Broadway plays, and overseas travel. But we never discussed this, a subject that mattered so much more.

Annette squeezed my hand. "I want what's best for you. And what's best for my grandson." She rubbed her other hand along her collarbone, weariness stamped on her lined face. "I've seen a lot of change in my life. I was born in a house with no electricity or indoor plumbing. It wasn't a matter of poverty. That's just how most folks lived in rural South Carolina."

She drew in a few drags off the oxygen tube at her nose. "My daddy farmed, and we had plenty to eat. I recall riding horseback, swimming in the river, reading every book I could get my hands on. But I also remember sitting in the back of the bus, drinking from a different water fountain, and taking my grandson to first grade in a segregated school."

"But things are changing." The sentence felt inadequate on my tongue. "Aren't they?"

"Yes, things are changing, but not nearly fast enough. Just like I want you safe from the past that hurt you . . ." The heart monitor's beeps increased, along with the fire in her eyes. "I need my grandson to stay safe from people in the present who would still do him harm for looking at you the way he does."

I wanted to reassure her that I understood we couldn't have a future for so many reasons, my past being high on the list. But I also recognized this was a moment I needed to listen. "Thank you for talking to me, for being patient with me. I hope you know, I'm really trying."

"I do recognize that." A smile flickered across her face, along with a wince as she shifted in the narrow bed. "But there's going to come a time when people like me are going to get tired of carrying the burden of helping white folks *trying* to understand."

Rather than risk saying the wrong thing, I settled for the one pure and simple truth in my heart. "The last thing I want is for Russell to be hurt because of me."

"Then make sure he's not," she said with a firm nod, then motioned for me to lean closer. "Now let me fill you in on how our network operates."

⁂

2025

Although Bailey Rae wanted to become a beach girl, right now she was grateful to be exactly where she stood in rural South Carolina. And she was especially thankful for country boys who loved their blazing off-road lights, because Libby had wandered off into the woods right at sunset. Not for the first time. Except tonight, her disappearance put everyone on edge, given the fisherman's mysterious death and the uptick of squatters breaking into foreclosed homes.

Keeping pace alongside Keith on the wide walking trail, Bailey Rae brushed away a low branch, releasing a shower of leaves and pollen. In the distance she heard the shouts of other search teams. Martin had helped the police in organizing most of the town to turn out with flashlights, water bottles, and bug spray. They'd checked the obvious places in town and now were shifting their focus into the forest. This trail had been a favorite of Libby's, with its earth packed and cleared from four-wheelers and dirt bikes.

Still, fears for Libby multiplied, beyond just the regular worries about wild pigs and snakes. She could be injured and unable to call for help. Or worse yet, someone may have preyed on her vulnerability. Sure, everyone in Bent Oak knew her, but the market would have brought strangers to town. And there was also the problem with drifters.

Bent Oak at night wasn't nearly as friendly looking as daytime. As a child, the twisted oak trees with Spanish moss reminded Bailey Rae of Halloween and haunted woods. She really needed to talk to Councilman Tyler about installing more streetlamps.

How far could Libby have gone in a wheelchair, for heaven's sake? Even if she'd managed to use her walker, she wouldn't have had the stamina to continue for long.

Keith stopped at a fork in the wide walking trail, looking left and right, then sagged against a tree trunk. "I don't know how to keep her safe anymore. Her memory loss is a struggle in more ways than one."

Bailey Rae chugged her water bottle to swallow down tears. "Alzheimer's is challenging, and you've been a great son."

Pushing away from the trunk, Keith set off along the trail on the right. "Sometimes I wonder if it's Alzheimer's or if the memory loss is because of some pretty severe blows to the head she took in the past."

Shocked, Bailey Rae recapped her water bottle.

"I didn't know." She'd read about athletes who'd sustained brain injuries from multiple hits, even when wearing a helmet. She didn't want to assume the worst but had to ask, "Do you mind if I ask what happened?"

Keith's jaw flexed, his boots hammering the ground harder. "My dad was bad news. He was abusive to Mom and me. We couldn't even blame it on booze or drugs. He was just a mean son of a bitch."

Bailey Rae stopped in her tracks, halting Keith with a hand to the elbow. "I'm so sorry."

His gaze skirted around the forest until finally meeting hers. "Mom did her best to protect me. This one time, when I was five or thereabouts, we could hear him outside, picking an argument with the guy in the next apartment over something stupid, like his taste in music. Nothing really. Except it wouldn't stay nothing. So Mom scooped me up onto her hip and grabbed a loaf of bread. She said we were going to feed the birds. We fed those birds all night long."

"I can see why you and your mother wanted a fresh start in Bent Oak after he died." She rubbed along his upper arm.

"Do you mind searching with Martin for a while?" He gestured to the game warden's truck parked about a football field away. "I'm gonna meet up with June and Thea, brainstorm some of the old haunts where Mom might gravitate."

Bailey Rae's head spun at the rapid shift in Keith's mood. Although emotions *were* running high. She held her silence and fell into step behind Keith as he led the way to wave down Martin's truck. The floodlight attached to the roll bar shone like a beacon across a field. Night critters croaked and buzzed from the river in the distance.

Before she could catch her bearings, Keith bolted back into the woods, leaving Bailey Rae shifting from foot to foot. She needed to shake off the awkwardness. Libby's well-being mattered most.

"Sorry that Keith dumped me on you while you're on the clock." She couldn't even bear to think about the riverbank on the other side of the field. "I don't want to interfere."

"It's an all-hands-on-deck event. Just stay close and keep your eyes peeled for snakes." Martin picked his way through the ankle-high overgrowth.

Bailey Rae shivered and clicked on her cell phone's flashlight for extra illumination along every suspicious glint from the high grass. Empty food wrappers from burgers and chips. Beer cans and soda bottles. Common items. Like at the riverside. Just teens escaping authority? Or more squatters? She shivered again.

Martin palmed her back. "How are you holding up? I've been worried about you the past few days, after what shook down at the river."

"I got your messages." She didn't know how to explain the need for distance when they weren't even a couple. Boundaries weren't her strong suit. Walls were more her style. "I'm okay. Really."

"So you said in your text." The floodlight from the truck cast his face in shadows. "I've been in your shoes. I recognize a brush-off peppered with denial when I see it."

His kindness in the face of her borderline rude dismissal left her feeling so very small. "Are you ever anything other than perfect?"

A half grin kicked a dimple into his cheek. "I thought I was a jerk because of the ticket for fishing without a license."

"Fair point." She paused at the end of the field, the river's current whispering in the distance. The muggy breeze against her cheek had shifted from steaming to warm with the setting sun. "Thank you for what you told me about when you were in the military. I know that couldn't have been easy to share."

"Well, the shrink the army made me go see told me it wasn't good to keep stuff bottled up," he said with a wry smile. "He would be glad to know I finally listened to him."

"You haven't spoken to anyone about it before?" She couldn't have heard that correctly.

"No one other than the shrink, until I told you." He cupped her shoulder in a broad hand. "But don't overthink that. It just felt like the right time."

She should have guessed what his riverside confession cost him, but she'd been so focused on her own pain. "Are *you* okay?"

"Better than I was before. Not done yet."

As she studied Martin's eyes to reassure herself, the night swirled around them, their pocket of the search quiet for the moment. She traced the furrows in his forehead, his bronzed skin warm to the touch. She swiped away the beads of perspiration, then pressed her mouth to his. Just a simple kiss. One that lingered a heartbeat too long for casual.

Angling back, she bit her bottom lip. "That wasn't a good idea."

"Probably not," his deep voice rumbled, his hand still on her shoulder while his thumb stroked her jawline.

She wondered for a moment if he was going to kiss her back, regardless of the wisdom or the timing. But the radio clipped to his belt squawked, jolting them apart.

Martin tugged the receiver up to his mouth. "Officer Perez here. Over."

"Sir"—a voice crackled through the speaker—"we've found Mrs. Farrell."

CHAPTER THIRTEEN

2025

Thanks to the flashing light bar on top of his truck, Martin made good time in driving Bailey Rae to the library after Libby had been found—confused and refusing to budge from the back stoop. Later, he would unpack the implications of that kiss from Bailey Rae. For now, he operated in business mode, calling off the search while Bailey Rae sat in the passenger seat texting Keith nonstop for details about Libby's state of mind before she went missing.

As Martin turned into the library's back lot, he switched off the light bar so as not to risk disorienting Libby. His headlights swept across her on the back steps, with her walker discarded to the side. A small cluster of teenagers from the volunteer search parties stood beside Libby with their phones out. Frail and curved in on herself, she took up so little space it was a wonder anyone had noticed her in the dark.

Tonight, more than ever, this town reminded him of a place stuck in time, of a gentler, more trusting era. He couldn't imagine anywhere else that a woman with dementia could ditch her wheelchair for her walker, ramble all around town, and come to no harm. Except this wasn't the past, and there were dangerous undercurrents swirling in Bent Oak.

Even though he was no longer an MP, those cop instincts were tough to shake, and those instincts insisted these people needed a larger police force. Bailey Rae and all her pseudo-mamas drew out his protective instincts. More than that, though. He cared about them, with their generous hearts, quirky ways, and an unerring ability to land in the middle of a storm time and time again.

He pressed the brake, but before he could even shift the truck into park, Bailey Rae flung open her door, letting in a gust of muggy summer air. She called back to him over her shoulder, "Keith's only a few minutes away. I'm going to sit with her. When I phoned the EMTs, they said it might take a while to arrive since they're slammed with calls . . ."

Was she running to Libby or away from him and the aftermath of the spontaneous kiss?

Either way, Bailey Rae leaped from the truck and raced to the older woman's side, half acknowledging the teens with a wave. Martin parked and thanked the cluster of high schoolers too before they piled back into a sedan with mismatched quarter panels. He checked his watch, wondering how far out Keith had gone in his search and how long it would take him to arrive. Would they be better off driving her to the ER now? Bailey Rae knew her best, so he would take his cue from her.

Gripping the rail, she sat gently on the concrete step beside her. "Mrs. Libby, the library's closed for the day. How about we take you home?"

"Shhh." Libby held a finger to her mouth. "Loose lips sink ships. We don't want anyone around town to hear us. I'm just handing over the paperwork, but they're late."

Frowning, Bailey Rae hugged her tanned legs. "What paperwork?"

"From the paralegal," Libby whispered, tugging at her loose denim pants absently. Compulsively. A sure sign her agitation was growing. "A birth certificate and Social Security card to replace the old ones."

Bailey Rae patted Libby's hand until the nervous fidgeting slowed. "I'm sure the old papers aren't lost. I bet Keith has them filed away."

"I do *not* lose things, you know." Frustration leaked into Libby's voice, her volume increasing. "I just have to be careful to remember my name. That's tougher than it sounds."

Martin crouched in front of her in hopes of de-escalating the older woman's stress. "Mrs. Libby, how about I stay with you awhile? Then you won't have to sit here alone in the dark."

"No need, young man. I should get home to my son." Libby frowned, plucking at her sleeve. "Who are you again?"

Bailey Rae slid an arm around Libby's shoulders. "This is Martin, the game warden. He's with me."

Libby's feet started tapping, like she was running in place. "I don't know what to do. Where am I supposed to go next?" She patted her pockets, her voice rising. "I can't find my papers. What did you do with the envelope?"

Martin struggled for what to say, hating the feeling of helplessness, all the while knowing the emotions churning in him didn't come close to what Libby must be experiencing.

Bailey Rae pointed toward Main Street, distracting Libby. "Look over there. That's your ride. Your boy is almost here with the van, and he will have all the answers."

Martin pushed to his feet, glad to have a way to help rather than just hoping for the right words. "Mrs. Libby, I'll get your walker and escort you to your ride."

Since the wheelchair wasn't in sight, he assumed she must have been more mobile today, making her way over with the walker. She had to be exhausted.

Keith's minivan sped into the lot, tires spewing gravel as he swept into a parking spot. The vehicle jerked to a stop, and he didn't even turn off the engine before hopping out of the driver's side.

Martin stopped him short and said softly, "She appears physically okay, but disoriented. Bailey Rae called the EMTs, but they haven't arrived. You may want to take your mom to get checked out by a doctor."

"Thanks, man." Keith nodded, then jogged to his mother's side. "Mom, why did you wander off like that? I was really worried."

Libby's eyes went wide, and she tried to scoot back on the step, only to cry out in pain. "Fred, I'm sorry. I was coming home soon. I promise. I just, um, wanted to go to choir practice."

Fred? Martin looked to Bailey Rae for answers, but she just shrugged, looking as bemused as he felt.

Keith clasped her hands gently. "It's okay. I've got you now."

"Please forgive me," Libby said, her whole body trembling. "You know I love you. I swear I'll never take off like that again. Please don't make me stop playing the organ at church."

Martin could almost smell the fear radiating off her. A deep unease crept through him as he realized her trembling reminded him of Gia's from that day at the market. As if she were speaking to someone who frightened her. Was her son guilty of elder abuse? Except her son's name wasn't Fred. Maybe a memory of her dead husband?

The sound of a creaking car door cut short Martin's concerns as June eased out of the passenger side and activated the vehicle's side panel with the wheelchair ramp. "Libby, honey," she called, "it's time for us to go. We aren't needed here tonight. Everything's under control."

June's calm words worked their magic. Libby took a shuddering breath and reached for them to help her stand until they could maneuver the walker in front of her. Keith hustled double time to get his mother loaded up before the bubble of calm June had created popped.

Libby scooted the walker along the concrete walkway. "We have to pick up Keith from the principal's office. I don't want to make us late."

June cupped her shoulder. "Of course you want to be prompt. The sooner we get in the van, the sooner we can be on our way." She continued her litany of words as she shepherded Libby along. "We can have a glass of sweet tea and talk all about it when we get back to your place."

As June and Keith loaded his mother into the van, their love for the woman shone through in their patience and calm. The same way Martin's sister cared for their aging parents. Standing here now, he felt guilty for not doing more, for diving so deep into his need for peace that he'd isolated himself.

He'd thought more than once about himself as an outsider, an observer of an area different from where he'd grown up. Could that be the reason he'd taken the job in Bent Oak, far removed from anyone or anywhere familiar, where there was less chance of emotional connection?

If so, he hadn't taken Bailey Rae Rigby into account.

Just thinking her name had him noticing her aloe scent on the night air, inconvenient when he had other concerns that needed addressing first. The best path forward? Tuck away the attraction to Bailey Rae and focus on what had happened here tonight.

The quiet intensified as the rumble of the van's engine faded.

Martin stuffed his hands into his pockets. "Bailey Rae? I need to ask you. Is Libby safe at home? With her son, I mean."

Bailey Rae's eyes went wide with surprise. "Yes, absolutely. He's dedicated to taking care of her. Libby's husband abused her, though. I don't know the full story, but it was bad enough she took quite a few blows to the head."

Martin cursed under his breath as she confirmed what would have been his next guess. He closed his eyes, scrubbing a hand along the ache pounding in his forehead. "So her disease took her back to when she'd suffered that abuse. What a nightmare."

Bailey Rae touched his shoulder lightly, then clasped his hand. "Thank you for bringing me here to her. You did a great job keeping Libby calm until Keith arrived. That military cop training served you well tonight."

"Glad to be of help. This is my town now too." He paused. "Or maybe I'm not allowed to say that since I didn't grow up here. That's a Southern thing, right?"

"Thea didn't grow up here either, yet she's a part of the community." Bailey Rae slumped back against the brick library. "I'm the one who's leaving. You're staying. The way I see it, that officially means you belong in Bent Oak more than I do."

Standing only inches away from her, he could only look at her and the way the moonlight glinted on the golden streaks in her auburn hair. He waited for her to pull away, but she simply stared back. Unmoving. Except for her thumb moving along his wrist.

The moment made him want things he couldn't have. Reminding him he needed to say something about what had happened between them.

He cleared his throat. "About the kiss earlier, if things were different . . ."

"No need to say anything more about it," she said softly, still staring back at him. "Please, let's focus on getting through the next week without creating regrets."

Her words were welcome, even as he acknowledged a hint of disappointment too. But since he was already living with a bellyful of regrets, he couldn't agree with her more.

⁌

1979

I'd learned more from Annette in the past twelve months than I'd learned in all of finishing school. Of course, I yearned for this education far more than I'd ever wanted to master the skill of table setting for an eight-course meal. Who really needed to know about a pickle fork when I was literally changing lives?

Every time I drove my Dodge Dart out to her cabin, I knew I was about to take that education to the next level. Of the dozen or so operations in a year, my role had increased over the months, with Annette supervising me. Details were usually coordinated at the library.

However, Annette reserved her home for more time-intensive elements or bigger secrets. And I wanted to be a part of those things. Saving the day felt good. Knowing why, though, left a hole in your heart that always felt empty.

Like the mother-daughter duo who'd needed to start over. At first, I'd assumed the mother escaped a bad marriage, but I quickly realized the thirteen-year-old was running from her soon-to-be husband.

Then, the eighteen-year-old who took her five-year-old sister away in the middle of the night after she figured out her mother was going to sell the child to settle a drug debt.

And so on, and so on. Each situation reminded me all the more how outright lucky I'd been to land on my feet with a job, home, and wonderfully reliable, albeit ugly, green car.

I parked Olive under a sprawling oak beside Annette's wood-planked cabin, where she'd brought up her son, then Russell too after his parents died. Annette and I hadn't openly addressed the "relationship" subject since her time in the hospital, but I also hadn't stopped seeing her grandson. Annette and I tiptoed around the subject without either of us giving ground.

Russell and I had started openly dating, more than just picnics by the river and dinner at the local barbecue joint, instead adding town hall meetings and high school plays. We became close—in every way. For those intimate moments, we met at my boardinghouse rather than his barn apartment at his grandmother's farm. I worried about alienating Annette. But the prospect of losing Russell saddened me more. I didn't take any of my happiness for granted, as I'd done before coming to Bent Oak.

Reaching into the back seat, I hefted out an overburdened canvas bag and hitched it onto my shoulder. The muggy air outside wrapped around me like a still-damp blanket warm from the dryer. Inside wouldn't be much better with just window AC units that went on the fritz more often than not.

Today, Annette sat on the front porch with a box fan plugged in. A tabby cat napped with his belly exposed to the gust. Instead of one of her smart work suits, she wore a paisley housedress with her hair in a wrap. "Come on up so we can talk. I have an extra glass of lemonade."

I slung the bag of supplies onto the end table between the rockers. An oversize canvas bag was far less conspicuous than a suitcase. "I found everything you requested. Change of clothes, size eleven. Shoes, size nine. Toiletries. I added a nightgown and a novel, something lighthearted. Plus a honeybun and a pack of crackers."

"Well done," Annette said as she inspected the contents of the sack, then slid a small wallet inside, "and just in time. I need you to ride along with her to the next handoff."

Me?

She wanted *me* to make the road trip? Panic splashed through me like an icy shower in the boardinghouse I shared with far too many people. I vowed the place had the world's smallest water heater, but it was home. The thought of leaving Bent Oak terrified me. "Are you sure I'm ready for that? Maybe Thea would be better suited."

Thea had nerves of steel. Nothing ever rattled her. Other than the time she'd lost her favorite gloves.

Annette leaned back in her rocker, gripping the armrests. "Winnie, Thea's not ready, and Libby is, well, she's fragile. That may sound harsh, but this isn't the time for polite niceties. We try to have a woman ride along anytime the driver is male. It puts everyone's mind at ease."

I absolutely understood the need for a woman's presence. Except how could I explain my sheer panic at the idea of being the one to travel beyond the town where I'd grown a new life? "I have to disagree with you about Libby being fragile. The way she's held on for her son surpasses anything I've had to do. If we're being brutally honest, I can't..."

My voice trailed off, trembling as the anxiety gripped me at leaving my safe cocoon.

"You're unable to leave the county limits," Annette said simply, gently. "I know. And I understand. That doesn't mean you can't play a vital role today."

She knew about my phobia? But then nothing got past Annette. "What am I doing?"

"Riding along with Russell, just to the county line to pick up the young woman."

With Russell?

My panic shifted to shock. I couldn't have heard her correctly. And if I had, then that brought a shock that far surpassed the other. "With *Russell? Russell* is the driver for this transfer?"

I'd long wondered how much he knew about the operation, never suspecting he might know . . . everything?

"Oh, so now you want to pretend like you don't know him?" Annette asked, closing the bag and tying the hemp strings. "The two of you will drive her across the county for the next leg to pick her up. Anyone who sees you will assume you're out on a date. It's the perfect cover."

The truth sank in. *My* Russell was a part of Annette's organization. He'd never given me the slightest hint that he knew anything about it, much less played an active role. I struggled for what to say. To her now. To him later. "Is this a different part of why you warned me away from your grandson?"

"What does that matter? There's been no stopping either of you," Annette said as she dabbed perspiration from her forehead. "I figure you've both been twisting yourself in knots with your secrets for long enough. Maybe you can use the ride over to have a little talk."

A little talk? The revelation was so far beyond a simple conversation, I couldn't even imagine where we'd begin to discuss it.

All these years I'd tortured myself over keeping secrets from him as we deepened our relationship, even becoming lovers this past year. Guilt had plagued me over technically still being married to Phillip. And yet, Russell had been keeping secrets of his own. Even knowing we had to protect the anonymity of the network, I still couldn't shake the sense of betrayal that Russell hadn't said something, anything, even a hint to put my mind at ease. How well did I really know him if he could keep such a huge secret so easily? I felt catapulted back into a time I'd been gaslit, manipulated into feeling bad about things that weren't my fault.

I knew Russell was a hundred times more of a man than Phillip could ever dream of being. Yet somehow, that only made the heartache all the worse for having placed him on a pedestal.

༄

An hour later, as Russell and I turned off Annette's dirt driveway onto the narrow back road, I still hadn't come close to resolving my hurt and anger. And we had at least twenty long, awkward minutes in the vehicle together before we reached our pickup location.

I very well might explode before then.

Annette had no reason to share about Russell's role, but her omission over the years stung. It was one thing to shield the identity of people in other towns, but why keep secrets here? I'd trusted Annette with my life, and right now, it felt like she didn't trust me in return. Not fully.

Now we had Annette's blessing to discuss that big fat secret between us.

Which quite possibly also included Annette's blessing for us as a couple too. If only her endorsement hadn't come at just the moment I feared Russell and I might not have a future after all following this "little talk."

He wasn't driving his Chevy tonight. Instead, he sat behind the wheel of a station wagon I'd seen in the shop at his family's gas station. The vehicle all but hollered domesticity, even sporting a high school bumper sticker. A truck with one headlight out swooped past. Then two motorcycles. Those who knew us would guess rightly that the car came from his family's gas station. And those who didn't recognize us would assume we were a couple.

Right now, I had no idea what we were. The only thing I knew for sure? Russell's lies of omission hurt worst of all. Maybe that was hypocritical of me to think, given that I hadn't told him about my identity prior to Bent Oak. But I thought I'd been protecting him by not speaking.

Russell cast a sideways look my way, his arm draped along the back of the seat as he powered down the two-lane country road. "According to Granny," he said, his fingers threading through my hair to stroke my neck, "it's time for us to quit dancing around how much the other knows about her operation."

Another pinch of betrayal made me wince. He was talking now only because of his grandmother's permission. I wanted to shout at him, to rage, all reactions I knew to be unhealthy and wrong. Especially at a time when I couldn't bear to have another man label me an out-of-control, crazy female with over-the-top emotions. Truth be told, wouldn't anyone get a little loud if they weren't listened to for years?

"That's pretty much what she told me." I eased my head away and picked at the fraying hem of my jean cutoffs. I'd hacked these myself after busting a hole in the knee. Given I used to spend a small fortune on a similar look in my past life, I was quite proud of the end result. "You'll have to pardon me if I'm slow on the uptake right now. My head's still reeling. Is your whole NASCAR gig some kind of elaborate plot for you to travel in support of your grandmother?"

So much for words being stuck in my throat. The floodgates had been opened, and my bitter accusations had spilled out. At least I wasn't shouting.

"The pit crew job is real," he said tightly. "As is my NASCAR dream. The truck driving for the mill, however, gives me a reasonable cover to help out where I can."

Processing that snippet, I hooked my elbow on the open window, sucking in drags of muggy night air in hopes of clearing my spinning head and strengthening my resolve. More than anything, I wanted the joy and excitement of his arms around me, but I needed answers. I thought of all the times I assumed Russell was wrung out from a long haul for the mill, but I could see now it was more than just the extended hours. His journey, the mission, had taken an emotional toll.

I cared so deeply for this man, and he'd vowed the same to me. Yet we'd kept such a wall between us, one we were only now scaling because

Annette made us. How much longer would we have held our secrets? Forever? No. Because there wouldn't have been a forever for us under the weight of such deception. "All this time, you knew I wasn't just the average new girl in town, and you never even hinted."

He stayed silent for so long I thought he wasn't going to answer. Then I realized he was just searching for a wide-enough shoulder on the side of the road where he could pull off without sliding into a ditch. Finding a safe patch of dirt, he put the station wagon in park and turned to me.

"There's nothing average about you." I couldn't miss the intensity in his words as he toyed with a lock of my hair. He didn't touch me again, yet the strand still made a whispery link between us. "To answer your question: Yes, I knew something bad must have happened to you before you arrived. I don't know the specifics. Granny has a strict code about not sharing anyone's past, and out of respect for her, I honor that. I'm still stunned she okayed our conversation tonight."

I closed my eyes as a tidal wave of relief threatened to swallow me. I hadn't realized until that moment how deep down I'd hurt at the possibility Annette might have shared about Eloise Carlisle Curtis. The betrayal would have been more than my scarred heart could take.

Although it sure would have been nice if she'd arranged for this little conversation a while back. "If you suspected, why haven't you asked me before now?"

"That decision had to be yours and yours alone. Granny understands that too, although I have a strong feeling that by putting us in this station wagon together, she's hoping you'll tell me the rest on your own."

His eyes were so intent on mine, hopeful and wary in equal measure. Something in his expression brought home all the secrets I'd kept from him too. Some of my anger at him seeped away.

Now that the time had come to spill my truth, I struggled with where to begin. There were a million things I needed to tell him. Important things. Like about my miscarriages and my stillborn daughter. My parents. The time in the hospital. Except I needed to start with the most important.

"Russell, back in my other life, before I moved to Bent Oak, I was married to another man. A man who betrayed me in so many unimaginable ways." Even saying this much out loud for the first time in eight years made my chest go so tight with anxiety, I feared my ribs might crack. Then I looked into Russell's golden-brown eyes and saw *him*, seeing *me*. Noticing me. Knowing me. Valuing who I was deep down inside even as I sat there in jean shorts cut off all unevenly. This man was more than I could have dreamed I wanted and needed. "But, please know, that in spite of all the ways my husband tried to crush my spirit, I am completely, hopelessly in love with *you*."

CHAPTER FOURTEEN

2025

Bailey Rae hugged the porch post, watching Martin drive away from the cabin, lightning bugs speckling the night. Their parting had left her feeling hollow. More than it should for someone so new in her life. Still, she couldn't remember when she'd felt so alone.

Which was ridiculous, really.

Bent Oak was so small, she could swear all she had to do was sigh and people would show up on her doorstep offering help. But it wasn't the same without Winnie, a loss made even worse by the increasing realization that she may not have really known her aunt as well as she'd thought.

Sinking onto a step, she watched Martin's taillights along the lengthy drive. Would he park at the top of the drive and watch her house through the night again? He'd insisted she keep Skeeter close and set the security system once she got inside, but there'd been no kiss when he left. They'd both agreed on that earlier, hadn't they? So she had no cause to feel this disappointed.

Besides, she had other problems on her mind.

She was tired of those close to her speaking in riddles. Tonight wasn't the first time Libby had called her son Fred or Freddie. Each time it happened, Keith, Thea, or June hustled Libby away. At first, Bailey Rae had assumed they did so to protect her dignity, and that likely played a part in their behavior. Still, there was no denying something more was at play. The references to papers and new birth certificates. Different names. A million other little things made her question the secrets of the tight friendships in Winnie's circle.

And the answers must be here, somewhere.

She shot to her feet and whistled. "Come on, Skeeter. I've got half of a hot dog in the fridge with your name on it."

Skeeter galloped across the yard and up the planked steps, his tongue lolling out the side of his mouth.

Once inside, she set the security system and sagged back against the door, looking at the cabin through different eyes. In a place full of ghosts to escape, had she been so busy trying to leave town that she'd missed clues about Winnie's life? Now she took deep breaths and forced herself to search for the evidence of memories—good and bad.

She skimmed her fingers along a line of photos on the wall of Skeeter number one, two, and three—a shepherd mutt, an American bulldog, and a spaniel mix. Winnie had said naming the dogs the same thing made it easier to remember, but now Bailey Rae wondered if there might have been a shadow in her aunt's eyes when she said that.

Padding across the wood floor, she moved on to the marks on the pantry door. Each notch chronicled the beginning of a new school year until ninth grade, when she'd stopped growing. Winnie always vowed if the house caught on fire, she would rip the door off the hinges on her way out.

Time etched in that fashion was so sequential, logical, and not at all the way dear Libby recalled her life anymore. If only her memories scrambled by dementia could be organized back into their proper linear order. Maybe then Bailey Rae would have been able to make sense out of whatever Libby was trying to reveal.

Bailey Rae's gaze skated to the vintage sewing machine where Winnie had cranked out costumes for school reports on Amelia Earhart and Marie Curie. Strong women, Winnie had declared, encouraging her to aspire. On the one hand, the challenge had excited Bailey Rae as a child. On the other, it stirred a deep sense of unworthiness. Of being that homeless kid in the back of her mother's station wagon, sticking her hand into the very bottom of a jar of peanut butter, then sucking on her fingers.

Not that Winnie had ever judged her. She taught her instead. Like the time Bailey Rae had been caught sneaking in late as a teenager after drinking with friends by the river. The next morning Winnie had woken her at six to start snapping green beans before canning them. She hadn't rolled out a lecture about Yvonne's battle with alcoholism. Winnie hadn't needed to. By the end of the very long day canning beans, Bailey Rae had received the message loud and clear. Working hungover would make it very difficult to hold down a steady job.

The weight of those memories threatened to choke her with a tangle of emotions that knotted tighter the harder she pulled, like a ball of yarn batted about by a couple of Winnie's barn cats. Would she ever be able to untangle the mess, the secrets, to weave something beautiful that paid tribute to the way Winnie's intervention had saved her life?

Bailey Rae clenched her fists, determined to find at least one answer to the undercurrents no one else seemed willing to acknowledge. She tore through the cabin in search of anything she might have missed as she packed up the place with donations and items to sell. The filing cabinet would be too obvious, and she'd already been through that front to back after Winnie died.

Next, she charged down the corridor to Winnie and Russell's bedroom, only to stop short. Even the prospect of walking into their space made her ache missing them. This was the one room she hadn't boxed up or marked anything for sale.

Stepping into the paneled space, she yanked open the jewelry box but found only a smattering of costume pieces—hoop earrings, a floral choker, a mood ring—and an old car key tagged as "Olive."

Nothing more, since Winnie's wedding band had been on her finger when she died. Bailey Rae swallowed the emotion clogging her throat. That ring had been a sign of Winnie's continued commitment to Russell after his death, even if they hadn't been legally wed.

Moving on to the closet, she searched the pockets of the remaining clothing and tried not to inhale the familiar vanilla scent of Winnie lingering on the fabric. The search turned up nothing of worth, only a couple of receipts and a tin of breath mints.

Fueled by determination, Bailey Rae dragged a chair over and ransacked the closet shelves, tossing one thing after another to the floor. Again, nothing but a pile of sweaters, hats, and an old pair of gardening Crocs.

Breathless, she put her hands on her hips and surveyed the mess around her, deciding where to search next in the cabin. Skeeter sat in the doorway, wide eyes studying her with a sympathy that seemed to say he understood well the benefit of zoomies.

"Come on, Skeeter. I still owe you that stale hot dog," she said, returning to the kitchen and tossing the dog's treat into the metal bowl.

Might as well tackle the kitchen. She yanked open the pantry and burrowed a spoon into the leftover baking goods, peeking into the spices, dumping three junk drawers. No luck. Stepping back, she scanned the familiar room from the battery-operated wall clock to the opaque milk jars on the shelves. She grabbed a broom and toppled a jar over, catching it before it hit the floor, and finding . . .

Money. Twenty-dollar bills rolled together. Fifteen of them.

Surprise swelled through her, then galvanized her. She tipped over another bottle. Tens and ones this time. One hundred dollars.

Deep in her gut, she knew that wasn't all. Somehow, she'd found the tip of the iceberg in this mystery. She scrambled up onto the counter and stood, grabbing one bottle after another, tilting them. So, so much cash rained out, drifting to the floor like leaves from tree branches.

Her pulse roared in her ears. She jumped off the counter, bills crackling under her shoes, and started her search in earnest, only to find money stashed in so many places. Rolled in a pill bottle. Buried inside a puzzle box. Underneath Monopoly money. Tucked in a box of tampons.

Heartbeat throbbing in her ears, Bailey Rae dropped to the braided rug in the living room and counted out close to $7,000. That didn't even take into account what she might have missed or inadvertently sold to someone at the flea market. Imagine buying a jar of peaches only to find silver dollars tucked inside.

Winnie had always told her a woman needed to have money of her own. So Bailey Rae had been surprised at the low bank balance after Winnie's death. Now it all made sense.

As she stacked the cash in neat piles in front of her, sorted by denominations, she wondered if there might be a floor or wall safe too. Right now, she wouldn't discount anything. Pushing to her feet, she moved furniture and rolled up rugs, peered under the beds, and checked behind all the pictures. Again and again, she came up dry.

She stood in the middle of the room, pivoting for inspiration until her eyes landed on Skeeter nosing his dog bed, pawing and circling as he always did before napping. Maybe . . .

Bailey Rae rushed across the room and shooed Skeeter away. She lifted the cushion to unzip the liner, then stopped cold. The wood flooring had a discolored section about twenty by twenty inches. Dropping to her knees, she ran her fingers along the edges until finding a groove.

A tiny trap door popped open. A small fire safe rested inside the cubby, the kind with a keypad. She groaned in frustration as she lifted the small safe and punched in the same code as the security system. Then her birthday. Winnie's. Russell's. Still nothing.

The safe wasn't necessarily a strange thing. But taken in context with all this cash lying around, she had questions.

She wasn't sure why those answers should matter so much. Winnie was gone, Russell too. If the riddles had been important, Winnie would have made mention of the money in her will, wouldn't she? Or maybe just the opposite. That the secrets were too big to contain in one document.

She had only one way to find out. First thing tomorrow, she needed to go straight to the nearest reliable sources.

Thea and June.

⁌

During her early months in Bent Oak as a child, Bailey Rae had assumed Libby, June, and Thea were somehow related to Winnie. They went just about everywhere together, ate meals at each other's homes at least a couple of times a week. They'd felt like family. Not the family Bailey Rae had known for her first six years, but the type she thought only existed in books or on television.

And family could drop in unannounced. By morning, frazzled and frustrated, she'd decided to start with Thea.

With the rising sun dappling shadows through the tunnel of oak branches, she steered her truck along the lengthy driveway. A level road with no potholes, the drive curved until the sprawling home came into view—with Libby's minivan parked in front, which meant June or Keith must be there as well.

At least three times the size of the cabin, Thea's two-story brick house sported wraparound porches and balconies. A stately home befitting the heir to the paper mill, Bent Oak's main source of employment. Thea also lived on the river, but with a cleared lot and a dock with a pontoon boat on a lift.

The spread offered quite the contrast to June's condominium on the refurbished second floor above a law office. And it seemed a world away from Libby's modular home on an acre of land deeded over to her by Russell. These ladies took care of each other, that much Bailey Rae knew from the earliest of her days in Bent Oak. She just hoped they would see her as a proxy for Winnie and pry open the vault to their secrets.

Literally and figuratively. Bailey Rae rested a clenched hand on the small safe perched on the passenger side of the bench seat. The knot in her stomach grew tighter as she drew closer to answers.

Stopping beside Libby's minivan, Bailey Rae threw the truck into park and stepped out in the summer morning, eighty degrees and climbing.

From the porch, Thea waved her over, a wide-brimmed hat shading her face. "Hey there. What perfect timing for you to stop by. Come join us for sweet tea and hummingbird cake."

Bailey Rae hefted the small safe from the passenger seat and kicked the door closed behind her. She followed the paver stones, the walkway lined with hostas and hydrangeas. Thea had the prettiest yard in all of Bent Oak yet refused to join the garden club, in spite of her mother-in-law's repeated invitations over the years.

The women had gathered in a far corner of the porch at a wrought iron table and chairs, ceiling fans swooping overhead. The friends had congregated there so often that once Libby's mobility waned, Thea's husband had installed a ramp along the side of the porch.

Bailey Rae plunked the mini-safe onto the wrought iron table beside a four-layer hummingbird cake. "Look what I found in the floor of Winnie's cabin. Any idea of the combination or what she's hiding inside?"

Thea glanced up from pouring tea into cut-crystal glasses full of ice. "In the floor of Winnie's cabin? Maybe that's from Annette or Russell's day."

Bailey Rae dropped into a chair. "It's not dusty—and it wasn't when I found it either."

June sliced through the cake with undue concentration, sliding a piece onto each of the gold-rimmed plates. "That's quite a mystery."

For once, Libby had nothing to say. She simply plucked at her overlong lemon T-shirt. Clothes with buttons were becoming a thing of the past since she'd started to undress in the middle of the grocery store shortly after Winnie had died. The doctor had indicated disrobing at inappropriate times sometimes happened to a person with dementia, especially during times of stress.

June passed a ball of cornflower-blue yarn and a crochet needle to Libby. "Honey, here's the baby blanket you've been working on for Thea's new grandson."

Bailey Rae waited through the distribution of plates and filling of drinks, all in silence. Was it her imagination or were they avoiding her eyes? "So that's it? Nobody's going to say anything else about the safe?"

Thea met her gaze for the first time. "What do you think the safe contains?"

"Secrets." The word fell out of her mouth as she sat forward, determined to find answers. "I also found thousands of dollars in cash stashed all over the cabin in the strangest places. I get the feeling there's some kind of mystery in Winnie's past. Maybe it's none of my business, but Winnie was all I had in the world, and I thought—I know—I was important to her."

Thea reached to clasp her hand, the warmth of her filtering through her lightweight glove. "You were the child Winnie never had. She loved you. Anything she kept from you came out of a need to protect you."

Except Bailey Rae wasn't a child any longer. "What might I find in the safe if I opened it?" Frustration bubbled up and out. "You can tell me now or wait around for Libby to spill the beans later down the road. I'd really rather hear it from you."

June gestured toward Libby engrossed in her crocheting. "Bailey Rae's right about that. Since we're all alone here, maybe this is the right time to give her the basics."

That last word—basics—hinted at a pared-down accounting when Bailey Rae wanted the full scoop. But she would wrangle for more along the way. At least this was a start.

Thea pushed her dessert plate to the side. "If we tell you, you need to promise you won't say a word to another soul."

"Of course," Bailey Rae said, pressing a hand to her chest, her heart already speeding in anticipation. This was almost too easy. "You know that you can trust me."

Nodding, Thea glanced over her shoulder before she said, "You're sure you want to know, even if the truth makes you uncomfortable?"

"You're my family," Bailey Rae answered without hesitation. "We may not be blood relatives, but you are the relatives I choose. That comes with messy parts as well as the good."

"Family first." Thea's throat moved in a long swallow and a deep breath. "Winnie didn't just help you and your mom. There were others. Lots of them."

"Yes. And?" Bailey Rae tried not to snap in frustration at being put off with an obvious response. "I lived here. I noticed all those 'friends' coming through, people we didn't see again. There's more. I know there is." She looked from one to the other. "June?"

The youngest of the friends, June folded her hands on top of the safe. "You've made Winnie proud with the way you helped Gia and Cricket. That was your aunt's legacy, helping women and children at risk."

Again, a nonanswer. "I'm a testament to that. Now, I need some answers, because I'm about at the end of my 'respect your elders' rope."

With a final look at Thea, June continued. "I don't think you understand what I'm saying. She didn't just help people struggling in life. She built them a whole *new* life."

Bailey Rae wanted to shout a great big *I know* to the heavens but settled for a calmer response. "Yes, she was so committed to that goal she packed the barn full of thrift shop finds for people to set up a new home. June, didn't you even tell me once how she gave you an encyclopedia set when you came to town?"

"You still aren't hearing me," June said softly, firmly. "She created whole new *identities*."

Identities? "Like assisting the Witness Protection Program?"

Thea shook her head, leaning forward to whisper, "She worked through unofficial channels, helping those that the system failed."

Collapsing back in her chair, Bailey Rae struggled to believe her ears. The prospect sounded right and crazy all at once. But there was a calm logic to Thea's and June's words. "I'm listening."

Thea took the lead. "It wasn't just simple word of mouth. She was a part of an organized effort. If you tell anyone about it, that could be problematic for others."

"Why?" Bailey Rae asked. "Now that Winnie's gone, there's not a secret to reveal . . ." Realization seeped in. "She's not the only one here in town creating those identities. The four of you did everything together."

Libby smiled, without looking up from her crocheting, the pale-blue blanket pooling in her lap as her fingers flew. All those confusing things Libby had been saying lately made sense. Her decline was getting worse, though, and secrets wouldn't stay such for much longer.

June followed her gaze to Libby and nodded in silent understanding of Bailey Rae's thoughts. "She needs one of us with her at all times. We're handling it."

Bailey Rae grabbed her sweet tea and gulped down half before setting her glass back on the table. "And that's all there is to it?"

June shrugged. "What else could there be? Since Winnie's gone, we've stopped our involvement and just work at keeping a low profile."

A wry smile tugged at Bailey Rae as she gestured toward the fresh streak of sapphire added alongside the purple one in June's hair. "For someone trying to fly under the radar, you sure do a lot of things to bring attention to yourself, changing that every month—sometimes even less."

Laughing, June twirled the blue lock. "But I bet you can't remember my real hair color."

Thea clapped her gloved hands together. "Mission accomplished."

How could they be so glib about this? "What about Gia and that cookbook? She insisted it was the key to getting help."

Libby looped the yarn around the hook for her next stitch, chiming in without looking up. "Thea has a talent for creating codes."

Bailey Rae gripped the seat of her chair, the world increasingly unsteady. "Like for computers?"

"No," Thea said, winking. "Like cyphers, used to send secret messages. It began with my grandmother. She was a codebreaker during World War II. She used to play games with us as kids, teaching the grandchildren."

Bailey Rae shuffled all the puzzle pieces in her mind. "Uncle Russell told me about a relative of his who did that for the government too . . ."

"Russell and I were distant cousins," Thea confirmed. "Annette helped me start over in Bent Oak. Creating a code for secret communications was part of my contribution."

More confused than before, Bailey Rae asked, "So Russell's grandmother asked you?"

"Actually, Winnie was the one who helped me find a creative outlet for my, uh, talents." A grin played with Thea's mouth as she smoothed a napkin over condensation from her glass. "Let me tell you, developing a way to disperse our message saved my sanity in those early days, when the boredom just about leveled me."

June blurted, "And we used it in the cookbook. We found ways to send complimentary copies to women we'd heard might need to find a way out."

"Along with a carefully worded letter," Thea added, smiling to herself.

That seemed complicated for simply helping a few people. Those puzzle pieces were shifting while leaving big holes in the picture. "The cookbook that Gia insisted had brought her to Bent Oak? You knew all along why she'd come here? Then why didn't you help her when she asked?"

"We wanted to." June blinked back tears. "Winnie is gone. She was the glue."

That was it? No help without Winnie? Her incredulity must have shown, because Thea tipped her head toward Libby.

"As you already mentioned," Thea said dryly, "someone isn't exactly a vault when it comes to keeping secrets any longer."

Fair point. Bailey Rae opened her mouth to ask how long this had been going on if Annette had been gone for more than thirty years—

Except Thea shot to her feet and set the safe on the floor just as a fishing boat floated into view out on the river. "I'm going to get more lemon slices for the tea."

And just that fast, the window to asking questions closed. Walls she hadn't even noticed before were erected again. June began talking about her class "Beauty and Power" being offered in the fall session. Even Libby crocheted faster, her forehead furrowed in concentration that defied interruption.

Yet maybe it was just as well she had some time to process what she'd just learned. To reconfigure her own memories now that she knew about Winnie's past. Uncovering the fact that her aunt had been involved in a highly sophisticated—highly illegal—activity blew her away.

Bailey Rae picked up her fork and tucked into the hummingbird cake, sugar and pineapple soothing her taste buds. Even easing her frustration. Not so much, though, that she would lose sight of her goal to find out when Winnie started her secret dealings. Or why her aunt had hidden thousands of dollars in her cabin.

And what was tucked away inside that little safe.

CHAPTER FIFTEEN

1981

Two years had passed since I told Russell I loved him. Since he assured me of his love in return. And during that time, we'd become partners in more ways than one. We united in our goal to help his grandmother as her health deteriorated.

Some days, it felt like a lifetime ago that we'd lost Annette. I kept turning around expecting to see her at the library's checkout desk. I tried to keep my grief inside for Russell's sake. After all, she was his grandmother. Not mine.

Continuing her work helped us both, but Annette had made it all look so seamless—so well planned—in those final years of her life she'd spent teaching me how to take over the network when she died. Person comes through. Person leaves with next ride.

Not the case, though, on the overheated June evening as, once again, I sat in the station wagon, parked on the shoulder with Russell waiting at the county line for the newest arrival.

This time in the pouring rain.

Between two washed-out roads.

With a broken air conditioner.

At least the eight-track player worked, piping Fleetwood Mac through the speakers. I fanned myself with a notepad, sweat making my legs stick to the seat, nerves stretched taut. I just wish our maiden voyage in helping out could have been a better tribute to Annette, who'd died in her sleep six weeks earlier. We'd barely had time to grieve her death and get our bearings in the organization.

Somehow Annette had always managed to be on time, while working her library job and pitching in at the family gas station. But I'd managed to miss an all-important call about the timing. Then Russell had to make an emergency repair on the station wagon after the radiator overheated. Summer beach traffic had been rerouted through our little town because of road construction, which slowed us down even more once we got on the road. How fitting that the storm clouds then unleashed a wall of water. Even now the scent of radiator fluid clung to the vehicle, reminding me how close we'd come to failing tonight.

I touched Russell's arm lightly. "Would you like a Coke? I've got a couple left in the cooler. Or maybe some snickerdoodles? They're Annette's recipe."

"Nah. I'm good. Save them for the kid."

"You're right, that's what Annette would do."

Her funeral had packed the church, with people overflowing into the streets. Children had come up to the altar, donating favorite books to the library with handwritten messages inside. The stacks in front of the casket had been a beautifully heartbreaking tribute. I just wished there had been a way to celebrate all the other lives she'd touched who needed to remain anonymous.

So, in honor of Annette, it was up to Russell and me to handle tonight's operation—a sixteen-year-old girl, the youngest I'd ever known to come through without a family member. I hadn't been given many details, other than that her teacher and a pastor had reached out for help. After both of her parents went to prison, she'd been sent to live with distant relatives who thought nothing of pimping her out. Social services had been contacted multiple times, with no luck.

Our network was her last resort.

And we sat in the hot car like drowned rats with our windows open to keep from suffocating.

Russell swiped drops of rain off the face of his watch, his normal calm fraying. "We're not gonna make it to the connecting pickup in time. She'll have to spend the night."

At least he didn't blame me for throwing the schedule more out of whack by searching for Libby when she'd failed to show at the library. She'd been "off" since imagining she saw a ghost wandering around town last week. When pressed for details, she'd been hazy—simply saying everyone had a double in the world. Although she'd been forgetful lately. We were all struggling and mourning in our own ways.

"Russell," I sighed, wanting to kick myself, "I don't know when we'll be able to set up another transport for the next leg. Who's going to trust us after how we botched this meetup?"

"Don't ask me," he said over the din of rain hammering the roof. "I'm wondering how Granny pulled this off on her own for so long."

"She had a lot more practice. At least that's what I keep telling myself."

Russell's cheeks puffed with an exhale. "We both need to take a breath. We'll figure it out. Even Annette had occasional hiccups in her plans."

None that I'd ever noticed. "You're only saying that to make me feel better for chasing around after Libby."

"I'm being honest. And while we're being up-front, we both know when things derailed today."

He left the words unspoken.

But he wasn't wrong. Keith had skipped school. Again. He'd become increasingly a handful, and Libby had spent her morning looking for him, only to find him back home in his room. He'd been playing the Atari video system Russell had given him two weeks ago for his birthday. The teen refused to say where else he'd been, still angry over not being allowed to get his driver's license. Libby had gone for a walk to cool off and never returned.

Russell plucked at his sweaty T-shirt. "Do you have any thoughts on where we should put this girl tonight? And for however many days it takes us to work out another plan?"

There weren't a lot of temporary housing options in Bent Oak, and the few that existed were far from private. Discretion was everything in the network.

"The cabin maybe? It's out of the way. If anyone asks, I'll say she's my cousin." Even thinking about Annette's cabin made my heart squeeze in my chest. We hadn't made much progress in sorting through her things with the pain of losing her still so fresh.

"That's probably the simplest solution." He scratched his eyebrow. "Except..."

I sighed. Hard. "It breaks Annette's cardinal rule. Never use the cabin for a leg of the journey. Except Annette lived there then. It's empty now. How about we decide when we see her? We'll trust our instincts and take it from there."

"Okay, I can see your point about letting the girl stay there temporarily—if our instincts tell us she's not a risk. At least Granny's house would be put to good use." He skimmed back a strand of my hair that had slid loose from my ponytail. "Of course, if you became my wife, we would have a ready-made home."

My gut knotted. We'd been over this a half dozen times already. I loved him. He loved me. Why couldn't that be enough?

"You know about my past. I can't." After telling him about my marriage, I'd revealed more snippets over time, gauging his reaction, waiting for the moment he would pull away from me. Because I wasn't divorced. I couldn't give him children—even if our lives magically became safe.

Or because I'd been placed in a psychiatric hospital.

Telling him that part had frightened me most. Except he deserved to know, to understand who I was and all those reasons why I couldn't marry him. After each confession, he'd held me against his broad chest and told me again how much he loved me, whether I was Winnie or Eloise.

Now he linked hands with me, rubbing his thumb over my ring finger. "We don't have to do the official wedding thing. I wouldn't want to risk your safety, and that extra paper trail at the courthouse could be a problem."

The way he cared for my well-being meant more to me than I could express, but I couldn't be selfish. "You deserve so much more."

"How about you let me decide what I deserve. What I want." He cradled my face in his broad hands. "I would like for us to wear my grandparents' wedding bands. If even an unofficial exchange of vows is too much for you, I don't need the paper to feel married. My heart is committed fully to loving you for the rest of my days on earth."

This man.

This *everything* man.

Tears blurred my vision more than the gush of rain outside our vehicle. I didn't know if I could accept his offer of a life together—I still struggled with how unfair that would be for him. But Russell carried such a calm confidence, I could almost envision our future.

My hands fluttered to his chest just as headlights pierced through the torrential night, breaking our intimate spell.

He glanced at the approaching van, then back at me. "Just think about it, my love. We'll have time to talk once we've got our guest settled at the cabin."

"All right. Later." That was as close as I could come to accepting his proposal, even an informal one with no paper trail. "Now, let's focus on this poor little girl who needs us."

His arms slid around me, and he drew me in for one of those wordless hugs of understanding that I needed, even though we were sticky with rain and perspiration. He knew I had a soft spot for the female children, each one reminding me of the daughter I'd lost.

I steeled myself for the familiar ache in my heart, the yearning to hold my baby even though she'd been stillborn. The longing to see her face. Phillip had told the doctors to take her away and spare me that pain. With each year that passed, I hated him all the more for that. Peace was hard won on most days.

On an evening like tonight, it was all but impossible.

Russell grabbed an umbrella from the floorboards and circled round to my side of the station wagon. Together, we walked toward the van, only the headlights of our two vehicles offering relief from the blanket of darkness.

The side door of the van slid open, and a figure swaddled in dark clothing stepped out—black jeans and a baggy shirt, with leather bracelets and a spiked choker. Probably no more than five feet tall and ninety pounds soaking wet, the teen eyed us with disdain as thick as her eyeliner. Her hair was shaved short on one side, the rest gathered into a ponytail, dyed coal black like her clothes.

My knee-jerk reaction shouted not to let this girl near our house. Could she be trusted not to lead someone back to us someday? Russell's shoulders tensed, and his set face indicated he had the same reservations. More, even.

But I also knew, odds were that the girl's hostile appearance was honed from the long practice of distancing herself from people determined to harm her.

So I stepped out into the rain, water plastering my hair, and called, "Come on, young lady. There are snacks in the car, and we have a place ready for you until we can arrange the next leg of your journey."

Russell wasn't happy with me.

He didn't outright scowl, but he held the steering wheel in a death grip that went beyond just careful driving in a thunderstorm. The tic in the corner of his eye had broadcast his frustration since the moment I'd ignored our decision to trust our instincts and had invited this troubled teen to stay in his grandmother's cabin. The place where he wanted to make a home for us, wearing his grandparents' wedding bands. My heart squeezed at the prospect.

Rain drummed on the roof in time to the Fleetwood Mac eight-track. I hated that we had two disagreements at once hanging between us—the proposal and the teen's lodging. Although now I wondered if I'd suggested the cabin to avoid having to discuss the other. If so, that wasn't fair of me. Russell deserved a more honest and up-front response.

Later, though. I would apologize, but first things first.

The cabin was our best—truly our only—option for the teen's temporary lodging. Even if we could locate Libby, I couldn't ask her to take in this girl, not with Keith under the same roof. And Thea lived in a one-bedroom efficiency apartment, although she spent more nights than not with her new boyfriend.

I glanced over my shoulder to check on our passenger. She *appeared* to be sleeping, slouched with her arms crossed, except her jaw kept flexing and her breathing was too rapid. She was alert underneath all that attitude.

This didn't seem to be the right time to tell her she'd already broken the number one rule two mile markers ago by telling us her real name—Destiny Nelson, from Atlanta, Georgia.

Although she wouldn't have a new name until her final destination, she still should have been warned to maintain her anonymity. For heaven's sake, I hadn't even told Libby my real name, just as she'd never shared hers or Keith's. Only Russell knew who I was before Bent Oak. But I reminded myself this girl was young—not even a fully formed adult and already on the run.

As Russell turned into the driveway leading to the cabin, the station wagon jostled and skidded in the muddy potholes, water sluicing off to the side.

Destiny shifted in the back seat. "This is it? Looks like the kinda place where that guy from *Friday the 13th* jumps out of the woods with a chain saw."

I stifled a twinge of irritation, reminding myself the attitude was a shield. "Well, then lucky for you he won't be able to see you with all your black clothes."

The kid would likely reject sympathy, but it still made me sad to think how she wouldn't be here—in this *Friday the 13th* place—at all unless she was running from something much worse. I started to apologize for my comment, then saw her smirk in the rearview mirror.

Only a few more minutes, twenty tops, and we would have her settled. Then Russell and I could have a sit-down discussion, the kind of mutual exchange I'd never experienced with Phillip.

As the station wagon bounced along another pothole, I saw a thin light piercing the darkness from Russell's apartment over the barn. Strange, since Russell was always a stickler about not running up his power bill. Another of those idiosyncrasies I'd learned over the years about the man I loved, like how he preferred his coffee with two sugars and that he put the milk jug back on the refrigerator shelf even when empty. Yet there was still so much of myself I couldn't give to him.

Because I always had to be careful and never forget the people who'd been angered by my relocations. "Russell, did you happen to leave a lamp on?"

Frowning, he squinted into the murky night. "And pay for the lights when nobody's home? Nope. I turned everything off."

In the back seat, Destiny stretched upward until I saw her face in the rearview mirror, like an apparition, given all that goth hair and makeup. "Is something wrong? You two screwed up, didn't you. I knew this was too good to be true. I'm gonna file a complaint with whoever runs this rinky-dink operation."

I ground my teeth. Destiny and I were going to have a serious conversation about manners and the importance of safety soon—once we solved the lamp issue.

Russell slammed on the brakes as the headlights swept over a rusty pickup. "Were you expecting anyone to meet up with us here after we finished?"

My skin prickled with anxiety. I could just barely make out Tennessee plates on the muddy truck. "No. I would have told you."

And he would have told me.

Russell threw the station wagon into reverse, swinging the vehicle around. The back end fishtailed until he righted the car again, powering forward. I knelt on the seat, twisting to check Destiny and look back to make sure we weren't being followed.

The open barn doors framed a shadowy couple, a man and a woman I didn't need lighting to recognize.

"Stop," I screamed, my hand wavering as I pointed. "It's Libby. He's got Libby."

The station wagon jerked to a halt, flinging me into the dash. My ribs exploded with pain. But it didn't change what I saw. The man eased out into the rain, with his fist in Libby's long hair. Her legs pedaled as she thrashed alongside him. Was he somehow connected to her? Or one of the other women who'd come through Bent Oak over the years?

I clawed at the door handle, desperate to get out. To help Libby. To save her. I didn't know how, but inaction wasn't an option.

Russell gripped a hand on my arm. "Wait."

Pivoting, I slapped at his arm. "Let me go. We have to do something."

"Stop," he said softly, his voice low and reasonable. "We need to think, not just react."

His words made sense, although the logic still made me mad. How could I do anything other than react? "Fine. I'll get him talking while you come up with a plan."

I lunged out of the door with barely a glance back at Destiny. My feet slid on the mud until I landed hard on my bottom. My teeth slammed together. I clamped a hand against my ribs, the pain so excruciating I saw sparks behind my eyelids. Or maybe more lightning. Through the sheeting rain, I took in the man about fifty yards away, mid-height with hair darkened by rain and his face full of hate.

Libby grabbed at his soaked shirt until she regained her footing, her eyes pleading with me. "Winnie, get Keith out of the barn. Take him."

She had to know I couldn't just leave her here.

The man shifted his attention to me, and as much as I tried to hold my ground, I backed up a step.

"His name is Freddie," the man growled. "Fred Gordon Jr."

My stomach dropped at the fury in his tone.

Russell's voice cut through the night, calm, reassuring. "Sir, let's get out of the rain, and you can tell us all about what's on your mind."

The man yanked that fistful of hair harder. "Listen, buddy, this is none of your concern. This is between me and my *wife*."

His words stole the air from my lungs. So this was Libby's husband. Fred Gordon Sr. Rain hid tears streaming down my face for my friend and what she must have endured. How difficult it had to have been for her to escape. The harsh reality of how quickly we could be found sent ice through my veins.

The monster in front of me made Phillip look like a choirboy. This man was pure evil. The violence in his eyes alone made my throat sting with bile.

And he held sweet, gentle Libby up by her hair with one hand, a knife glinting in his other. Even in the dark I could see the surrender in her eyes.

"Fred," she pleaded, "just take me. Let them go."

Fred shook his head, hauling her around in front of him. He pressed the knife to her throat, the jagged blade glinting. "A son needs his father. Nothing would keep me from finding my boy."

Should I run to Keith? I didn't know how to help, and I was terrified of doing something to make this man even angrier.

Keith stumbled out of the barn, his hands trembling as he reached toward his parents. "Mama, I'm sorry. It's my fault—"

"It's okay, baby." Libby choked out hoarse reassurance, her voice gurgling from rainwater, maybe, or from whatever violence had been done to her before we arrived. "I love you." Then she mouthed the word *Run*.

Her order launched Keith into action. He bolted past his parents, sprinting toward the station wagon. Rain slicked over him, plastering his hair over his eyes. The station wagon began rolling, gaining momentum, and for a moment my heart went into my throat until I realized Destiny was behind the wheel.

She leaned out the window and shouted at Keith, "Get in."

Keith only hesitated for a moment before diving into the passenger side. Destiny floored the gas, tires spinning, spewing mud. Finally lurching free with the taillights winking in the night.

At least the teens were safe. Two less people to worry about so we could focus on Libby.

Fred backhanded her, once, twice. "See what you made him do?"

A scream of denial tore from my throat, mingling with Russell's growl. Calm was fading fast. He strode forward with measured, determined strides. His gaze locked with Fred's as the man arced his fist upward again. And I realized he'd dropped the knife. Russell was making his move.

He ducked a shoulder and charged Libby's husband, catapulting him backward into the barn. Russell's shout carried on the wind. "Winnie. Go. Get Libby out of here."

Lightning sliced through the sky, and the crack of thunder snapped an instant later. Followed by another burst of jagged light that split the massive oak. Half of the tree stayed upright. The other half split away, falling toward the old barn with hints of fire skipping through the branches. The station wagon's taillights swerved, fishtailing out of control as they struggled to avoid the falling limbs, until the land barge of a vehicle spun doughnuts on the lawn.

Broadsiding the remainder of the ancient oak.

My heart cried out in fear for the teens, and for Russell too, but I didn't have time to think. My focus had to be on getting Libby to safety. I half carried, half hauled her across the muddy yard, torn up all the more with tire tracks. I lost a shoe in the mud and kept going. She moaned in pain, one eye swelling closed. She was alive, but not much else. Her wet hair hung heavily on her face, and I was pretty sure the dark patch on her scalp was blood where a chunk of hair was missing.

I gasped and tugged, her feet dragging until I collapsed onto the muddy earth with her, safely between some bushes and the cabin. Still holding on. As if my grip could keep her anchored to this side of heaven.

Away from the side of hell that Fred had just shown me.

My mind filled with nightmare images of what her life must have been like before Bent Oak. I'd suspected, but being faced with the evil she'd endured shook me to the core. An evil Russell faced even now. Gasping for air, I peered through the downpour toward the barn, searching for Russell.

Another bolt of lightning lit the sky, immediately followed by a crack of thunder. Sparks showered upward from the heavy branches lying across the barn roof. My gut twisted with fear for Russell. What if the sparks grew to flames, trapping him inside?

I untangled from Libby, laying her back the rest of the way on the ground. After crawling my way to my feet, I sprinted toward the fallen tree. Pain shot up through my one bare foot as I clambered over the protruding roots. Smoke curled from the roof and through the open doors, stinging my nose.

Panicked, I weaved my way faster through the smoky labyrinth of boughs. Until finally, I saw Russell. Illuminated by a growing flame. Trapped under the weight of thick branches. Unmoving. I didn't see Fred, and in that moment, the threat of him faded to nothing. I only cared about reaching the man I loved.

A heartbeat later, I dove forward, ripping branches and boards with my bare hands. Sparks burned my skin. I became the madwoman Phillip had once accused me of being, one thought pulsing through me with each breath.

Was this the price I would pay for tangling my life up with Russell's?

CHAPTER SIXTEEN

2025

Bailey Rae hadn't imagined seeking answers about the cash and the safe would only bring dozens more questions.

Yet here she sat on Thea's veranda, head still spinning from hearing her aunt had been part of some secret network to help at-risk women. They'd dodged sharing any more information, instead simply eating cake and talking about pruning bushes, book club reads, shelling pecans. Anything other than revisiting the conversation about Winnie until Thea had ducked into the kitchen, locating Tupperware for a to-go dessert. June had stepped off the porch to take a work call from the college. Real or fabricated? Who knew?

More than anything, Bailey Rae longed for the sound of Winnie's voice to explain the shifting reality, to tell if the stories she'd shared about her own childhood were true. Such as how her father had taken her to the beach, where they'd built sandcastles together. Or how her mother had taught her to bake pound cake and sew Halloween costumes. Was there a grain of reality in those? Timelines and memories were hard enough after those chaotic first years with Yvonne.

Bailey Rae refilled her tea and Libby's as well, while the older woman crocheted and the ceiling fan fought a losing battle with the rising sun.

Libby loosened more of the cornflower-blue yarn from the skein. "People assume my hearing went along with my memory. But that's not the case."

"I'm sorry." Wincing, Bailey Rae placed the pitcher back on the table. "I would never want you to feel discounted."

"No need to apologize." Libby tapped the safe with her crochet hook. "I can give you some insights into the cash and what this might contain if you would like."

Bailey Rae sat up straighter in the wrought iron chair.

"Please, yes," she said, not holding out much hope, but wanting the dear woman to feel heard and valued, however lucid her words.

"The answer is simpler than you would think. More money. When Winnie and I were your age, we women didn't have as much control over our finances." Libby looped stitches with each word. "The first time I tried to leave my husband, I went to the bank to get a credit card. My application was denied unless he cosigned. Ironic, since in those days, I worked in a textile mill and earned more than he did. When he worked. Which wasn't often."

A textile mill. I looked at the yarn in her hands, another piece of the Libby puzzle sliding into place. "I'm so sorry you were devalued that way."

"That's in the past." Libby waved a dismissive hand before resuming her crocheting. "When Winnie and I each arrived in Bent Oak, we opened an account for those bills that required a check. Using cash, though, became easier than dealing with a banking system that didn't respect us. And we socked away what we made at the market selling her canned goods and my crafts. I used to hide mine in my cowgirl boots. Boot cash is 'I gotta leave my man' money."

Listening with a new understanding, Bailey Rae heard the shades of pain and struggle in Libby's past.

"If the stacks of money lying around the cabin are any indication," Bailey Rae said dryly, "that was a lot of canned peaches and rag dolls."

"We were frugal," Libby said with a flickering smile, her narrative clear. She seemed to be having a good day to relate the details of the past so well. "We were preparing in case we had to run again."

Again? We?

Had Libby meant to use those words? Keith had talked about his violent father, but what would have made Winnie hide? Bailey Rae thought about pressing Libby on the point but worried she would clam up. Or worse yet, grow stressed and agitated, losing the conversational thread in the tangle of dementia.

The need for answers had to take a back seat to concern for this fragile lady. "Winnie sure did know how to pinch a penny and track expenditures. I remember recording sales for her in elementary school as a way to practice my math tables."

Libby chuckled, her face animating at mentions of the past. "She was always looking for ways to keep you occupied and out of trouble. You were a sweet child, although it was tougher to see at first because of all the acting out. Kind of like June did when she first arrived as a teenager."

And there it was again, the hint of something different in the past from what Bailey Rae had been told. "When June came to Bent Oak as a teenager?"

"That's what I said," Libby answered smartly. "The night the old barn burned to the ground."

Now that story she remembered. A massive summer storm had blown through with lightning striking a tree and the barn. Uncle Russell had been critically injured. Winnie had hated discussing that dark time in their past. "Such a tragedy they didn't know there was a drifter sleeping in the hayloft."

"A drifter . . ." Libby's gray eyes flickered with shadows of confusion, like cataracts coating her memories and making them hazy. Until one day, they would fade altogether. "Russell kept us safe from him, though. Like you did too. I mean, like Winnie did. You're not her."

Her words tumbled on top of each other, and she trembled until she dropped a stitch. Her face creased in confusion, and she fidgeted in her chair.

Bailey Rae rested her hands on top of Libby's. Guilt pinched over pushing too hard and upsetting the delicate balance. "You don't have to say anything more."

"Yes, I do." Libby's gaze settled, locking in on Bailey Rae's. "Winnie loved you. I hope you know that. She may have had you call her 'aunt,' but she considered you the daughter she and Russell never had."

Bailey Rae nodded, her throat too tight for words. She missed Winnie with a sort of homesickness that would never go away. "She was the best thing to ever happen to me."

"To many of us." Libby held up her crocheting. "They thought this was a baby blanket for Thea's grandson, but it's really a vest, like the kind they wore back in the '70s. I made one for Winnie to wear on a date with Russell. I thought you might like one for the next time you see that nice young man . . . Officer . . . Um, Officer . . ."

And just that fast, Libby was fading again as she struggled to remember Martin's name. Still, Bailey Rae treasured the moment of connection all the more for its rarity. Losing Winnie had taught her too well not to take an instant for granted. "I would love to have one." Bailey Rae angled forward to kiss her cheek. "Thank you. He's not my boyfriend, though."

"That's what Winnie used to say about Russell." Libby tucked away her yarn. "Now let's have some cake."

Rather than remind her they'd already eaten, Bailey Rae cut another slice. She'd come to Thea's home in search of answers, not expecting Libby to fill in surprise details. And again, those answers spurred more questions. Not the least of which was, what had brought Winnie and Libby to Bent Oak decades ago?

And why did it feel crucial to get answers before leaving?

By suppertime, Bailey Rae had finished restoring order to half of the cabin, if not her thoughts. In replacing books and knickknacks, she'd uncovered another $1,473. The little safe—tougher to break open than expected—held another $10,000. No paperwork, though, that gave a clue to Winnie's life before Bent Oak.

Maybe if she searched the barn again. Bailey Rae grabbed the bug spray on her way outside. Libby had grown agitated when discussing the night the old barn was struck by lightning. Could there be a clue in that somehow? The new structure had an apartment and office in back. Bailey Rae had searched the files and letters there, but not with her newfound insights—and questions. She made a mental note to scan the papers later to save space when she moved into the Airstream yet keep them available for reference.

Halfway across the yard, she caught sight of an unfamiliar sedan turning off the back road onto the long drive. Unease whispered through her, and she hated whatever had disturbed the sense of safety she'd felt here growing up.

"Skeeter," she called, then whistled. She pulled out her cell phone in case she needed to text for help. In fact, maybe she should do that anyway.

Her fingers flew across the keyboard, messaging Martin and sending him a photo of the vehicle. She'd lived without fear for so long, thanks to Winnie and Russell, she'd almost forgotten how quickly security could be ripped away.

As the silver sedan drew nearer, she saw the rental car plate on front. Gia sat behind the steering wheel.

Bailey Rae puffed the bangs off her forehead with her sigh of relief and texted Martin a follow-up. She tucked the cell into her back pocket and walked to the sedan just as it parked under a tree.

Gia stepped out from behind the wheel and slammed the door. "I hope you don't mind my stopping by. I promise not to keep you."

"Of course it's fine. What can I help you with?" As she stepped closer, she could see the mottled yellow of the fading bruises on her face.

Gia held out a baggie with some kind of treats inside. "It's not much. Just peanut butter fudge as a token of thanks for everything you and your friend did for me—and for Cricket."

"Thank you so much. I love peanut butter fudge." Bailey Rae took the bag with a smile, her gaze skipping to the sedan and finding it empty. No child hid under a blanket. The past threatened to push through. "Where is your daughter?"

Gia tucked her hands into the back pockets of her jeans. "Cricket's still at the day care provided by the women's shelter. They've been such an incredible help. They even lined up a job for me at a church day care where I can bring Cricket at a discount."

"That's wonderful. I'm so glad for you."

"I have an apartment and a no-contact order on Ian." She rocked back on her heels, chewing her lip. "It's the right thing to do, but it's scary knowing the risk of him harming us increases right after leaving."

The woman's worry mixed with wary hope was unmistakable. Bailey Rae smiled her encouragement. "You've accomplished so much in a short time."

"You pointed me in the right direction at the market, then afterward too," Gia said, her voice soft. "But more than that, you believed me."

"Of course I believe you," Bailey Rae rushed to say. Had her own mother been wary of speaking her truth? Was that what had kept her from seeking help before coming to Winnie? Except even then, Yvonne had left and returned to Winnie's more than once. The cycle was tough to break. "I just wish I could have done more."

Enough that she wouldn't worry about Ian finding Gia and Cricket someday.

Gia blinked back tears. "More? You did a world more than anyone else. My friends, even my own family, insisted it couldn't be that bad. Or had a bunch of suggestions for how I could work on our marriage. Telling me to examine my blame because relationships are fifty-fifty . . ."

"Until they're not," Bailey Rae said softly, understanding too well. Gia's eyes softened with sympathy. "There's a man in your past too?"

Thank heavens, no. To keep herself safe she'd held back so much of herself from anyone. She wanted what Winnie and Russell had shared, but at the same time, that kind of connection terrified her. "In my mama's past. So many bad men, just like my grandmama had before her."

Her mind winged back to the fights and the bruises, the time her mother *had* tried to break the cycle by fighting back. Bailey Rae couldn't remember the man's name, just a shadowy image of a big guy with dirt under his fingernails who'd demanded red beans and rice. Then exploded that he hated them.

He'd ducked into the pantry and started hurling cans at her mom, shouting all the other foods she could have prepared. Yvonne had ducked behind the refrigerator and freezer doors. A sad move on her part since there never was much in the way of fresh food in the apartment. Still, she gave it her best effort with a gallon of expired milk and some frozen peas. The whole time, Bailey Rae had sat under the dinette table watching the dog lick milk off the floor.

She still couldn't stomach the smell of red beans and rice. "Your plans sound solid. You deserve to be proud of yourself."

"I don't know about solid," Gia said, rolling her eyes, "but certainly better thought out than showing up with a cookbook in my hands."

Bailey Rae laughed softly. She couldn't argue with that. Still . . . "You took that first step. It's tougher to do than people realize." She didn't share anything more about her mom. This was Gia's moment. "I hope you have the most wonderful life."

Blinking fast, Gia pulled her hands from her back pockets. "Do you mind if I hug you?"

"I don't mind a bit." Bailey Rae folded her in a tight hug before stepping back and watching Gia drive away to launch her shiny new future.

Was this how Winnie had felt over the years as she and her friends helped others? Warily hopeful. Excited. Humbled. And yes, even a little bit proud.

Although it sounded as if her aunt had done far more. The secrets weren't in the money, the safe or filing cabinets. Not really. Winnie's story was about the individuals she'd gone to great lengths to help. Bailey Rae had been so focused on unraveling a mystery, focused on her own grief and need to know about the past, that she hadn't taken time to marvel at all Winnie had accomplished.

Standing under the bower of oak trees that had served as her playground, her haven, she struggled with guilt. And confusion. She'd thought she was honoring Winnie's memory with her plans to leave Bent Oak and fulfill one of Winnie's dreams. But was that really what her aunt would have wanted? Was that a good way to honor Winnie's legacy? She truly didn't know. In fact, she had no idea how to proceed next.

୬

Martin ducked under the curtain of Spanish moss as he trekked out of the marsh to his truck. He smacked a mosquito feasting on his neck. Annoying and uncomfortable, but at least he'd had a welcome respite from thoughts of Bailey Rae.

He'd been deep in the woods following up on another case of a mutilated animal. He suspected a ring of deeply disturbed teens were responsible, but he couldn't discount some kind of religious cult too. There was no shortage of crime hidden out in the swamps where the average person wouldn't dare venture.

Sweat dripped from his forehead as he peeled off his hip-wader boots and tossed them into the back of the truck. He hadn't bothered taking his cell phone into the wooded bog since there wouldn't be a signal. He barely had one bar at the truck. If work needed him, they could reach him on the satellite phone clipped to his belt.

Sliding behind the wheel, he reached into the cooler on the floor and snagged a sports drink. He chugged with one hand and reached for his cell phone with the other to power it back up. Message after message loaded, including two from Bailey Rae. Now that caught his attention. No surprise, since that woman turned him inside out.

He set aside the empty drink and thumbed open the text, scanning through her alarm about a strange car approaching, followed by her assurance it was only Gia. He wished he could have taken comfort from that, but his pulse still hammered. A shower and supper would have to wait.

"Siri, call Bailey Rae," he said into the phone while cranking the engine. The ringing transferred to the truck's speakers. Although even if she answered, he would still worry until he'd laid eyes on her. He peeled out, gravel and mud spewing from his tires as he floored it toward the cabin.

The phone rang, and rang until finally . . .

"Hey, Martin," Bailey Rae answered breathlessly. "I'm sorry to have alarmed you. I'm fine."

"Okay," he said, somewhat assured, yet still gunning it down the two-lane road with lights flashing, "but I think we need to come up with a safe word. Because until I see you, I'm going to worry."

"Safe word?" She laughed softly. "Like red beans and rice?"

He welcomed her answering chuckle. "As far as safe words go, that's pretty random."

"I hate that dish, so the odds of me ever saying it are low. Less risk of sending out a fake alert."

"Note to self. You hate red beans and rice."

"Ugh, stop. I'm going to gag."

A smile pushed through. Man, he liked her spunk. "Well, I'm almost at your place, so you can tell me all about what Gia said. Or is she still there?"

"You should check your messages more often. I sent that text a half hour ago."

"I'll talk to my cell phone carrier," he said, even though he already knew. He didn't want to discuss the horrific details of the case he'd been investigating. He waited for her to answer, only just realizing how much he'd missed talking to her.

He kept driving. Toward her.

She cleared her throat. "Are you almost here?"

Thanks to breaking land speed records through the forest, yes. "Am I welcome?"

"I wouldn't mind the company." Her voice grew hesitant with an unusual vulnerability. "It's been a really challenging day."

"I'm turning into the drive now."

As he steered the truck off the road, his tires crunched on the gravel that would lead to Winnie's cabin. He soaked in the sight of Bailey Rae standing on the porch with Skeeter sitting beside her, leaning against her knee. Her legs stretched from her jean shorts, tan and long, and he wondered what band tee she wore today.

He stepped from the truck in the hot afternoon. "Are we having red beans and rice for supper?"

"No, sir. I made my award-winning pimento cheese. Winnie's recipe, actually. Which you're getting none of," she said with a teasing smile, then swept an arm wide. "See, I'm totally okay and alone. The place is clear. But thank you all the same for coming so quickly. Kinda like a knight in shining armor."

He strutted closer and propped a boot on the bottom step, taking in her Eagles T-shirt as well as the curves inside. "I feel confident you can slay your own dragons, but I'm happy to lend aid."

She nodded toward the mud on his boots. "Did you encounter any of those dragons at work?"

Was that a hint of worry in her eyes? "Nothing worth noting. Just regular old wading through the swamp for a few hours."

"Oh my, that sounds miserable. Come on into the air-conditioning." She snapped for Skeeter and opened the cabin door.

"I won't argue with you. I've even got a change of clothes in the truck," he said as he jogged back to snag the T-shirt and jeans.

Once inside, Martin closed the door behind him before following her directions to the bathroom to change. The intimacy of the moment wasn't lost on him, or the ease in her offer and his acceptance.

"Are you hungry?" Her voice wafted through the door as he shucked his grungy uniform.

He was starving, hollow for her and food, but he didn't want to pressure her on either front. "I carry snacks and drinks with me in the truck."

"Snacks aren't nearly enough," she admonished. "I've had a change of heart about sharing my award-winning pimento cheese with you. I still have a loaf of homemade bread left for sandwiches. And hummingbird cake."

"What's hummingbird cake?" he asked, the flowery scent of her shampoo permeating the small bathroom now that he'd ditched his swampy clothes. He washed his hands and splashed water on his face.

Laughing, she answered, "Well, it's not made of birds. I promise. We really need to work on your grasp of fine Southern cuisine."

He tugged on his jeans and a game warden T-shirt, leaving his boots and uniform in the shower stall for now. He swung open the bathroom door and padded on bare feet through the living room toward the kitchen. "You still haven't introduced me to chicken bog, so I'm not a hundred percent certain if you're pulling my leg—"

Whoa. He stopped short at the sight. Papers littered the floor. Kitchen counters were covered in opened spices and baking goods.

Concern kicked right back into overdrive. "Did someone break in?"

"No. That's all me, and it looks better than this morning," she said, slicing into a loaf of bread. A Mason jar of pimento cheese rested on the edge of the cutting board. "I was looking for something, and the mess got a little out of hand."

"A little?" The place looked like a tornado had hit. "Do you need help cleaning up?"

"I'll just sweep it all away and put it in the dumpster." She passed him the cutting board and nodded toward the kitchen table.

"What did Gia have to say?" he asked, placing the sandwich makings on the table.

Bailey Rae joined him with napkins and two cans of Coke. "She's got a job and a place to live. She even took out a no-contact order against her husband."

"That sounds like good news." He tapped the worry crinkle between her eyebrows. "What made this day difficult?"

She hesitated for so long, he wondered if she would even answer.

Shaking her head, she took a seat. "I just know how often those good intentions fall apart."

"Because of your mother." They'd come a long way in getting to know each other since the ticket incident. Working together to help Gia had shifted something between them.

It had shifted something inside him too. Something that had been closed off since he left the military. He took his seat, his knees brushing hers under the table.

"Yes, and after watching my mom," she said, slathering pimento cheese on bread, enough for three sandwiches, "I understand there's nothing more I can do."

"Winnie would be proud of the way you've taken what happened to you and helped make sure it didn't happen to another child." He rested a hand on hers, pausing her busyness.

Her gaze snapped to his and held for three slugs of his heart against his ribs before she leaned forward to press her mouth to his. The feel of her soft skin under his touch, the flowery scent of her shampoo swept away a dark workday.

She eased back, her hands on his shoulders. "Thank you for saying that. It means more to me right now than I even know how to explain." She drew in a shaky breath. "Now let's have some supper and I'll tell you all the ingredients in hummingbird cake."

As the warmth of her voice filled the space between them, Martin couldn't ignore the truth any longer. He'd considered traveling to Myrtle Beach to see her once she left town, making an effort to maintain their growing connection. But the kiss told him how much he was fooling himself. His heavy heartbeat and undeniable hunger for her had him realizing he didn't want only an occasional meeting.

He wanted her to stay in Bent Oak. The very thing she'd made clear wasn't anywhere on her agenda.

CHAPTER SEVENTEEN

1981

Russell was still alive. I told myself to think positively, but for so long my escape had felt too good to be true. What if his life was the price fate exacted for my freedom?

I dug my fingers into the pleather of the emergency room's industrial sofa and bit back the urge to scream. Not only because the nightmare at the barn still held me in its grip an hour later, but also because I was in a hospital again, staring at the sterile walls, having no control of my life.

Libby and Russell were both in ER exam rooms. Russell hadn't regained consciousness, but he hadn't died during the attack from Libby's husband. That was something—everything.

Keith and I managed to drag Russell into the station wagon just as the barn burst into flames. More than anything, I wanted to cradle his dear head in my lap, but someone had to drive. Libby was too heavily concussed, and I wasn't trusting either of the teens behind the wheel, even though Destiny had offered.

I'd forced myself to stop trembling and drive while Libby sat in the passenger side cupping her battered face. We'd agreed to tell the doctor she'd been injured by a falling beam. Destiny and Keith piled into the very back. Fred had almost certainly died, and reaching him in the burning rubble would have been impossible. Calling for help had been out of the question since the phone had been disconnected in the cabin when Annette died, and Russell's barn apartment was being consumed by the flames.

By the time we'd raced down the driveway, the barn had collapsed, showering the vehicle with sparks and rumbling the ground beneath the tires. We didn't start off with an official pact not to tell anyone about Fred Gordon being in the barn. It just unfolded that way. First, there was nothing we could do for him, while Russell and Libby needed urgent medical attention. If—when—the police or fire department questioned the body in the barn, we agreed to mention that drifters sometimes sought shelter in the haystacks.

Another secret that bound us even tighter together.

The hospital had assumed all the injuries came from escaping the barn. Again, we decided to stay silent.

Now Libby was getting X-rays and possibly a CT scan. A nurse had given us a brief rundown on the care Russell would receive. But the way they'd wheeled him back quickly told me it was serious. Then came the news that his right arm and shoulder had been shattered and a lung punctured. Plus whatever was causing his loss of consciousness.

He had to live. No matter what I needed to do, I couldn't face the thought of a world that didn't include Russell.

The antiseptic air stung my nose, and the corner television did little to drown out the PA system and rattle of medical carts. Luckily, there wasn't much traffic this late at night, just a couple sleeping tucked against each other and another person listening to music on a portable cassette player with headphones.

I'd called Thea from the nurses' station to have her look after Destiny, leaving me here with Keith. He huddled in a chair across from me, his hair slickened and dark from the downpour. Our drenched clothes had been so covered in soot and mud, one of the nurses had given us green scrubs to wear. Part of me hadn't wanted to change, like keeping my own outfit was a way to deny this whole nightmare had happened.

Focusing on comforting Keith would be easier than sitting in my own worries. I moved the stack of old magazines from the seat next to him and settled into the chair, keeping my voice low. "I heard what you said back at the barn, but I want you to know none of this is your fault." Didn't kids often blame themselves for adult problems? I wouldn't allow him to carry any guilt for what Fred had done. "This lays firmly on your father's doorstep."

"And now he's dead," Keith whispered. "Because I called him."

Shock stunned me silent for a moment. "You did what?"

"I called him a couple of weeks ago," Keith confessed, each word growing more and more breathless. "It was my birthday. I gathered up all the change in the house and I went to a pay phone. I called directory assistance for his number and I dialed it." His eyes were huge. Pained. He scrubbed his hand over his chest, as if there were an ache too big to soothe. "I did this to Mom. To Russell."

Keith hung his head, gasping for air, panic and guilt coming off him in waves. To the receptionist checking in patients, he looked like a son worried about his mother.

And he was, of course. But there was so much more to it than that. The poor kid.

"Okay," I said, rubbing my palm along his back, "take deep breaths. Slowly."

I needed the reminder as much as he did. How had Libby and I grown so complacent that we hadn't seen something like this coming?

Keith turned to look at me, the nightmare still fresh in his eyes. "I didn't give him the address. I swear. But I forgot that the pay phone call might be traced through his telephone carrier when he got his bill. Or maybe I let something else slip. I don't know anything other than it's my fault."

We'd been so careful to keep our location a secret. I'd worried about the new girl giving us away, but the leak had been closer to home. I couldn't bring myself to blame Keith, though. The weight of our secrets was tough enough for an adult to carry. I should have thought more about the burden for a child. People said kids were resilient.

I wasn't so sure about that.

For now, I needed to focus on talking this through with the teen who'd just seen his father die and now was worried about losing his mother. "You're right that was a mistake, and it's one you'll carry with you." Saying otherwise would discredit anything else I told him, and he needed to understand the importance of security in the future. "But it has to be a secret that remains between us. Forever. Because sharing it with the rest of the world out of some need for forgiveness will only put more people at risk. Including your mother."

After tonight, with the body in the barn, there was no going back.

Keith scratched his jaw, scrubbing along the peach fuzz. "I didn't think of that."

Now came the reassuring, sympathetic part he deserved to hear. "Life hasn't been fair to you, Keith." I still remembered him from the first day so long ago, a small child losing himself in his shiny red View-Master. "You've had to grow up fast more than once, and today is the biggest of those times."

"As long as my mom and Russell are okay, nothing else matters to me."

I squeezed my eyes closed to will back tears before continuing, "I owe you an apology for something I said to you not too long after you arrived in Bent Oak. I'm sorry for telling you that dragons aren't real."

He nudged my foot with his toe, then patted my knee in one of those rare teenage shows of affection. "It's okay. I like the world better your way, where there are people who fight back."

I struggled for what to say. I wasn't at my best. But my heart ached for the frightened boy he'd been and the troubled teen he'd become.

The double doors from the exam area swished open, pushing aside all other thoughts from my mind as a doctor walked out in his scrubs that matched ours. A random thought. But my mind was pinballing out of control.

"Family of Russell Davis?" the doctor called.

I didn't hesitate. I stood. "That's me."

A flicker of confusion whispered through the physician's eyes before his face shifted into professional neutrality, but I didn't have time to educate him about interracial relationships, so I opted to cut straight to the chase. "I'm Mr. Davis's fiancée."

I rested my right hand over my left to hide the bare finger that should have been sporting Annette's ring, a regret I would face later, provided Russell and I would have a later.

"Of course," the doctor said, then nodded toward the nurse standing behind him with a clipboard. "We need a relative to sign the surgical consent forms."

"Surgery?" My voice quavered. In my mind, I could hear false medical advice from my former husband, and I felt sick. "He doesn't have any living relatives."

"All right." He exhaled, taking a seat and waiting for me to sit as well. "Mr. Davis is still unconscious, and we can't wait for him to regain consciousness. We need to stop the internal bleeding and repair the damage to his lung before we can set the broken collarbone. I wish I had better news or more time to answer the questions I know you must have. But I need to scrub in while you fill out the paperwork."

"Thank you," I said, standing, trying not to assume this man who held Russell's life in his hands might be like Phillip.

"I'm going to do my best for him, ma'am." He patted me on the shoulder before he disappeared back through the double doors.

My legs folded, and I couldn't breathe. I thought I might be having a heart attack, because my chest felt so tight. I leaned over to put my head between my knees.

I felt a hand on my back and saw the nurse's shoes as she crouched beside me. "Breathe in, breathe out, slowly. Smell the flowers. Blow out the candle. Smell the flowers. Blow out the candle."

She continued chanting until the dizziness eased and my breathing slowed. I hadn't felt this out of control since I lost my child. I'd survived that, barely, but would I be able to withstand another blow? The fear of losing my world—losing Russell—leveled me when he needed me to be strong.

I squeezed my eyes closed and straightened with another deep inhale. "Okay, let's fill out those papers."

The nurse with kind eyes and a tight red perm stood, motioning toward the corridor. "I'll show you both the way to the surgical waiting area."

Both . . . How had I forgotten about Keith? Worse yet, how had I let concern for Libby slide to the back corners of my mind? "And Libby Farrell? How is she?" I asked the nurse. "This is her son."

"They'll be moving her up to a room when one becomes available. Then you'll be able to see her." She hugged the clipboard to her chest. "I'm so sorry about the fire at your place. Thank goodness you're all alive."

I slid an arm around Keith's shoulders, feeling the shudder rack him. Guilt gnawed at my already ragged nerves. I'd let my friend down by not looking after her child. Yes, I loved Russell, with all my heart, but a mature heart should also have room for friends and family. Had I fallen into old habits of letting my love become obsessive? I hoped not, because that dishonored my friends and Russell.

I owed him my best. I just prayed he would live to receive it—and place that ring on my finger.

◯

An hour, then two ticked by on the wall clock with no news about Russell's surgery. Already three other families had left and another had come in to wait. No matter how many times I told myself that no news was good news, I worried over the length of the procedure.

Thea had shown up to bring us food from the cafeteria with Destiny in tow. Keith had stepped in to see Libby with a meal for them both.

Meanwhile, Destiny sat as far away from me as possible and tore into the cafeteria fried chicken like it was five-star cuisine.

I cradled a Styrofoam cup of coffee in my hands but didn't do more than inhale the scent. Eating wasn't an option for me either. My stomach was in turmoil.

Thea tapped a pack of sugar into her cup of hot tea. People in town joked about Thea's gloves, calling her the Queen of England. The fitted skirt-and-jacket sets didn't help. I wondered if Thea would ever let go of her worry of fingerprints being traced. But then the past could be hard to shake, especially on an evening like this.

"Thank you for coming up here," I said, grateful that all the decision-making didn't rest solely on my shoulders. My confidence had taken a serious hit. "I appreciate you picking up the pieces tonight."

"Of course. You just focus on yourself and Russell." She blew into her tea and took a sip before setting it aside.

I got her point, but after the way I'd all but forgotten about Keith, I needed to pull myself together. "You're all dressed up. Please tell Howard I'm sorry for cutting short your date."

"Don't give it another thought." She waved off my concern, her eyes tracking the staff as they walked back and forth along the corridor, shoes squeaking.

Thea never missed much. No doubt she wouldn't have missed the phone call and lost track of Libby. At that moment, I felt defeated, like I should throw my hands up and pass over the whole operation before someone else got hurt.

"Thea, I am so afraid." I'd never uttered those words out loud. Not even in my previous life.

Thea gave me her stern look that was somehow laced with caring. "You are the bravest person I know. The way you and Russell have built a relationship in this convoluted existence of ours is nothing short of incredible . . ."

"You might want to rethink that. Russell has been proposing to me, and I keep telling him no. In fact, I turned him down again this evening."

"Honey, I'm so sorry." She slid a gloved hand over mine and squeezed. "Do you mind if I ask why?"

"So many reasons." I realized that I'd never shared anything about my past with her. Thea had every reason to assume my life was just as I'd told her. That my secrets only involved the help I gave Annette. "Do you understand I landed here in much the same way that you did?"

"I wondered," she said with a sigh, "but I didn't know for sure."

"Russell understands too and says it doesn't matter to him . . . The legality of a marriage . . ." My voice cracked on the last word, out of fear and regret that I may have missed my chance with him. Instead, I focused on Thea. "Were you single—before coming here? You don't have to answer if you would rather not."

"Is that the reason you won't make it official with Russell? Because you have someone out there?"

I looked around to check again that we wouldn't be overheard by Destiny or anyone else, then measured my words carefully all the same. "According to the courts, I'm legally dead. So anyone who may have been attached to me in some way is free to move on."

"Why not go ahead, then?" Thea's eyes held no judgment. Only caring.

"That's exactly what I'm asking myself." I rubbed the empty place on my ring finger and called myself ten kinds of a fool. It was one thing to deny myself happiness. But it wasn't fair of me to deny Russell's when he'd been nothing but wonderful to me. I glanced back at Thea. "What about you and Howard? You two have been dating for quite a while."

"He has plans to run for town council one day, maybe even be the mayor. If I tell him, I'll put him in an awful position. If I don't tell him, that could blow up in my face too."

How well I understood. "You could walk away from him."

"That's the one thing I can't do. I've lost so much. I won't lose him too." Her dark eyes flashed with a fire that reminded me what a formidable woman she was.

"Then you'll have to follow your heart on how best to handle that." The words sounded hypocritical to my own ears. If I had followed my heart, I would have accepted Russell's proposal.

"Thank you for the advice. I have to admit, I'm better with logic and math than I am at trusting emotions." Thea patted my hand again before nodding toward Destiny. "If you're okay staying here with our bottomless pit over there, I would like to pop in and check on Libby."

"Of course," I said. "Yes, please. And give her my love."

Thea nodded as she rushed to catch up to a nurse in a crisp uniform, who then pointed the way. Thea clutched her fake pearl necklace as her heels clicked along the tile, a little slower than normal. The foundation had been rocked under all of us, and I wondered if we would ever be able to recapture our secure little utopia.

Maybe if we'd all been more upfront with each other about our pasts, we might have navigated the stresses better. Libby could have had more support with Keith's challenges.

My glance slid over to Destiny, currently cracking apart a chicken wing to get every bit off the bone.

"You can have mine too if you want," I offered. "I'm not hungry."

"Okay." She slid the extra Styrofoam container off the end table and tucked it under her backpack as if saving it for later.

I shifted to a closer chair and stretched my legs out in front of me. "We should start a fashion show for these scrubs. Sorry they don't come in black."

Destiny grunted. Then mumbled, "Thanks for the food."

"Sorry your time with our 'rinky-dink' organization hasn't run smoother." When she didn't laugh or snap back, I ducked to meet her eyes. "I'm really sorry you had to go through that tonight."

She pushed her dyed hair back from her face. "I've seen worse."

I hated that we'd added more trauma to her load.

"I had a daughter," I confessed, not altogether sure why. "Before I got to Bent Oak. She died." Those sparse few words about my stillborn baby made my throat burn.

Destiny met my gaze fully for the first time. "What was her name?"

I thought long and hard about whether to answer. Sharing about our pasts could be helpful but also dicey. I didn't want to launch into this without thinking. It was one thing for me and Thea to share a few benign details, but I also needed to be careful not to set a precedent for this teen as she tackled a new beginning.

A secret beginning.

Yet taking in her terrified blue eyes and her freckled young face scrubbed fresh from the rain, I realized reassuring her meant more than the concerns. Giving her a stable start—and a friend—would serve her best.

I understood all the risks in sharing, but I told her anyway. "Her name was April, because she was born on a beautiful spring morning that month."

Phillip and I had been debating names, never settling on one. When our little girl had come early, seven months into the pregnancy, stillborn, he hadn't wanted to use his preferred name. He'd insisted on saving it for a live child and told me to pick whatever I wanted for the casket and tombstone.

I'd been gutted even before his callous words. Afterward, I understood how profoundly alone I was in my marriage.

My depression had been deep, and truthfully, if my husband had institutionalized me then, I'm not sure he would have been wrong to do so. But he hadn't. He'd just left me to cry alone for ten months in a postpartum fog of despair. It wasn't until another year later, when I was at my strongest in such a very long time, when I had begun to make plans for adoption, that he locked me away.

I'd never been so terrified. Until tonight.

The teenage girl beside me fidgeted with the tie to her scrub pants. "Is your daughter the reason you helped me?"

That question I could answer without hesitation. Because even though Russell was right that I had a soft spot when it came to girls in need, I still saw each person as an individual. A special soul worthy of the best life has to offer. "I helped you because you needed it. You're not a substitute for anyone. *You* matter."

I could see Destiny would need time to believe in her own self-worth. Part of me regretted that I wouldn't get to watch her come into her own someday. She'd made a big impression on my heart in such a short time, showing up for Keith—and by extension, for Libby and me—without a thought for her own safety. She'd been so brave. Would the people at her final stop look past the dyed hair, thick makeup, and bravado to the spirit sparkling inside her? Would they understand that her black clothes would shine light on them if they looked close enough?

And in an impulsive decision I refused to question, while I understood she wasn't a substitute for my daughter, I also realized I wouldn't be sending her to another outpost in the network. I didn't know how I would secure a future for a troubled sixteen-year-old girl who didn't even have her high school diploma yet. But I knew one thing with an unshaken certainty.

Bent Oak would be her home.

"Would you like to choose your new name?"

Her eyes went wide. "I can do that?"

The gratitude over something so simple affirmed I'd been right in my decision. I would work out the details later, with Thea's help this time.

"Since you arrived sooner than expected, we don't have the paperwork complete." I'd planned for her to be in transit for another couple of weeks. "As long as you don't choose something like Jodie Foster or that Blondie singer Debbie Harry, we should be fine."

She laughed, a rusty kind of sound, while tugging at her coal-black locks, which had dried in clumps. "Now there's an idea. I could bleach my hair like Blondie, or dye it all sorts of colors, just to throw people off the trail. Maybe even rub lemon juice on my freckles."

"That's the spirit," I said, even as I grieved inside that this girl couldn't be a regular teen instead of thinking of ways to hide herself. But I could give her control over this one thing. "Have you decided on your name?"

She stared at her combat boots, so at odds with the surgical scrubs, clicking her clunky heels together while thinking. Yet it called to mind her own odd sort of Dorothy clicking her way out of Oz.

Destiny looked up with her eyes taking on the first light I'd seen in her, all the brighter for shining through the darkness.

"June," she said, simply. "As in the month. Because my life starts today, on June the first."

CHAPTER EIGHTEEN

2025

Bailey Rae pushed open the door to the Fill 'Er Up Café, the bell chiming its signature gas station–style tone. She scanned the packed noontime crowd full of familiar faces but didn't see Martin. Her lunch date.

Even though the Fill 'Er Up was the logical place to meet him, she also appreciated the opportunity to say a quick farewell of sorts to the place that held such special memories of Russell, with all the stories he'd told her about his family's time owning the place—until he and Winnie needed to sell it off to pay Russell's medical bills after the barn fire. Maybe his injuries presented yet another reason Winnie had hoarded cash.

Bailey Rae paused at the register, rusty road signs on the wall calling to mind old landmarks. "Kinsley, have you seen Martin Perez? The game warden? I'm supposed to meet him here for lunch."

So far, Bailey Rae had done a good job of avoiding overlong goodbyes or too much nostalgia as she packed up her life in Bent Oak. The tug of melancholy now surprised her, in the place where she'd worked for years.

Behind the counter, the teenage waitress looked up from her phone. "He's at an outdoor table by the river. I didn't think we would see you in here before you moved."

"I can't resist one last dish of fried catfish before I leave town," Bailey Rae said with a smile as she snagged two menus.

Her heart squeezed as she threaded her way around the tables toward the door leading to the outside seating area. A wall of warm air hit her, made bearable by the strategically spaced misting fans. A dock stretched out back, where clientele were invited to walk down the planks and pitch leftover hush puppies and fries to fatten up the catch for another day, drawing in schools of bluegill, largemouth bass, and of course, catfish. Winnie had taught her to throw in a line here when the place was still a gas station.

She'd sworn the best fish were caught using a good old-fashioned cane pole, like the kind used by the two teens dangling their feet off the end of the dock. Bailey Rae curled her toes in her sandals. Winnie had taught her how to bait her own hook and cheered with the first catch.

They'd eaten fried catfish for supper that night, surprising Russell who'd driven into town for a checkup. His arm had been giving him trouble, and there had been talk of another surgery. Years later, Winnie had told her how fishing together that day had helped distract her from worrying about Russell since he'd insisted on driving himself.

She would miss the restaurant. She'd told herself she would be carrying the spirit of the place with her, but the plan felt muddier now. As a child, she'd found it easier to leave a place by distancing herself ahead of time.

Not the healthiest of coping strategies, but it was too late to rewire her synapses now.

Martin waved to her from a picnic table closest to the water's edge, standing as she drew nearer. "I went ahead and ordered tea and fried pickles. I'm learning to like them."

Laughing, she tucked onto the bench and unrolled her napkin from around the silverware. "Before you know it, you'll start speaking with a drawl."

"I'm not so sure about that," he said, one eyebrow raised. "Hey, since Gia came to see you yesterday, I stopped by the police station this morning and asked around about Ian Abernathy, just to check if there's been any headway on his location."

"And?" She gripped the picnic table until splinters dug into her palms.

"Authorities had hoped Ian would show up for his brother's memorial service, but no luck." He tapped a packet of sugar into his iced tea. "Rumor has it that Ian and his brother Owen had a big falling-out before he went fishing. The police are investigating if it might not be an accidental drowning after all."

So much turmoil and violence in one family. Thank heavens Gia had broken free. "She mentioned staying away from the service too. How sad that she and Cricket had to miss it out of fear of Ian."

He reached across to ease her hand loose and link their fingers, his thumb circling the inside of her wrist. "You did a great job helping her make a fresh start. If you ever decide to give up the restaurant business, you have a real calling. There sure are plenty of people in need of assistance around here."

The words landed like a brick in her gut, mirroring all the ways she'd second-guessed herself lately.

She squeezed his hand until his thumb stopped moving. "Martin, I'm leaving Bent Oak. You know that."

Frustration flickered in his deep brown eyes, and he leaned closer. "What about whatever is happening between us?"

Did he really think she was like some lovestruck girl putting aside her dream college to follow him? She understood he wasn't a bad guy. In fact, he was very much the best of the best. Even so, she couldn't stem the disappointment at his pressure. She'd intended to keep her personal vow not to be like Yvonne.

"Martin, I have my future mapped out. If you're coming to the Myrtle Beach area, let me know. We can see the sights, go out. I don't want to lose touch, but I am leaving." She kept her voice kind, but firm. "Now, what were you planning on ordering for lunch?"

1981

Libby's battered face looked worse now than it had in the barn. That nightmare was still too close to the surface, physically as well as emotionally. As I stepped deeper into her hospital room, I stifled a gasp and tried to school my features not to let the horror show. For an instant, I even stopped worrying about Russell as I took in her eye swollen closed and the shaved portion of her head with at least a half dozen stitches. I had a million questions I wanted to ask but knew I'd have to limit myself since my friend was in no condition for an interrogation.

Still, maybe we could clear up a few things. A quick check of her roommate confirmed the woman was sleeping and on some kind of breathing machine. Libby and I could talk freely.

As soon as that uncharitable thought crossed my mind, I winged a silent apology to the poor woman and pulled the privacy curtain between the beds. "How do you feel?"

"Like my life fell apart," Libby croaked, her voice barely more than a whisper with each word tugging at her split lip. "At least it takes my mind off all this." She motioned to her face, two of her fingers splinted together.

If I'd ever required assurances that what we did at the network was important work, I had plenty of it right here in my poor friend's condition.

"You're alive and you're free. Focus on that." I still measured what I said on the off chance someone might hear something, anything.

"How is Russell?" Libby asked, a tear teetering on the edge of her one open eye.

Tears weren't too far away for me either. I only just managed to hold them back, saving them for the shower later where I could wash away the acrid scent of smoke and terror.

"Doing well. They set his collarbone, and he's resting comfortably." I knew I had to give her a snippet of information to keep her from probing, but I left out any mention of his punctured lung. Libby had enough to worry about. The rest could wait until emotions were less tender. "The nurses' station said I can visit him in a few minutes. I just wanted to pop in to tell you I love you, dear friend, before you go to sleep. Thea is going to look after Keith and the new girl. She is committed to staying awake and keeping a vigilant eye on both teens."

Libby let out a weak laugh. "Thank you." Her chin began quivering. "I'm so sorry. This is my fault. I thought I saw Fred around town recently but convinced myself I'd imagined him. That he was just a ghostly figment of my guilty conscience."

A ghost. I'd discounted Libby's worry over seeing a "ghost," growing complacent. Another thing Annette never would have let happen. Lesson learned.

Run like hell from ghosts.

I placed a careful hand on her arm, opting to keep her calm for now. We could unpack our mistakes later. "After so many years, who would have thought he would find you now?"

"I should have realized he wouldn't give up." Her feet twitched under the sterile white blanket, as if running in place. "A month before I left, he took my boy and barricaded himself in a hunting shack. He swore if anyone came in, he would shoot them, himself, and my son. Eventually, he calmed down and came out, but I knew in that moment I couldn't take the risk again, not with my child's life. That's when I started planning to leave in earnest."

"Libby, I'm so in awe of how brave you were then and now." Even as Libby shared the chilling moments from her past, the words stirred a memory of my own.

My mother once told me—in a lighthearted tone—about the time she wanted to kill herself. But she didn't want people to see her messy house. So she cleaned. Then she worried about how she would look when people found her, so she showered, changed, and styled her hair.

Next, she wanted to make one more special moment with her daughter and sat with me on the sofa to read a book. As we explored the Velveteen Rabbit's urge to become real, she realized her house was clean, she looked her best, and her little girl was such a quiet toddler.

And my mother's urge to take her own life faded.

She would tell the story jokingly, a drink in one hand and a cigarette burning to ash in the stone ashtray. Everyone would laugh. I would join in.

Why had it taken me so long to see her hidden message to her daughter and any other females out there? Maintain a clean house, stay pretty as a peach, and keep your children quiet. The stakes for doing otherwise were high. Life or death.

I couldn't figure out if her warning was for me to carry into marriage or if it was meant as a warning to toe the line as a child so Mommy didn't want to off herself.

Either way, it wouldn't pass the sniff test with any decent therapist. If I'd dared share the memory. And I hadn't. Not even with Russell. "You said you thought you saw Fred here in town? Where was that?"

If Fred had revealed Libby's and Keith's true identities to someone, what would that mean for them in regard to that body in the barn? Might our cover story about a drifter be blown?

"I thought I saw him coming out of the post office." She pressed a trembling hand to her forehead. "The postmaster knows everyone. Fred said he showed photos of me and Freddie."

Back at the barn Libby's husband had talked about "Junior," but I'd been so filled with fear, I hadn't processed much more than survival. Now my mind returned to that first day in the library, when Keith—*Freddie*—had struggled to respond to his name. While all these years I'd realized that it must have been difficult for the child to adapt to so many secrets, a part of me hadn't fully grasped the magnitude of that until this moment. No wonder he struggled.

It felt wrong to ask Libby to reveal more of her story—to expect that level of trust on a night I'd learned just how horribly her trust had been broken in the past.

So I gave her my trust instead, allowing her to rest while I shared something of myself. "My name is Eloise. And I left my husband after he convinced the world I was crazy and locked me away in an institution."

My gut knotted over saying even those few words. What if Libby assumed I truly was insane? What if I lost her friendship? I wasn't sure I could bear it. Telling Russell had been easier since he had kept so many secrets for his grandmother over the years. And Annette would have been able to vouch for me, as she always investigated those she took in. I'd learned over the years that while Annette gave her help generously, she didn't bestow her assistance easily. Secrets were sacrosanct.

But just as Annette had led the Bent Oak arm of the network, I wasn't her, and my way would have to be different, more of a small group co-op style with Russell and my friends who I trusted with my life.

Libby extended her hand and clasped mine in greeting. A new spark glinted in the eye that wasn't swollen shut. "Hello, Eloise, I'm Mary Jo, and for the first time since I turned eighteen, I'm not afraid Fred will kill me."

༄

Libby's—Mary Jo's—words still echoed in my mind as I walked in to see Russell. For now he was in a private room, a blessing, because more than anything I needed to curl up against him, and heaven help any staff member who tried to evict me from his side. "Russell, my love."

I couldn't choke out anything more. Not yet. I was too close to tears.

He extended his good arm to me, his movements slow from either pain or the remnants of anesthesia. Maybe both. I ran to his bed and clutched his hand, raining kisses and tears over him.

"Winnie, lower that bedrail. I need to hold you," he said, his voice raspy from the fire and intubation during surgery.

He didn't have to ask me twice. I dropped the silver railing and eased onto the narrow bed by increments, carefully, until I settled against him. Home. "Let me know if I'm hurting you."

"It would be worth it."

He drew me closer to his good side, and I nudged the neck of his hospital gown enough that I could press my cheek against his warm brown skin. I listened to the steady thud of his heart in his chest, the beat echoed by the machine behind me. I had to restrain myself from hugging him tight. My fear of him dying overwhelmed me, and I needed to anchor him to this world.

The love of my life.

His hand cupped my shoulder, his chin resting on my head. Everything I could have wanted even before I'd known a relationship like ours could exist.

I closed my eyes and treasured the moment as I embraced our future. "I would like to wear your grandmother's ring."

He exhaled in relief, burying his face in my hair. "I'm glad you've come to your senses."

His answer pried a much-needed laugh from me, but then Russell had that gift—knowing just how to help me shed my fear and relax into the joy. I angled back to look at him, and his smile was the most beautiful thing I'd ever seen. "Russell Davis, I hope you know how much I love you."

"Sure do, and I can't believe I get to tell you how much I love you every day for as long as I draw breath."

I wished I'd never given him cause to doubt me. But I was also learning to look forward. I lost track of how long we lay together in that bed, letting the depth of our feelings and commitment saturate our souls. There was a special kind of beauty in moving from the tumultuous part of "finding" each other to the peaceful assuredness of our future.

His fingers circled lightly on my shoulder. "How's Libby?"

"Doing better than you are, actually," I answered against his neck. "The doctor said she can go home in the morning. They're only keeping her overnight because of the concussion."

He nodded against my hair. "I guess I'm going to be laid up for a while recovering."

"I'm here for you," I promised without hesitation. "Whatever you need to heal and get back onto the racing circuit." I couldn't bear it if my mistakes cost Russell the pastime that brought him so much joy. I didn't know how I could have foreseen Fred Gordon, but guilt hammered me all the same.

"Honey," he said, his voice soft and rumbling against my ear, "I'm probably not going to be racing anymore. The doctor believes the nerve damage in my arm is extensive, and I need quick reflexes behind the wheel."

My brain would not compute his words. This couldn't be happening.

"Then we'll find other doctors, better ones," I insisted, as if I could heal him through sheer force of will. "I'll drive you to those specialists myself." My stomach went queasy at the thought of leaving my cocoon here in Bent Oak, but I would wade through alligator-infested swamps barefoot to get Russell whatever he needed.

"Hold on, Winnie girl—I hear you and I'm thankful. We can talk about options more with the surgeon later."

I could tell he was just pacifying me, but he had the upper hand here, being the patient. "Russell, you should rest. You're right. We can discuss it when you're feeling better."

"Just so that you know, even if the wonders of medicine somehow magically cure all the damage, that brush with death tonight pulled the world into sharper focus."

"What do you mean?" The sheets rustled as I shifted to get a better look at his face.

"I helped my grandmother for years, but more as a way of assisting her. If her passion would have been woodworking, I would have been in the workshop sweeping up sawdust." He drew in a ragged breath, his eyes haunted. "Until tonight, I didn't fully feel the weight, the desperation, of these women and children. Tonight, I really registered their helplessness, just as I'd seen it in people while I was in Vietnam during the war. People who'd lost control of their world."

The connection he made caught me by surprise, but there was no denying Libby had lived in a domestic war zone. "You don't talk about your time over there very often."

"I was lucky not to see much in the way of combat. But my deployment made an impression all the same as we helped deliver Red Cross supplies."

"Like you've been driving aid here at home." I promised myself I would dig deeper into his experiences overseas, but later.

"Yes, and tonight was the first time I looked into the eyes of the evil the women we transport have faced. It changed my perspective." There was no mistaking the intensity and conviction in his voice. "I don't think I can go back to my old ways, pursuing a finish line for the thrill of it. I have a new dream now that is very personal, and one I hope you'll join me in bringing to life."

"And I hope you know that you can count on me. I can't wait to hear more."

Whatever he might have said in response was delayed a moment as the PA system crackled to life with a sudden, frantic call for a doctor to the emergency room. The insertion of that tense voice into our quiet conversation reminded me of the life-and-death battle we'd already fought tonight. We needed time to recover from what had happened, and the hospital was a poor place to settle anyone's nerves.

Before my brain could spiral down that unhealthy path, Russell's voice was warm in my ear again.

"I want to honor my grandmother's memory by expanding her network."

His words stunned me silent for a beat, shock scrambling my thoughts.

"You what?" After tonight's debacle, I could barely wrap my brain around continuing, much less expanding. I'd spent the last hours looking for ways to scale back and, even then, enlist the aid of my friends with the smaller operation. For now I tried to sidestep a discussion. "We don't need to decide anything tonight, about that or your career."

"Winnie," he said, squeezing my shoulder, "I'm a pretty easygoing fella, but when I decide something, I'm focused. Like the first time I saw you. I knew you were the only woman for me, and I was willing to wait however long it took."

I skimmed my fingers along his bristly jaw and thought of all the years I'd wasted out of fear. I wasn't sure what I'd done to deserve this man, but I didn't intend to squander this second chance we'd been given. "I'm sorry it had to take me so long to realize we should be together."

"You're worth the wait," he said. "You're my lightning in a bottle, that once-in-a-lifetime event. Difficult. Challenging. And exciting beyond belief."

"We're in the South," I reminded him. "So that should be lightning in a Mason jar."

His chest rumbled with his laugh, hoarse from the smoke but so very wonderful and familiar. "True enough. Now kiss me good night so we can rest up. We've got work to do."

CHAPTER NINETEEN

2025

Packing up decades of memories made in the cabin got tougher rather than easier the higher Bailey Rae stacked boxes to take to the July Fourth farmers' market. But this would be her last load, for her last market. Motown music played on the porch, a cassette unearthed, along with memories of Russell spinning Winnie around the kitchen. Tomorrow, she would sell the remainder of her wares. Everything else remaining inside the cabin would go to charity—a few well-loved pieces of furniture, the curtains Winnie had sewn, and for good measure, a cookbook left on the counter.

After a final scrubbing of the place, she would be on the road.

Skeeter cast a woeful look her way, sprawled on top of his dog bed. He sure knew how to work the soulful hound dog eye while hiding the icy-blue other one.

June knelt to place a bowl of water beside him before sitting on a sealed box of soy soaps and candles. She fanned herself with an old magazine. "Take a breather, girl, until Keith gets back from the dump with the truck so we can load up for tomorrow. Is there a bee in your bonnet sending you into such a frenzy?"

Bailey Rae traced a finger along the growth marks notched into the doorframe, a safer subject than the reason for the unsettled feeling that had plagued her since her lunch with Martin. "I wish I could have a do-over on so many of those years that I gave Winnie grief. I wasn't the easiest child to love."

How tough it must have been for Winnie to raise a surly teen while protecting her from the harsh realities of the lives she'd touched.

June's fan kept a steady pace to make up for the air conditioner wall unit on its last legs. "I think you were spunky, which was charming. But I understand your point. My early years in Bent Oak were much like yours. I was angry at life and my parents. Winnie was a seasoned veteran when it came to 'spunky' by the time you came around."

Bailey Rae sat on the wood floor, the braided rug already rolled up against the wall for charity. "I always assumed you were an orphan."

"A more appropriate statement would be that my parents were dead to me." June forked a hand through her hair. "My folks were heavily into drugs and the whole 'free love' scene. Large parties. Guests passed out all over our apartment. Occasionally, one would wander into my room . . ."

Bailey Rae gasped. "I'm so sorry."

She'd suffered her fair share of abuse from Yvonne and her boyfriends, but never that.

Skeeter nudged June's knee, and her hand drifted to rest on his spine. "At times different relatives would take me in for a while. I tested boundaries often. Sometimes for fun and sometimes to see if the love and protection being provided was conditional."

"Did you go into foster care?" Bailey Rae asked. "Sorry if I'm being too nosy."

"Not at all, kiddo," June answered with a bittersweet smile. "After my parents landed in prison, I was shuttled back and forth from a group home to relatives who pimped me out to pay their rent. The cycle continued until a teacher took notice. I had an early miscarriage in the tenth grade, just before a history final exam."

Her jaw jutted on the last part, her hand stroking Skeeter faster and faster. Bailey Rae wanted to reach out and hug her hard but understood how sometimes comfort kicked holes in walls that needed to be dismantled one brick at a time. She hugged her own knees instead and stayed silent, listening.

"I told my teacher everything after she found me having a panic attack in the girls' bathroom. She reached out to a pastor in town with connections to the network." June motioned at the cabin. "I ended up in Bent Oak. Winnie and Thea helped tutor me until I was ready to take the GED. I got into college . . . and here I am."

Her GED? And now she taught college? "You sure did turn your life into a tribute to that teacher who saved you."

June angled forward, closer. "It wasn't always easy or smooth. I can't count how many times I've wanted to let you know I understand the anger inside you. Winnie and I discussed it but ultimately decided we couldn't risk telling you."

"I wouldn't have said a word." She would have appreciated knowing she had something in common with June. But would she have let something slip in a childish mistake?

"I trust you, but this is a heavy secret to keep, and you already carried so much." June's gaze shifted to the growth chart etched in the doorframe. "Winnie wanted you to grow up free to move forward rather than be stuck in the past."

"But you all have had to tote those same burdens . . ."

"We didn't have a choice," June explained gently, her teacher voice coming through in her tone. "You do."

∽

2006

Mama had told me that marriage was work. And I believed her. But I hadn't realized that while marriage was work, it shouldn't be a chore. Loving Russell taught me the difference.

There were days I grieved that I couldn't give him a child. Even if I'd been able to carry one to term, even if I hadn't needed a hysterectomy, the lies in my past would have stopped me. Thea felt differently, and I respected that. I'd celebrated the birth of her son and daughter with Howard.

Russell and I found our own way to build a family, though, first by helping Libby with Keith. Then by bringing June into our home. Tutoring her through her GED and first year of college had been an ironic joy as I finally put to use all that high-priced classical education. Russell suggested I might be coming to peace with a blended identity of Eloise and Winnie.

And I thought he could be right.

We trusted each other's insights that way. So when he telephoned that summer day asking me to drop everything and come up to the gas station, I hadn't hesitated. I moved the pot of preserves off the burner, grabbed a sun hat from the hook by the door, and drove my truck right over.

Russell waited in front of the garage, both bay doors open and full with a pickup in one bay and a rusted-out station wagon on a lift in the other. He raised a broad hand, motioning for me to pull over on the side of the building with the bathrooms. Seeing him, I winged yet another prayer of thanksgiving that Russell had survived the fire. The nerve damage in his right arm had been worse than expected. He'd shifted from driving long hauls to managing the gas station and supervising the mechanics.

If he regretted the loss of a NASCAR career, he never showed it. He'd stayed true to his word about turning his full attention to growing his grandmother's network with the help of me and my friends.

We'd found a safe home for a dementia patient who'd been abused by her adult son in a hurry to obtain his inheritance. There'd even been a housewife who'd gone "missing," her cult-leader husband pleading on the news for her safe return. Except she'd been locked in the cellar with no heat for weeks for any behavior he deemed unacceptable.

We'd made a difference for people, and I finally felt like I was living with purpose.

I parked by the air pump and dumpster, but before I could turn off the engine, Russell slid into the passenger seat and pointed the air conditioner vent toward his forehead. I tried not to worry about the exhaustion on his face and how heavily he perspired. The damage to his lung was more apparent in the brutal Carolina summer.

He swiped a bandanna over his face, then the top of his head, his hair buzzed shorter these days as his hairline receded. "Thanks for coming over so fast."

"What's the scoop?"

"Well, this young mother—Yvonne—isn't looking for a new identity. She said she just needs her station wagon repaired and a tank of gas, then she'll be on her way to some place she heard is looking for waitresses." He nodded toward the gas station "lounge," where a woman puffed away on a cigarette in spite of the NO SMOKING signs I'd placed all around to help protect Russell's respiratory system. "I should fix her busted radiator, give her the gas and a twenty, then send her on her way. But it looks like she's living out of her station wagon, and she's got this kid . . ."

He rubbed along his collarbone absently, his eyes tracking toward the dock behind the garage. A scrap of a kid sat on the edge, dangling her feet in the water. Now I understood why Russell had stayed outside. Not because of the smoke, but because the mother let her child run around unsupervised.

Russell shifted his attention back to me. "I didn't want to make a decision without running it by you. But I'm not sure how we can walk away. That kid was huddled under a blanket in the back seat of the station wagon with no working air conditioner, trying to make herself as small as possible. Those wide green eyes got to me."

I didn't hesitate.

"That's all I need to know. How about I go talk to her so she doesn't run off—or fall in—and could you give Thea a heads-up to start checking records to make sure that woman is really the child's mother?" The internet had been a godsend when it came to verifying backgrounds, although with each year that passed, it made staying off the radar all the tougher. "Then Thea can find a job for her at the mill."

We wouldn't be able to count on the factory for a steady stream of jobs much longer. Paper mills had shrunk by over 50 percent in the past couple of decades, which left a substantial part of the Bent Oak population out of the workforce, reinventing themselves at only ten years shy of retirement.

But the fate of dying small-town America was a problem for another day.

Russell tunneled his hand under my hair and cupped the back of my neck. "Lord have mercy, I love you, woman."

Then he kissed me, one of those familiar kisses that couples share after years together, when they know there will be more. A "goodbye for now, see you soon" kind of kiss.

"Love you too," I said, then adjusted my hat and stepped out of the truck, hitching my canvas sack on my shoulder since I always carried snacks around. The kid might be hungry.

Taking my time as I picked my way along the weedy path, cockleburs sticking to my canvas shoes, I made plenty of noise to keep from spooking the child. Underfed arms and legs spiked out of a shorts set already a size too small.

Heavens to Betsy, she was a mess, with tangled red hair in need of shampoo and a good brushing. My hands itched to give her Pippi Longstocking braids to go with those freckles. And not because she reminded me in any way of how I'd envisioned my own daughter. I'd certainly never imagined my child would be sitting on a dock throwing rocks at passing boats and metal signs.

No Trespassing.

Private Property.

No River Access.

Ping. Ping. Ping. Defying authority with rocks. She had good aim. And why wouldn't she? Her mother didn't seem to be a trustworthy authority figure as far as I could tell.

"Hey there," I called down the length of the dock.

The girl bolted to her feet, even shorter than I'd expected. She couldn't have been more than six years old, if that. Still, she wore decades of jaded attitude layered over hungry wariness. "I ain't doing nothing. Just waitin' on my mama."

"I know. My husband and I own the gas station. I'm just checking on you. I thought you might like a pack of peanut butter crackers and a bottle of water."

I kept those on hand for when Russell grew overtired. Once upon a time, I would have packed them in case I needed to run. I didn't worry about that so much anymore. Peace had found me before Phillip could.

The girl stared at the pack of crackers like it was a whole bag of Halloween candy but picked at a scab on her knee instead. "If you try to take me, I'm gonna yell fire."

"Why not shout stranger danger?"

"People don't always care when you say that."

I gave her a simple nod, my throat a little tight. "Staying safe is important. If you squint you can see the back of your mom's head from here, so I'm sure she would hear you if you yelled." I lied about that last part, but it didn't feel right to speak disrespectfully about her mother— her very neglectful mother. I shouldn't judge. The woman might have been doing her best, and since we were working to keep her around, I would have the opportunity to learn more about this Yvonne, as Russell had called her. "What's your name?"

"Bailey Rae. Mama said Baileys is her favorite thing to drink, and Rae was her daddy's name." She scratched the scab until a trickle of blood leaked.

The way she kept scraping at the wound reminded me of a nineteen-year-old who'd once told me cutting brought her relief from stress.

"Okay, well, I think your mom might be staying here for a while." I opened the packet of crackers and passed one over. Then took one for myself too, trying again to set her at ease. "Your car's gonna take a while to fix, and since your mom's already looking for a job, maybe she'll take one here."

Grunting, Bailey Rae ignored the cracker and me. She pinged a stone off a tire swing dangling from a branch over the still water.

I finished off my cracker before saying, "Bent Oak is a great place to live."

Bailey Rae shot a skeptical look my way before tossing another rock toward the swing, sending it sailing through the opening this time to plop in the river.

But I wasn't that easily dissuaded. "Don't let that 'No Trespassing' sign worry you. Since the gas station belongs to my husband and me, we let youth groups from Scouts and church go swimming and fishing."

"I can't swim, and I don't know how to fish." The girl hurled another rock with unerring aim at a slow-moving johnboat.

Time to try a different approach before some fisherman pulled a firearm out of his tackle box. "I bet you can't hit that cypress knee over there."

Her little jaw thrust out, and she nailed that jutting root dead-on.

"Nice." I applauded, while dusting crumbs from my hands. "I bet you'd be killer with a slingshot."

"Why do you care?" Bailey Rae turned the full power of her flinty green eyes on me. "My mom's not gonna stay here. She never does. You're gonna wake up one day and we'll be gone, with all your crackers and the money outta your wallet."

As if to emphasize her point, she snatched up the remaining crackers and stuffed them into her mouth one after another. Her cheeks puffed wide as she chewed.

I made a mental note to hide my purse and lock the cash drawer. "Well, if you'll be leaving, can I have one of those rocks to remember you by? I keep a jar in the window of my kitchen. It's full of stones from special times in my life that I want to remember."

She gulped down the food and swiped the crumbs from her mouth with the back of her wrist. "Why would you want to remember me?"

It was all I could manage not to hug her. But she still radiated so much defensiveness, I figured affection would make her run rather than risk letting the kindness bring tears. Anger was easier than vulnerability.

So I settled for a safer way of reaching out. "Because you have the best aim I've ever seen. With that great arm of yours, I bet you'd be a whiz at casting a line."

She sat up straighter. "What's casting a line mean?"

I'd piqued her interest. I held back a smile. "It's throwing the fishing line in as far as you can. Since it's gonna be a bit before the car is ready"—and while Thea figured out a job for the woman—"how about I show you our collection of cane fishing poles? If you like it, we'll drop a line in and catch some supper. Lucky for you, kids under sixteen don't need a fishing license."

It about broke my heart when her eyes narrowed for a moment. The hardened gesture spoke volumes about the kind of life she'd led so far. But it made the reward of her nod all the sweeter when it came.

"All right, then," she agreed, tilting her chin at me. "I'll try."

༄

2025

Martin tossed his citation booklet on his kitchen counter, worn out in a way that had nothing to do with work. He'd been agitated since his lunch with Bailey Rae the day before. He'd had such high hopes for persuading her to stay in Bent Oak at least a while longer, just to see where the connection between them might lead. But she'd cut him off at the knees. Sure, she'd mentioned going out for a meal with him if he was in the area, but he couldn't miss her determination to leave. The rejection stung more than he would have expected.

His restless feet carried him around his efficiency apartment over the hardware store on Main Street. Not optimal for the long term, but the simple digs suited him for now. He spent most of his time in the office or out in the field anyway, so he didn't care much about where he rested his head at night.

Except today, the walls echoed with silence that felt suffocating.

He pulled up a playlist on his phone and dropped onto the sofa while Chris Stapleton's mellow voice soothed his soul. Maybe news at work this morning had triggered a callback to the shooting in the hangar. Evidence continued to stack up against Ian Abernathy and how unhinged he'd become since learning Gia and his brother Owen were having an affair. A second autopsy had been ordered to confirm the drowning may not have been accidental.

What a mess.

A knock thumped on the door—odd, because he never had visitors. He turned off the music and checked the peephole to find Keith and June standing in the corridor. Had something happened with Libby?

He unbolted the lock and swung the door wide. "Good afternoon, what brings you this way?"

Keith stepped aside to let June enter first, then followed. "Hope you don't mind us stopping by unannounced. Bailey Rae asked us to drop off some things you might like to have. Canned goods and a quilt with a wildlife theme."

Any other time, he would have been touched by the gesture. But right now, it felt like a slap in the face that she hadn't wanted to deliver the items personally. "That's thoughtful of her—and of you two to bring it over."

June placed a small basket full of jars onto his kitchen table, by his work cap. "We're trying to help her as much as she'll let us. She was clearing out the last things in the cabin and wanted to say thanks for everything you've done for us—for Gia and Cricket too."

Martin closed the door. "I would have come by."

June abandoned her unloading to face him while Keith draped the quilt over the arm of the sofa. "She's in 'flight mode,' hiding from emotions—just like when she was a kid. Don't take it personally, Martin."

Her insight fit well with his own perception of Bailey Rae, even if he didn't much care for the way she'd shut him out.

"Is that why she's leaving town?" And talking of low-key lunches when he'd just asked her to stay?

Sighing, June said, "She has it in her head that moving to Myrtle Beach is the best way to honor Winnie's memory. Bailey Rae just can't seem to grasp that Winnie would want her to live her best life. Wherever that may be."

After all she'd shared about her childhood, he could see why she might want to make a fresh start. As he had by coming to Bent Oak. Who was he to deny her a new beginning? "I'll be sure to thank her when I see her at the July Fourth market tomorrow. Well, as long as I don't get called into work." Martin scratched the back of his neck. "There've been some teens, um, up to no good out in the woods lately."

Keith dropped to sit on the sofa, making himself at home. "June and I weren't the best of teenagers, but we had good people on our side." He elbowed June lightly. "Remember when Russell taught us to drive? I thought for sure he was gonna have a heart attack."

Martin motioned for June to have a seat before pulling up a kitchen chair for himself. "I didn't realize the two of you grew up together in Bent Oak."

June tucked her colorfully streaked hair behind her ear. "I, uh, emancipated at sixteen. Russell and Winnie let me stay with them until I turned eighteen."

Martin reconfigured the histories of Winnie and her friends as he learned those details, trying to make all the pieces fit. At times, though, he felt like those histories kept changing.

Keith clasped his hands between his knees. "My mom and I moved here when I was six, the same day Winnie arrived as well. We showed up at the same time because of a big hiring fair at the mill. I spent evenings at Winnie's and Russell's whenever Mom had a late shift. I was there so much I even carved my initials into a windowsill at the cabin."

There was definitely a family vibe among the people Winnie had made her friends. He could see that all the more clearly now. The details didn't matter as much as the connection. And none of the people she'd pulled into her orbit had actually been related to her—a testament to the way people could build strong relationships with the friends they chose.

Bailey Rae had been lucky to land in such a supportive community. He had too, for that matter. Of course he wouldn't have gotten to know these people without Bailey Rae as a bridge of sorts. He would miss her when she left, but he also realized he would no longer isolate himself.

Time for him to reenter the world . . . he had Bailey Rae to thank for that. Something he intended to tell her when they said goodbye.

CHAPTER TWENTY

2025

Goodbyes were hard. But they were all the tougher when saying farewell to nothing but a tombstone.

Bailey Rae sat cross-legged in the graveyard beside Russell's headstone, tugging weeds and tossing them aside. When he'd died, Winnie had bought a double plot with her marker in place as well, already prepping for the day she would be reunited with the love of her life. No question, some of her spark had dimmed after Russell passed away.

Live oaks shaded the slabs, the twisted branches tangling together into a canopy over the familiar family names. Tyler. Watson. Davis. Underwood. And so on for generations. Winnie had brought her here periodically to leave flowers on Annette's grave for holidays and her birthday. Family connections weren't always made by blood, but however those bonds were formed, Winnie had taught her to cherish them.

Hugging her knees to her chest, she rested her head against the polished stone, warmed from the summer. "I wish I could talk to you and get your advice. I'm trying so hard to honor your memory, both of you."

Winnie had always told her to fight for her dreams and never give up. Wasn't she doing so by preparing to move to the coast? Now she wasn't so sure, and she was getting weary of fighting. At the moment, she wished the wind could carry Russell's quiet wisdom that brought order and peace to her life . . .

Mother's Day had been weird enough when Yvonne was around, but Bailey Rae had done her best to give a gift. From coloring a picture of a pretend house to stealing a candy bar from a vending machine. She hadn't realized, though, that the celebration would be even weirder after Yvonne bailed. Everyone in school had made a Popsicle-stick frame with a Polaroid picture inside. Bailey Rae had gone along with it, then pitched hers in the trash on her way to the school bus. Even if her mom showed up—which she wouldn't—Bailey Rae was still mad at Yvonne for forgetting her seventh birthday.

Now the bus chugged away from her in a stinky cloud of fumes, and she walked down the dirt driveway to the cabin. Her book bag bumped the backs of her legs as she dragged her feet. The straps were too long, and it held monster-big books she couldn't understand. She tried to remember that this place was better, with good food, a bed that wasn't on wheels, and people who didn't shout.

Uncle Russell waited for her on the front porch in a rocking chair, thumbing through one of those racing magazines he liked. The biggest fan she'd ever seen swooshed away beside him. Bailey Rae kicked a rock so it thudded off the bottom step.

"Where's Aunt Winnie?" They'd told her to call them "Aunt" and "Uncle" rather than Mr. and Mrs. She slipped her backpack off her shoulders, and it landed on the porch with a thump. Her shoulders hurt, and she fought back tears at the spelling test inside with a bright-red F on top.

"Winnie had some errands to run, so I came home from the gas station to make sure you got off the bus okay." He set a juice box and a cookie on the other rocking chair. He didn't ask her if she wanted it. Just left the snack there for her to decide. "Do you have any homework?"

Shaking her head in a big fat lie, she scooped up the snack, ate the snickerdoodle cookie in two bites, and sucked on the straw until the box made that empty sound. "Can I go watch TV with Skeeter Number Three now?"

She'd never had a dog before. She liked his floppy ears and wavy fur. Most of all, she liked the way he slept curled up on the end of her bed at night. As if keeping watch over her.

Uncle Russell pushed up to his feet. "In a little bit. Skeeter needs to run around the yard for a while." He started down the steps, gesturing for her to follow. "I know you had a mama, but I thought it would be nice for us to do something for Winnie on Mother's Day."

"Like what?" Her throat got tight as she thought about the gift she'd thrown away. "I ain't . . . I don't have any money."

"Winnie doesn't care about money," he said with that special smile he got when he talked about her. "She appreciates thoughtful deeds."

"Like if I wash her car?" she asked, trailing him across the yard. "Skeeter likes the hose too."

He motioned toward a patch of dirt all churned up over by the barn. A wagon full of plants waited in the middle. "I thought we could plant a vegetable garden for her."

She didn't know how to do that, and she didn't want to look stupid. "That doesn't sound very fun."

Russell raised an eyebrow. "Do you think Winnie had fun taking an afternoon off work last month to sit in the principal's office listening to how you headbutted Sissy Watson and chipped her front tooth?"

"She had it coming." The brat shouldn't have made fun of Aunt Winnie.

He lifted plants out of the wagon and set them one by one on the ground. "Do you want to tell me why?"

"Not really." It would make his heart hurt to hear.

"Kids can be mean."

His words gave her a sick feeling in her stomach, like when she ate too many cookies. Bailey Rae picked up a container from the wagon. The label had a photo along with the word tomato. "I know it wasn't nice, okay?"

He stood up straight, his brown eyes surprised. "I was talking about Sissy Watson. First time I saw that girl steal a candy bar in the gas station and try to blame it on her twin, I knew she was no good, and she hasn't gone out of her way to prove me wrong." He sniffed like he'd stepped in a Skeeter pile. "I'm not saying what you did was right. I'm just saying I understand there may have been a reason."

She wanted to pour her heart out and tell him so bad, but he'd just said how she should think about Winnie. And the way Bailey Rae saw it, she should think about Russell too. Besides, she'd also stolen candy bars out of vending machines, even if she'd never tried to blame anyone else. "What are we going to plant in this garden besides tomatoes?"

He lifted another plant, one with green spikes and tiny purple flowers on top. "These are chives, for cooking. I thought the little blooms were mighty pretty . . ."

The memory of that day was still so fresh in her mind the taste of that cookie and juice lingered. Bailey Rae traced the year etched in stone that she'd said goodbye to him—2019. How could it have been six years since she'd gotten her last hug from Uncle Russell? One of his gentle hugs that had taught her not to fear men. She could still hear the peaceful timbre of his voice, raspier near the end as he wheezed for air through the cannula easing oxygen into his nose.

She tipped her head back, blinking away the tears that blurred the oak branches and Spanish moss overhead. Once her vision cleared, she opened her backpack and pulled out a paper sack. She eased it open and withdrew the small plant.

Chives, flowering the most beautiful purple that would return year after year.

Sinking back on her heels once she had it well situated and watered, she reached into her pocket and pulled out two rocks, placing one on each marker before pocketing two loose stones from the ground. Bailey Rae surrendered to the battle with tears and said farewell to the only real parents she'd ever known.

2019

A part of me died the day Russell left this earth. I felt like one of those swans that mated for life, then grieved themselves to death after the loss of that partner. I'd known Russell and I wouldn't have forever, and that our time had been cut shorter by the accident that night of the fire. He'd lived longer than the doctors expected.

But I wasn't ready to let him go.

Over the past three weeks, I'd spent most of my time outside in the rocker because it made me feel closer to Russell. He'd wanted to see one more sunset, so I'd helped him into his wheelchair. We'd sat on our porch and fallen asleep under the stars, listening to hoot owls. When I'd woken that spring morning, he'd slipped away in his sleep.

Most days, I felt like I was sleeping too, caught in a fog halfway between this world and heaven. I hadn't been able to do anything. I'd stopped helping out the network. Quit tilling the ground for my garden. I barely ate when someone placed a plate in front of me. Thankfully, my friends were keeping an eye on Bailey Rae. They understood something inside me had broken.

A creak on the bottom step jarred me. My eyes snapped open, and my ears tuned in to the echo of a Carolina wren chirping.

Libby climbed the wooden stairs with a baking dish in her hands. "Spaghetti casserole. You can freeze it if you're overwhelmed with food from other people. I would have gotten here sooner, but when I finished at the grocery store this afternoon, I couldn't find my car in the lot."

"Thank you," I said, the words coming up my throat like shattered glass from one of my old projects. "Bailey Rae has been bringing food home from the Fill 'Er Up after her shift."

Selling the gas station had been rough for Russell, even more so than parceling off acreage. He'd worried about leaving me without an income. I told him I'd learned a long time ago how much more people mattered than money or things. I bit back a fresh sob that wanted out.

Libby ducked inside to put the casserole in the freezer before taking a seat beside me in the other rocking chair. She eased her graying braid from behind her and draped it over her shoulder. "It's a good thing you're sitting outdoors, because you need to take a shower something fierce, my friend."

I didn't even want to look in a mirror. I knew what I would see. A woman mad with grief. "Back before Bent Oak, when people said I was crazy, I knew deep in my soul they were wrong."

"They were," Libby said with surety.

"But I think this time . . ." My voice cracked, and I wrapped my arms tighter around myself, shivering in spite of the spring warmth. "I'm broken, and I don't know how to find my way back."

Libby grasped my hand as if to tether me to this side of sanity. "Winnie, you weren't crazy then, and you're not now." She squeezed my fingers, her gaze so fierce on mine I didn't dare look away. "You're just hurting. And you're sealing that pain up inside like okra in one of your Mason jars. Except that isn't gonna work. You gotta pour it out, sit in it for as long as you need, then step back into your life."

"Why? Why do I have to?" I was past the point of caring if I sounded pathetic. I just wanted to crawl into bed until . . . forever. "If you tell me to think of all the women who need my help, I think I'll scream. When will my debt be paid? I don't have anything left inside me to give them."

I couldn't imagine turning away from my grief. Because then I'd be turning away from Russell. It was easier to hurt than envision life without the only person who understood every facet of me. Russell knew every last piece of my soul. Good and bad. Even the oldest pieces of me that were still pure Eloise.

And he had loved me anyway.

"Of course you don't have anything to give the network. Because right now you need to focus on yourself and Bailey Rae. She needs you," Libby said in that quiet way of hers that commanded attention. "Yes, she's nineteen now, but she's still a teenager full of attitude and pain. Trust me, I know a thing or two about troubled teens."

My chest ached at the thought of Bailey Rae hurting too. I knew how much she loved Russell. She needed help that I couldn't give her.

"I love Bailey Rae. And because I love her, I know she's in much more capable—stable—hands with you, Thea, June, and Keith even."

This conversation was lasting longer than any I'd had in weeks, and it wore me out. "I know I can trust you to look after her."

"Of course we are always there for her," Libby said kindly. "But you are her mother, just as Russell was her father, and she won't survive losing you both at the same time."

"Well, aren't you a bundle of sunshine today?" I couldn't resist quipping. I even tried to pull a smile but apparently wasn't very successful.

Libby gave me a look in return that broadcast loud and clear I wasn't fooling her for an instant.

"Winnie, my friend," she said, her gray eyes as steely as her will. "Yes, Russell is gone, and my heart is absolutely broken for you and Bailey Rae. Perhaps the two of you can grieve together. And while you do, the rest of us are here to carry everything else."

Somehow her words managed to filter through, bringing a comfort I hadn't expected as she shouldered some of the weight and let me focus on myself and Bailey Rae. With my defenses down, I'd allowed old insecurities to creep in, whispers of Eloise. It wouldn't be easy to banish those ghosts without Russell by my side, but Libby was right. I needed to look toward the future.

I needed to be the woman Russell had believed in. The woman he'd trusted. Loved.

I pushed myself up out of that rocker, feeling decades older than a month ago. "Libby, do you have anything pressing on your agenda today? After I take a shower, I'd appreciate it if you could go with me to the hardware store. Bailey Rae and I need to plant the garden."

༄

2025

Bailey Rae filled Skeeter's water bowl and left a dish of dry kibble out for good measure. As much as she enjoyed having him with her, this Fourth of July market day promised to be a long one. Skeeter would be better off here at the cabin using the doggie door and resting up for the big move. He'd had enough upheaval with all the boxes, then most of the furniture sold or put into storage. She'd even slept on a mattress on the floor last night.

Not that she'd slept much, second-guessing her conversation with Martin. She still wasn't certain why she'd decided to give him Russell's fishing quilt. Chalk it up to another awkward farewell, except she didn't have Russell to guide her through it anymore.

Better to stay busy. She drained her cup of morning coffee and tugged her scrunchie tighter around her freshly washed hair before hefting up her insulated bag full of frozen water bottles and snacks to carry her through the day. Even though there would be food booths, she couldn't count on having time to leave her station.

Firecrackers popped in the distance, no doubt people getting into the Fourth of July spirit early. Or perhaps emptying their stash in case the forecast for thunderstorms came true.

All the same, she intended to err on the side of hope and head on over to the market. She swung open the front door to whistle for Skeeter.

"Hello?" A masculine voice carried across the yard, from a tall, slim man in his twenties, with a headful of dark hair and clothes that spoke of understated wealth. He stood beside a luxury SUV.

She didn't recognize him, but at least he didn't resemble Gia's husband. Still, he was a stranger, and she was out here alone. After the past few weeks of turmoil and strangers lurking around her property, she wasn't letting down her guard.

He held up a broad hand with some kind of college ring. "I didn't mean to startle you. I'm looking for the lady who lives here. Winnie Ballard? I've written her a number of letters and even spoke with her on the phone around four months ago about helping me with my search for my grandfather's wife."

Search for a missing wife? Bailey Rae's skin prickled like her nerves were on fire now that she knew about Winnie's help with the network to relocate at-risk women. She thought of all those letters she'd scanned in, planning to read them later. What had she missed? Could this guy have been the stranger who had been spotted around town and the lurker on her property?

Even though this wasn't Ian Abernathy, was this some other abusive husband in search of a spouse Winnie had helped to escape? How many more people like this would land on the doorstep? Since her phone was already in hand, she typed out a text to Martin.

Stranger at the cabin. Please come.

She hated how scared she felt in her own home. Although that made her think of all the women Winnie had helped, women who'd felt deeply afraid in their homes on a regular basis.

The echo of more firecrackers snapping carried on the wind, each gust picking up speed and swirling leaves. Flinching, Bailey Rae clutched her cell phone tighter. "Sir, unfortunately I can't help you. Winnie passed away three months ago."

Would that be enough to send him on his way?

"My condolences. She seemed like such a nice lady when we spoke. I came today to try one last time to find answers about my grandfather's wife." He started to walk away, but before she could so much as breathe a sigh of relief, he paused, then turned back. "Maybe you can help me."

The nerves shifted into all-out alarm. "How about leave me your number and I'll get in touch with you later. My friend Martin is due here to pick me up any minute."

She hoped.

The man raised both his hands and moved no closer. "I didn't mean to spook you. I should have explained myself better." He tapped his chest. "My name is Phillip Curtis III. I'm from Mobile, Alabama. My grandfather's first wife—not my grandmother—went missing back in 1971. I am almost certain Winnie Ballard is—was—that woman."

Bailey Rae grabbed a porch post, her head swimming. "You must be mistaken," she denied automatically. "Winnie was my aunt."

Not really. But she felt like the Lord would forgive her this little lie.

"Just hear me out," he said. "Please?"

If she told him no, would that make things worse? Anger him? Should she run into the cabin? Her gut told her to keep him outside while waiting for Martin. If this Phillip fellow was dangerous and they went indoors . . . "I'm listening."

"I came across an article in a publication discussing the history of paper mills in the United States and how they're closing at a rapid rate. They ran a photo taken at the Bent Oak facility in 1972. The woman looks exactly like my grandfather's first wife." He picked up a manila envelope off the hood of his car, took slow steps toward her, and carefully placed it on the bottom step before backing away again. "Inside is the article, along with a photo of my grandfather's wife—Eloise Carlisle Curtis."

Curiosity got the better of her, and she snatched up the envelope. Her heart hammered hard in her chest as she pulled out the newspaper clipping first. The local paper mill was easily recognizable, as was the image of Winnie standing beside an oversize roll of paper. Bailey Rae tugged out the glossy picture next.

And that woman looked exactly like a younger Winnie.

Bailey Rae went dizzy again and blinked to clear her vision. Still, the truth was right there in front of her. A truth that would have made no sense a few months ago, but after learning about the way Winnie and her friends helped women at risk?

The identity of Eloise Carlisle Curtis—Winnie—was clear. Winnie had been one of those women escaping a dangerous homelife.

Yet for some reason when the man had questioned Winnie in their phone call, she'd denied it. She had wanted to keep her life, her name, and her history safe here in Bent Oak. That reason had been important enough for Winnie to hold her secret for decades.

Which made Bailey Rae's response simple. "I'm sorry, but this isn't my aunt." She shrugged. "They say everyone has a doppelgänger."

"I can understand why you may be cautious, your aunt too. My grandfather was not a . . . kind man." Wincing, he rubbed a scar on the corner of his bottom lip. "My grandmother was actually his third wife. His second wife killed herself. Which should have alerted my grandma, since he had his first wife—Eloise—committed to a psychiatric hospital before she went missing. She left a suicide note, but her body was never recovered. I think the odds of him having two wives die by their own hands are slim."

She kept a lock on her jaw so it didn't fall open to hear how close Winnie had come to an even worse fate. But apparently, she'd been through a special kind of hell in the first place to prompt the change of name.

Just like all the women she'd helped.

"I'm sorry you had so much turmoil in your life," she said gently, earnestly, her heart aching all the while over what kind of painful life Winnie must have endured before breaking away. "But this has no bearing on me."

"Except, yes, it does," he said. "Eloise inherited a substantial sum of money in a trust from her parents. I want to make sure the inheritance goes to her—and if not to her, then to her relatives."

More money raining from the sky like the cash in the cabin? The minute she unraveled one mystery of Aunt Winnie, another came around. The image of Winnie growing up in a wealthy family didn't fit, except in some ways it did. Her education. Her speech patterns. Dozens of other tiny things that in isolation meant nothing, but taken as a whole made sense. "Well, even if she was who you think, Winnie was a widow and doesn't have any children."

Nodding with resignation, Phillip Curtis sighed. "Just think on what I've told you, and if you need to reach me, my phone number and address are on the envelope."

The gentle hum of his departing SUV barely registered over the roaring in her ears, compounded by a screaming firework that had no hope of lighting the morning sky. Now that he had left, the weight of his words settled. Winnie had been in a psychiatric hospital and staged her suicide to escape.

Bailey Rae didn't think for a moment that Winnie had been anything but sane. Sure, she was eccentric, but she was also one of the most grounded, giving individuals who'd ever lived. Yet the visitor's story had called something else into question now.

Would a woman who'd faked suicide once ever be tempted to do it again? Bailey Rae wasn't sure if Winnie's drowning had been accidental or something far more tragic when faced with the past threat catching her.

Either way, Bailey Rae owed Winnie more than she could ever repay her for saving her life all those years ago, for giving her more than a future, but also a home and love. And she intended to honor Winnie's wishes.

With the same fervor that had driven her to sell everything and move to Myrtle Beach, Bailey Rae knew what she needed to do now. She closed the envelope and studied the phone number. She pulled out her cell phone full of all those scanned documents and typed out a text to Phillip Curtis III.

> This is Bailey Rae Rigby. We just spoke at my aunt's farm. Here's Winnie Ballard's birth certificate. I hope that clears up the confusion. Best of luck on your search for answers.

The whoosh of the sending message echoed her exhale of relief as she jogged back toward the cabin to check that she hadn't left any boxes behind. She willed away bad weather and dark thoughts. Dew brightened the grass, birds lifting their morning chorus with a woodpecker keeping the beat. The garden had been emptied of the last of Winnie's harvest, the earth churned by a hoe and ready for whoever purchased the property.

Nostalgia tugged at her as she entered the cabin, her steps echoing in the empty rooms. Her throat tightened, and tears she absolutely did not want to shed burned her eyes.

She ran back toward the front door, shouting, "Skeeter, get on over here right now so I can go."

Yanking open the door, she plowed through.

And slammed into the hard wall of a masculine chest, his T-shirt dirty and rancid with sweat. Nothing like the crisp and clean Phillip Curtis III. Dread and a horrible sense of foreboding filled her as Bailey Rae looked up into a face she recognized from photographs.

His blond hair darkened with perspiration and his eyes full of rage, Ian Abernathy gripped Bailey Rae's arm in a bruising vise and growled, "Where's my wife?"

CHAPTER TWENTY-ONE

"Your wife?" Bailey Rae struggled not to wince at the painful pressure on her arm. Wind from the incoming storm swept dust and grit through the open door and into her eyes. "I don't know what you mean."

Panic welled inside her. Frantically, she weighed her options, his grip tight on her arm. Heaven forbid that he might shove inside with her. So she pushed forward onto the porch, reaching behind her to close the door.

She'd been so careful all these weeks since Gia showed up at the market clutching the cookbook. Bailey Rae had activated her security system religiously. She'd kept Skeeter nearby at home. She'd had people stay over. And she'd reached out to Martin so often she feared today would prove one time too many. Although another part of her feared what might happen if he showed up after all and challenged the man snarling down at her, his fury barely caged.

"Stop moving or I'll have to use this knife." Ian pressed a blade tip into her side and yanked her arm up harder with his other hand. "I don't want to hurt you. I just want my family back. Now where are they?"

Fear sank into her, deeper than the knife. Skeeter pawed at the window from inside the cabin, letting out a couple of alert woofs that only served to make Ian's grip tighten.

"I can't help you," she gasped out.

He slammed her against the porch post while he ran his oily gaze over the yard as if searching for any hiding place between the overgrown azaleas and juniper thickets.

"You mean you won't." He smelled of sweat and something darker. Insidiously evil. "Do you think I'm stupid? I know you helped my wife run away from me with my kid. You and that cop friend of yours."

Now didn't seem the right time to correct his mistake about Martin's profession. Bottom line, he wore a uniform and a gun, and she desperately hoped he would arrive soon. She tried to ease away from the knife blade at her side. "Mr. Abernathy—"

"So you admit it. You do know who I am, who my wife is," he hissed, a dark smile tugging at his mouth. "I saw you visit her at the hospital. I've been tailing you for a very long time. Now tell me where you hid my family, and I'll be on my way."

Thank heaven he hadn't mentioned Gia's recent visit to the cabin. Bailey Rae suppressed a shiver. "Mr. Abernathy, I truly do not know where your wife and daughter are now. They have been relocated, and I'm not privy to those details."

"Privy?" He sneered. "Now aren't you all high and mighty? You better figure out how to find Gia or I'll have no reason to keep you alive any more than I did that traitor brother of mine who'd been banging my wife."

His words turned the blood ice cold in her veins.

The man who held her was a killer.

But she couldn't afford the distraction of thinking about that murder. She scrambled for something, anything, to get away or at the very least buy a little time in hopes Martin would arrive. Or so that she could get her hands on a weapon.

Maybe she could send another SOS to Martin. She inched her fingers toward the cell in her pocket. "Let me make some calls and see what I can find out for you."

"Do *not touch* that phone." The knife pressed deeper, the tip piercing her Pink Floyd T-shirt, stinging her skin just enough to strike terror.

A squeak of pain slipped past her lips.

"Shut. Up," he shouted, backhanding her across the face.

Pain exploded behind her eyes as she stumbled down the steps and slammed into a tree. Thunder cracked overhead. Skeeter nosed through the doggie door onto the porch.

A feral growl swelled as the hound launched off the steps.

Skeeter hit the ground running, closing the gap between them and sinking his teeth into Ian's jeans leg. Snarling, Skeeter held on, paws planted. He swung his head back and forth as he tugged on the denim.

Ian's knife sliced at the air. Glinting. Bailey Rae let out a cry of denial as Skeeter yelped. But the dog's jaws stayed clamped on the man even as blood trickled down his brown fur.

Heart pounding, she brushed through the pine needles littering the ground, crawling. Not to run away. But to find a weapon. She couldn't leave Skeeter behind with this monster. Desperation and adrenaline seared through her. Fueling her. Her hand curled around a wrist-thick branch, and she prayed it would be enough.

She launched to her feet and swung at Ian. Again and again, pummeling his back. He made a grab at the branch, and she dove forward, jabbing him in the gut. The wind howled, showering pine needles over them. Skeeter still hung on, dragging Ian lower. The dog held his ground despite the wound in his side.

Then a low whine sounded in the distance, growing louder into sirens. The police? A fire truck? Even as she heaved the tree branch down on Ian, she prayed her text to Martin could net a result this large when, in the past, he'd shown up on his own.

Ian thrashed and dodged, swiping the knife in a wide arc. "What do you think you're doing?"

"I'm stopping you," she screamed back, possessed by the need to stand up for herself. For Gia. For Skeeter.

Decades of pain poured out of her in a shout just short of feral. The child inside her who'd once fought to mask fear now harnessed every last drop of it to save herself and her beloved companion. She wasn't curling up under the covers to make herself small. She wasn't lashing out at her loved ones. And she wasn't waiting to be rescued.

She was doing what Winnie would have done. Taking a stand. Leveling that righteous rage at a very deserving target.

A pop split the air. Ringing in her ears. Another firecracker?

And then just past Ian's shoulder, she saw Martin, gun in his hands.

Since she didn't see his truck, he must have approached through the woods, his professional familiarity with the land giving him an edge. Her teeth chattered, and relief rocked through her so hard the branch fell from her grip.

"Freeze, Abernathy," Martin shouted with unwavering authority. "Or the next shot won't be in the dirt by your feet."

Ian went stock still—only his eyes darting around. Assessing his options? Then he raised his hands in the air, tossing the knife to the side with a flick of the wrist.

Still jittery, Bailey Rae kicked the blade toward Martin just as Skeeter lurched to his feet with a massive shake-off. Blood still oozed from his side, but he was standing and steady, ambling his way over to Bailey Rae to lean against her leg. She stroked his head, reassuring them both.

Later, she would ask Martin for details. Right now, though, she was just so very thankful he'd seen her text.

"Bailey Rae," Martin said softly without looking away from his target, "take Skeeter and move aside."

Touching her dog's collar lightly, she backed up until coming flush against the trunk of an oak. Only once she had that support did she realize how her legs trembled in the aftermath.

Sirens grew louder as two cop cars sped down the driveway toward them. No doubt called by Martin, who still stood with his sidearm trained on Ian. Abernathy wouldn't be able to slither out of the charges this time, not after the attack here and the one on his wife. Gia would be safe from her husband for years to come once Ian was in jail for murdering his brother. She wouldn't need a new identity like Winnie had.

Cricket, who'd already suffered enough trauma, wouldn't lose everything familiar to her.

How many times had Winnie faced down a similar threat for the good of others? Putting herself at risk to save others. A life lived with purpose.

For the first time, Bailey Rae not only understood Winnie's commitment, she embraced it on a soul-deep level. Pride filled her for the life Winnie had led, never needing recognition to do the right thing. How fortunate Bailey Rae had been to have such a role model.

At last, she understood exactly how to honor the woman who'd raised her. The woman who'd given her a sense of home.

The woman who'd given her a family.

The wind whipped harder, and tapping echoed overhead as rain pattered along the leafy branches, some drops trickling through, faster and faster. Bailey Rae tipped her face into the shower, feeling Winnie's presence in this place, in the memories they'd made together, all urging Bailey Rae to make the most of this washed-clean, fresh start.

Bailey Rae had barely found time to breathe all day, but not for the reasons she'd expected when rolling off the mattress this morning. Yet she couldn't think of a better end than this, sitting with Martin in the back of his truck, leaning against the pickup's cab while the fireworks arced overhead. The residue of adrenaline still tingled through her veins, but slowly peace and happiness were taking over.

Even if she hadn't spent hours giving her statement to the police and taking Skeeter to the emergency vet with Martin, she wouldn't have made it to the market. The daytime Fourth of July celebrations had been rained out. Luckily, the storm had passed in time for evening fireworks over the river at sundown.

The air hung heavy, thick with humidity and sulfur. Roman candles exploded in the inky sky while children skipped along the shore with sparklers. Girandoles spun upward with a shriek before exploding in an umbrella of sparks. A bonfire had been lit for attendees to roast hot dogs and marshmallows.

Just as the day had been marked every year since Bailey Rae had arrived in Bent Oak.

Except in the past, she'd watched Independence Day displays with Winnie or Russell at her side. Their absence was bittersweet, but today had reminded her to cherish every moment, a lesson Winnie and Russell had stressed often after welcoming her into their family. A great big family bonded by love, if not blood.

Beside her on the quilt spread out in the truck bed, Martin hummed along to a playlist on his phone, the best of the Eagles. Had he taken note of her preferences from her concert T-shirts? The thoughtfulness touched her.

Skeeter had been stitched up and appeared none the worse for wear, but the veterinarian was keeping him overnight for observation, sedated and calm. Fireworks could be stressful for dogs under the best of circumstances. Saying good night to Skeeter had been tough, but she assured him she would be there first thing in the morning with the very best treats.

Bailey Rae rested her head on Martin's shoulder, allowing the familiar refrain from "Take It Easy" to fill her. Wise words. "Thank you for coming to my rescue this morning."

"Looked to me like you and Skeeter had the situation well in hand."

Even though his voice was lighthearted, she heard the undercurrent of concern, felt the tension that hadn't eased yet from his muscles. This morning's close call would take time to process, to shake free of the emotions searing through them both.

A shiver rippled through her in spite of the muggy night air. "Skeeter and I sure didn't mind the backup."

During the frantic drive to the vet, Martin had explained how the instant he'd seen her text, he'd reached out to the police, but he hadn't waited around for them to mobilize. He'd sped over, except before he could turn onto the driveway, he'd caught sight of her through the trees. So he'd picked his way through the woods on foot for the element of surprise.

Martin slid an arm around her shoulders. "How much longer until you head for the beach? I was thinking of taking some of my vacation time. Dip my toes in the sand. No pressure. Whatever pace you're comfortable with. And if the day comes that we both want more, I'm open to relocating."

Stunned, she wondered if she'd heard him right, but the light in his brown eyes assured her. She appreciated his strides to compromise, more than she'd thought possible. As if he'd realized she needed to know her choice wasn't based on following a man like her mama.

Which made Bailey Rae's answer all the easier. "I think I'll stick around here for a while."

A pack of kids ran past the truck holding sparklers, their laughter reminding her of everything that Winnie had fought for.

Lives lived in peace. Happiness.

"Is that so?" His eyebrows raised in surprise. "I guess you do still have a final truckload of things left to sell."

"Actually, since I have enough money to buy a food truck, why not use it at the markets here?" She gestured to the gathering of Bent Oak residents. Her gaze skated over to Thea and Howard's tailgating party a few feet away with their adult children, as well as June, Keith, and Libby. She'd called them with the basics, and they'd agreed to meet in the morning to discuss in more detail. "There'll be other events too and some in surrounding towns, like for sports, fairs, festivals, weddings, and parties. Just to tide me over while I make a decision about my next step."

She would chase her own dreams. But she would chase a new one too. One that would make Winnie proud.

Martin toyed with a lock of her hair. "What about all the furniture you sold and gave away?"

"Lucky for me, I'll still have a little extra cash to replace the basics." Winnie had always been emphatic about saving for a rainy day. Bailey Rae just hadn't realized how deep the savings went. Most of the furniture had needed upgrading anyway. She realized her aunt had likely seen it as her last tie to her life with Russell. Bailey Rae had a host of memories connecting her to them both. "What do you think of my plan?"

"I think folks will line up to get a sample of that pound cake." He tipped her chin upward with a gentle knuckle, pressing a quick kiss to her lips before continuing, "And I'll be first in line every time."

༄

Industrial fan working overtime, Bailey Rae sat on the porch floor beside Skeeter, who was resting on a quilt. She'd picked him up the moment the vet had opened for business at the crack of dawn. "Sorry about the cone of shame, Skeeter."

He gave her a woeful hound dog look, clearly not a fan of the plastic cone that kept him from chewing his stitches. The six-inch gash along his side hadn't damaged any organs but still made her heart ache with the wide patch of shaved fur and painful red sutured line. The horror of yesterday morning threatened to steal today's peace, but she swept it aside. She wasn't living in the past anymore.

Ian had already been charged with murder. Between her statement about his confession and evidence connecting him to the crime, the authorities had enough to ensure he wouldn't be given bail while awaiting trial. Gia had texted Bailey Rae to thank her again. She'd even promised to send Skeeter a special peanut butter treat for his role in apprehending Ian. She sounded sincere when saying she didn't want to lose touch.

Bailey Rae understood all about the importance of connections with the special people in her life. Libby, Keith, June, Thea, Howard . . .

And yes, Martin too.

His workday promised to be busy after so many reports of vandalism in the marshy backwoods during the Fourth of July celebrations. He would come over later with supper from the Fill 'Er Up. She had a million tasks to tackle too, starting with unloading the contents of the truck back into the barn, then beginning the search for a good deal on a food truck trailer. Thanks to the money from Aunt Winnie, Bailey Rae had time to plan for her future in Bent Oak.

A honking car horn jolted her back to the present.

Standing, Bailey Rae shaded her eyes from the morning sun. An unmistakable minivan careened along the winding path on shock absorbers long past their expiration date.

The minivan slid to a stop by the front steps, a cloud of dust swirling. The driver's side door creaked open, with June behind the wheel. She grabbed the frame and hopped out. "Bailey Rae, honey, put on your dancing shoes. Your party has arrived."

"Not a minute too soon." Bailey Rae lifted her hair off her sweaty neck, nodding toward June's latest adventure in hair color. "Love the red-and-blue stripe for Independence Day."

June gave a sassy flick of her head. "Just celebrating freedom."

The side panel rolled away and the wheelchair ramp cranked out for Libby, a picnic basket on her lap and a cane hooked on the armrest. "Keith's putting in some overtime at the new construction job of his, but he sends his best."

Was she confused? Bailey Rae glanced at June, who shrugged, smiling. "Who knew Keith would be a whiz at construction? Guess he's a late bloomer."

Better late than never. Bailey Rae hoped, for his sake and his mother's, this could be his fresh beginning too.

The passenger-side door opened for Thea, who wore pink lace gloves. "We've brought chicken salad sandwiches, ladyfinger cookies, and sweet tea—"

Libby interrupted, patting the wicker basket. "I wanted Southern Comfort, but they said it's still morning."

June grasped the wheelchair handles, steering her toward the cabin's side ramp. "We're here to give you a proper send-off."

What Southern celebration would be complete without food? She would be glad to spend more time cooking Winnie's recipes in the weeks ahead, perfecting them for her food truck business. But for now, she couldn't wait to let them know this celebration was about to take a surprising twist.

"Well," Bailey Rae said with a grin, then blurted, "turns out I've decided to stick around for a little while longer."

All three paused, eyes wide with surprise, followed by an exhale of relief.

"Woo-hoo," June squealed. "Praise the Lord and pass the gravy."

Thea clapped her hands over her chest. "That's the best news I've heard in a month of Sundays."

Libby smirked. "I told you to let me bring the Southern Comfort."

Bailey Rae climbed the porch steps, motioning to the rockers and swing. "Let's have our picnic out here and keep Skeeter company."

The hound had drifted off to sleep, but she still wasn't ready to let him out of her sight for a moment.

June pushed the wheelchair up the ramp onto the porch, then set the brakes. "Did your change of heart have something to do with the yummy game warden?"

"Actually," Bailey Rae said, opening the basket and pulling out four Mason jars, "he offered to come see me and even look into job postings in the Myrtle Beach area."

June nodded approvingly, choosing the rocker closest to Libby. "An enlightened man. He has my vote."

Laughing, Bailey Rae poured sweet tea from the carafe into jars. "I decided I don't need to go to Myrtle Beach to feel close to Winnie. My very best memories of her are in Bent Oak."

"Hear! Hear!" Thea cheered, sitting in a rocker. "Will you return to work at the Fill 'Er Up? I'm sure they would be thrilled to have you back."

Bailey Rae passed the jars over one at a time. "I'm still buying a food truck. I decided to look into opportunities around the county."

Saying it out loud still felt a little scary, but exciting too.

"Brilliant," June declared, sipping her tea before continuing, "I can already think of ideas around the community college campus."

Thea waggled her fingers. "I know Howard will want to schedule you to come to the mill's loading dock for lunch and the occasional event."

Bailey Rae blinked back tears at their support. "I can't thank you enough for all the times you've been there for me."

"Honey," June said, leaning forward to pat her knee. "You're family."

Libby tipped her head back into the warm morning breeze. "This feels like the day Winnie and I arrived in Bent Oak at the same time. Full of promise, thanks to Annette and our new lives." She opened her eyes again. "But you don't have to trust my word. I realize I'm slipping. You can verify with Thea and June."

"I believe it," Bailey Rae said, taking a seat on the porch swing and cradling her jar of tea in her hands. "I only have one question. How did you manage the new documents, like birth certificates?"

Thea jumped right in, saying, "It's all a matter of who you know—having a connection with a paralegal, who then knows someone at the courthouse. Did we break the law?" She shrugged. "We did what we had to. Which brings me to our little bit of news."

"Your news?" Scooting to the edge of the swing, Bailey Rae couldn't imagine what other surprises life would have in store. "Please, do tell."

The three women exchanged excited looks before June and Libby nodded to Thea to take the lead. "As far as helping others find the freedom we have, we'd put things on hold after losing Winnie. We needed time to begin healing and figuring out what to do next. There's still more work to be done, but the path forward for us will look different. Less hiding, thanks to laws now that didn't exist then. Not perfect, but progress. It's time to step out into the daylight."

Libby gripped the arms of her wheelchair, her gray eyes animated and sharp. "We've seen firsthand how many people still need help, so many that the two shelters in this area don't have nearly enough beds. I've always wanted to open a shelter, the kind that helps families get back on their feet. The kind where folks don't have to keep secrets. It's tough enough for me to keep one set of names straight, much less two."

June cackled. "And it's not like I have to worry about anyone recognizing me now."

Thea tugged off her gloves. "The people looking for me died a long time ago. I kept quiet more for the others we'd helped, but I believe the time is right for me to spearhead some ideas about what services a shelter could provide with the right sponsors. What do you think of our idea, Bailey Rae?"

The bravery and generosity of these women took her breath away. "I can't wait to hear more and see your plans come to life." And as if Winnie whispered in her ear, an idea flowered as her gaze fell on one of her aunt's jars of collected stones. She'd poured so much love into the place, it was a shame not to share it. "If you're interested, we can talk about using this property in some way."

Thea blinked back tears, all the more moving from the normally reserved woman. "Annette, Winnie, and Russell would love that."

The rightness of building something lasting on this land settled around her. Details could come later, like piecing together a quilt.

Bailey Rae lifted her jar. "Shall we toast?"

And with the clink of four jars against each other, the thick glass refracting sunbeams, they sealed the deal.

EPILOGUE

Six Months Later

A big part of stepping out of the shadows included taking pictures, documenting, and celebrating. And today's photo deserved framing.

Standing on the cleared spot that had once housed the barn, Bailey Rae held a shovel, flanked by Libby, Thea, and June. Together, with their breaths puffing clouds into the cold winter air, they posed for the photographer from the *Bent Oak Weekly* documenting the groundbreaking ceremony for the Ballard-Davis Sanctuary House.

Bailey Rae still couldn't believe how smoothly the pieces had fallen into place to open a shelter for women in crisis. Perhaps because the need was so great. Or maybe because Winnie was smiling from heaven, punting any roadblocks out of their way—starting with the funding.

Phillip Curtis III had been persistent about reaching out, even after seeing Winnie's birth certificate. So much so, Bailey Rae worried he might stumble on the truth if she didn't give him some way to pass along Eloise's inheritance. She'd never seen someone so eager to unload a ton of money.

Well, no one except Aunt Winnie.

Finally, Bailey Rae had responded to Phillip's fourth inquiry and told him about the women's shelter she and Winnie's friends were opening. Would he be interested in making a donation? He'd been prompt in his response and in cutting a check.

A big check. She'd been taken aback by all the zeroes. Winnie truly had left behind a fortune. She must have been desperate beyond belief.

Admiration doubled for the woman who'd brought her up, who'd helped Bailey Rae through struggles and trauma, while managing to put her own in the past. Winnie had given her the greatest of gifts by teaching her to build a beautiful life centered around what mattered so much more than material possessions.

Friendship. Loyalty. Love.

Tears welled and Bailey Rae let them stream free, missing Winnie today more than ever. Although these days she didn't suppress her emotions. Good. Bad. Happy. Sad. She embraced them all.

Only a week after that chaotic July Fourth market, Winnie's body had been found, far downriver in a peaceful cove. They would never know if her drowning had truly been an accident or if Winnie had surrendered to her grief over losing Russell.

Either way, until that moment, Bailey Rae hadn't realized how, in a deep corner of her heart, she'd been holding out hope that her aunt would turn up on the doorstep with her bottomless purse and a family in need. Truth be told, she still liked to fantasize about Winnie riding a Greyhound bus along the coast, visiting beach after beach. Maybe even putting down roots in some sandy locale and selling blown glass to tourists.

Thanks again to Phillip III, a piece of Winnie's art would be displayed in the lobby of the completed shelter—a blown-glass creation of a mother and child nestled inside an oyster shell like a pearl.

Thea clapped her hands, in charge as their new de facto leader. "Don't forget we're having a pig picking over at the house tonight to celebrate. Howard has been out tending that pig in the roasting pit all night."

Pushing Libby's wheelchair, June cheered. "Party time. We'll bring the Southern Comfort. Right, Libby?"

Libby smiled up from her chair wordlessly as they made their way toward the minivan.

Martin stepped forward, looking too handsome in his uniform. "Bailey Rae, I'll get the heater running in the truck." He dropped a quick kiss on her mouth, squeezing her hand and whispering, "Great job here today."

She stroked his bristly jaw. "Great group effort."

They were all finding a niche. She'd already begun a soup kitchen from her shiny new food truck, a service that would expand upon the opening of Sanctuary House. June now offered GED prep classes, with Gia's assistance. Thea, of course, was already keeping the books. Keith had even managed to hold down his new job and would be working on the construction crew contracted to build the shelter where the barn had once stood.

In a poignant twist, Libby had a contribution as well. For decades, she'd been hiding her skills as a pianist, and while words faded for her more and more each day, her fingers had rediscovered the keyboard. The shelter would be filled with music for both adults and children.

The playground had already been constructed by the high school's carpentry class. Stepping stones that Winnie had made wound pathways through the equipment, a fanciful castle turret at one end and a row of swings at the other. Bailey Rae remembered well from her childhood the sensation of feeling safe under these very trees.

Taking one last instant to soak it all in, she traced the lettering on the rough-hewn sign proclaiming: FUTURE SITE OF THE BALLARD-DAVIS SANCTUARY HOUSE.

A tribute to Winnie, Russell, and Annette.

Their names said it all.

ACKNOWLEDGMENTS

This story has been percolating in my imagination for years, perhaps even for decades on a subliminal level. One of my most vivid childhood memories is of my mother—a brilliant, award-winning journalist—not being able to get a department store credit card without my father's signature. Thankfully, my father proved every bit as indignant on her behalf. Yet that moment stuck with me all the same, resurfacing at different stages of my life, prompting me to question. From those questions flowed *Lightning in a Mason Jar*.

Just as Winnie collected rocks to commemorate special times and individuals in her life, my heart is full of gratitude for the people who helped bring Winnie, Bailey Rae, Libby, Thea, June, and Annette's story to the page.

My deepest appreciation goes out to my editors, Danielle Marshall and Nancy Holmes, along with Krista Stroever and the entire team at Lake Union, for their vision, guidance, and enthusiasm for *Lightning in a Mason Jar*. As always, endless thanks to my agent, Barbara Collins Rosenberg of the Rosenberg Group, for championing my work over the years.

Thank you also to the amazing women around me who helped bring Winnie and Bailey Rae's story to life from the very first brainstorming to massaging the final draft. To my critique partner, Joanne Rock, who so generously shares her brilliance and friendship. And to early readers Haley Frank, Jeanette Vigliotti, and Denishia Stewart.

Even typing your names makes me smile and toast you with a glass of sweet tea.

Most of all, thanks to my family: My mother and my grandmothers, who nurtured a love of learning and stressed the importance of a woman being able to support herself. My father and grandfathers, who never said, "Girls can't." My four miraculous children, their wonderful spouses, and my even more miraculously wonderful grandchildren, who've cheered me on as loudly as I have cheered for them. My husband's children and grandchildren, who've shown me a whole new and lovely dimension of family. And to my husband, Jim, who helped me trust in the beauty of new beginnings. I love y'all!

DISCUSSION QUESTIONS

1. Does your name hold special meaning for you, or do you feel unattached to it like Winnie? If so, why?
2. Was Winnie being too cautious in holding so tightly to her secret? If so, how much should she have told Bailey Rae, and at what age?
3. What sort of challenges would Winnie have faced if she didn't have her group of friends?
4. Looking back on the women in your life, do you believe there was anyone who felt trapped by circumstance or lack of resources? What are ways we can help others feel comfortable reaching out?
5. How did Bailey Rae grow as a result of her discoveries about Winnie's past?
6. *Lightning in a Mason Jar* touches on several themes, including women's rights, family secrets, the resiliency of women, the resiliency of children, racial tensions, and dementia. Was there one theme that you were particularly drawn to? Why?
7. Russell and Martin both have military combat service in their pasts. How does that influence their subsequent career choices?
8. Keith and Bailey Rae experienced similar childhood trauma. Why do you think Bailey Rae grew and Keith continued to struggle?

9. Winnie and Thea each enter into committed relationships (Winnie with Russell, Thea with Howard). How do their approaches to happily ever after differ and why? Why do you think Winnie found it so difficult to marry again? Did you empathize with her reluctance?
10. How did the setting of the rural South play into shaping the story?
11. Martin is the only character in the story who is not from the South. How do his observations help showcase regional differences and idiosyncrasies? How has Martin used this relocation to avoid facing past trauma?
12. This book was inspired by the Equal Credit Opportunity Act (ECOA) of 1974, which took away the barriers women faced with getting credit cards in their own names. Why do you think it took so long for this law to be passed?
13. Winnie thinks in the opening pages, "we women aren't tethered to our names." She views that as something positive, considering she wants to hide her identity. Is there a flip side to this? What do women give up by not maintaining their birth names?
14. It took Bailey Rae some time to discover the darker reasons behind Winnie's friends' seeming eccentricities. How did each of the older characters—Thea, Libby, June—change themselves to adapt to their new lives? What did they each give up?
15. Early in the story, Winnie wonders if she will ever be close enough to the women she meets to learn their real names or their real stories. Do you feel you know your friends' deepest stories? Do they know yours? How does that deepen—or threaten—a friendship?

ABOUT THE AUTHOR

Photo © 2017 Rob Wilson Photography

Catherine Mann is a *USA Today* bestselling and award-winning author whose contemporary fiction novels have been published in more than thirty countries. After years of moving around the US, Catherine settled back in her home state of South Carolina with her Harley-riding husband. Empty nesters, they have a blended family of nine children, nine grandchildren, two dogs, and three feral cats, who all provide endless inspiration for new novels. For more information, visit www.catherinemann.com.